# THE DONOR

## JJ BURGESS

INKUBATOR
BOOKS

# FOREWORD

Following a change in the law by the UK government, all children conceived as the result of registered sperm donation on or after 1st April 2005 have the right to know the identity of their father when they turn eighteen years old.

There is currently a shortage of registered sperm donors in the UK.

The UK's National Sperm Bank closed in 2016 due to lack of donor recruitment.

Right now, there are over 4,000 private sperm donors advertising online. They are unregistered, which means they are not checked by the UK's government, hospitals or police.

# PART I

# PROLOGUE

He had bound her wrists with a length of chain and hung her up from the wooden rafters of his garage. She was lifeless, like a gutted lamb hanging in an abattoir, but he knew that she was just unconscious. A neat strip of duct tape covered her mouth, so the only sound he could hear was her ragged breathing through a bloody nose.

Her black blouse was ripped at the neck, revealing a thin strip of her white bra. Mud and grime covered her grey herringbone skirt. She wore only one shoe; the other must have fallen off as he dragged her through the car park and lifted her into the boot of his car. He wondered if they would find her lost shoe.

The garage was empty apart from a table against one wall. The tabletop was oil stained, and his small, leather bag sat on it. Within the bag he kept the tools that he used for such occasions, instruments of torture designed to cause suffering. On the floor near the closed garage door lay her handbag, which he'd thrown out of reach.

Slowly, he paced around the cold garage, moving silently

across the bare concrete floor. His eyes never left her. Because of the way she was hanging on her wrists, her hands had turned purple and looked painful, even to him. In stark contrast her face was pale and gaunt.

He stopped in front of her and stroked a strand of brown hair from her face so he could see her clearly. She didn't stir as he gently touched her mascara-streaked cheeks, his large hands caressing her skin. The urge to hurt her was huge, and it took all of his willpower to stop himself from getting his little stubby knife out of the leather bag.

"Not yet," he whispered. "Not until you are awake and we can enjoy ourselves together."

His fingers traced over her pale face. He stroked her eyebrows, then caressed the bridge of her nose before he gently pinched her chin. It was a face he had been watching for weeks, waiting for this moment to arrive.

Suddenly she stirred, and he took a step backwards.

Her eyes fluttered, and he watched as she tried to focus. She blinked rapidly, her eyes scanning the room before looking down at her own body. Eventually, she looked up, and their eyes met. Her confusion lifted, and he saw the exact moment when the situation hit her.

She tried to scream, but the duct tape muffled the sound.

"Hello, my princess," he said with a big smile. "Shall we begin?"

# 1

"Is there somewhere I can masturbate?" Doyle asked.

Anna and John looked at each other, both unsure how to reply.

John peered out of the lounge door towards the staircase, and Anna felt a sudden panic that her husband might invite this stranger to go upstairs in their house to masturbate. Before John could speak, she answered quickly.

"There's a bathroom by the front door."

Doyle seemed happy with this reply, and he set off back to the front of the house.

"Won't be long," Doyle called to them.

"Take your time," Anna replied.

John rolled his eyes at his wife, and she realised how perverted that had sounded, as if she were encouraging Doyle to enjoy it.

They heard the downstairs bathroom door close, and John let out a sigh of relief.

"Jesus Christ," he whispered, rubbing his face.

Anna slumped down onto the sofa and noticed her palms felt damp. She had wrongly assumed their new donor, Doyle, would have had a pot of his sperm ready for them before he arrived at their house. She hadn't even considered Doyle might need to masturbate in their home.

John looked up. "Can you hear something?"

They could suddenly hear the toilet squeak in time with Doyle's movements. Anna and John both looked at each other with wide eyes, as if their burglar alarm had just been triggered.

"Cup of tea?" John asked, his voice louder than usual.

Anna jumped up from the sofa. "That would be lovely, thank you," she said, her voice booming around the lounge as they made their way through the hallway and into the kitchen.

John turned on the kettle, and Anna set out two cups, the crockery clattering on the worktop. Thankfully, the noise of the kettle boiling filled the huge kitchen.

Anna was a lecturer at Bristol University, and John was a sales director. Between them, they were earning a six-figure sum, but even so, buying the house had pushed them to their financial limit. Because of the risk in the house purchase, Anna had questioned the estate agent on every aspect of the property, and armed with a clipboard and printed list, she had asked the agent over a hundred questions. But one she hadn't thought to ask was, 'If a stranger is masturbating in my downstairs bathroom, will I hear him from the kitchen?'

"There's no bloody tea bags! We're out of tea!" John's voice cracked with panic.

"Coffee, then. Coffee."

The kettle boiled, and they loudly set about making the drinks by slamming the fridge, clattering the spoon, banging the cupboard doors closed.

"Biscuit?"

"Yes, please."

The packet was opened and rustled. The coffee was

slurped, and the biscuits munched with open mouths. Despite their best efforts, an unwelcome silence descended on them.

Anna looked around the vast, cream kitchen, her eyes scanning for something to make a noise with. The kitchen was spotlessly clean as usual, and the only thing out on the stone countertop was her insemination kit, which had been lined up neatly to one side.

"I thought he was supposed to do it before he got here?" John asked, his voice a fearful whisper.

"Me too," Anna replied just as quietly. "Although the fresher, the better, I suppose?"

John couldn't help but wince.

"How long does it take?" she asked him.

"What?"

"You know..." Anna made a hand gesture at him, trying to demonstrate a man masturbating.

Despite the situation, John sniggered at her. "You calling me a wanker, mate?"

"You know. How long does it take to juice your load?"

John choked on his coffee and went red-faced as he tried to cough quietly.

"Juice?!" he rasped at her, trying to find his breath.

"You know what I mean."

Anna gave him another hand gesture, and he sniggered and coughed, his eyes bulging.

"Stop it."

After a moment, he could breathe again.

"Every man's different, I suppose. And I'm not an expert on it, before you say anything."

"Feels like it's taking a long..."

They heard the downstairs bathroom door open, and both straightened in anticipation. John opened the kitchen door to the hallway.

"We're in here, Doyle."

Doyle entered the kitchen and stood next to John. As the two men stood so close to each other, it was the first time Anna could see the differences between her husband and their chosen sperm donor. John was six feet and toned, but Doyle was taller and broader. Most people would agree John was handsome, but the same people would be drooling over Doyle. In that instant, Anna realised she had chosen an upgraded version of her husband to be their sperm donor.

Doyle handed over a small pot to Anna.

"Here you go," he said, his Irish accent sounding lyrical to Anna.

The sperm felt warm in her hand, and she couldn't bring herself to look at it. He smiled at her, and she again noticed his straight, white teeth and wide smile. Doyle had a flat pugilist nose and gentle blue eyes; it was an incongruous face, which gave him a slight air of mystery. She looked into those blue eyes and, despite herself, blushed.

"Thank you."

Behind Doyle, John folded his arms.

Anna picked up her insemination kit from the countertop.

"Well, I'd better get to it."

She left the kitchen and could feel both of them watching her through the doorway as she headed upstairs.

---

It suddenly felt good to be on her own, although Anna felt a little flutter of nerves as she closed the bedroom door. She had spent months researching about what came next, and it was strange for the moment to have finally arrived.

She and John had a large bedroom with cream walls and a ten-foot pastel painting hanging over a king-sized bed.

Opposite the bed was a wall of fitted wardrobes with mirrored doors. There was a large bay window on the far wall that looked out to the North Bristol countryside. The house itself was in Winterbourne, which was a village surrounded by so much greenery it felt like it was deep in the countryside, but within fifteen minutes, Anna could be in the heart of Bristol city. Through the window there came a soul-warming sun and the smell of freshly mowed lawns, made all the more special because it was the middle of September and the summer was ending.

She put the warm jar of sperm on her bedside table and opened the insemination kit on the bed. It was a yellow and white box, and inside there were ten syringes sealed in clear plastic, each one eight centimetres long and one centimetre wide. The whole pack had cost fifteen pounds, and there were a further four packs under her bed. She had fifty syringes for fifty pots of sperm.

Downstairs, Anna could still hear her husband talking with Doyle. Why hadn't Doyle left yet? She wanted quiet and privacy to help her relax, but the thought of him still being downstairs was unnerving.

It was usual for private donors to masturbate into a cup just before they arrived. They would do it in the back of their car or van outside the house, or in the toilet of a nearby service station. Even at their own house if they were local enough. Anna knew this because she had spent weeks online reading reviews and feedback from hundreds of couples who had also used private sperm donors. But she couldn't remember reading about anyone masturbating in the house where they were delivering the sperm.

Anna looked at the jar of sperm. It was small and plastic with a green lid, like something you would use to take a salad dressing on a picnic. Inside the jar, the liquid looked a yellowy grey.

How long should she wait for Doyle to leave?

Anna's feet padded across the thick cream carpet as she paced the bedroom, waiting for the sound of the front door to be opened and closed. She was tall and slim in an attractive way, but would occasionally slouch so that the beauty would slip off her, and she would become all elbows and knees.

She knew the quality of the sperm was dropping by the minute, so with a puff of her cheeks, Anna walked back to the bed and took off her knickers from under her skirt. Then she tied back her long brown hair with a hairband.

What were they still talking about downstairs? Surely John would have paid Doyle by now? The cheque was already written and waiting in the kitchen drawer.

Anna pulled on a pair of surgical gloves from the box on the bed and tore open the plastic wrapping on one of the syringes.

She picked up the pot of Doyle's sperm from the bedside table, and an image of Doyle came to mind. Tall and toned, great teeth and a warm smile. He was an architect with his own business. It had taken months to find the right sperm donor; with Doyle they felt they had the perfect man. Or at least she felt he was perfect. John had not been so sure.

Carefully, Anna opened the pot and received a faint hint of the sperm's odour.

The distant voices drifted up to her.

"What the hell are they talking about?" she said into the pot.

Anna put the syringe in the thick liquid and sucked it up into the plastic tube. Time was of the essence, the fresher the sperm, the better chance she had of getting pregnant. Anna couldn't wait any longer.

The empty pot went back onto the bedside table, and she rolled over onto her back. The skirt fell to her waist as she parted her naked legs.

With a deep breath, she inserted the syringe.

It felt surprisingly cold and hard.

Anna gave the plunger a gentle squeeze with her thumb, and the sperm shot into her. Before she could stop it, an image of Doyle entered her head. She could hear his Irish voice, 'Here you go'; he had smiled at her.

"Everything alright in there?" John's muffled voice called through the bedroom door.

It made her jump in shock, and Anna's heart pounded in her chest.

"Yes," she squeaked back.

There was a mumbled reply, and she heard John's footsteps retreating from the bedroom door.

Inhaling steadily to slow her breathing, Anna smoothly slid the spent syringe out of her. It was recommended that she lie with her legs in the air for at least ten minutes to let gravity do its work, so she gently rocked backwards, making sure her hips were thrust up into the air. Her bare backside felt cold.

It was strange knowing she had another man's sperm inside her, and she was hit with a pang of guilt at the idea of it. Anna had been with John for eighteen years, and they had been married for twelve, so it must have been years since she'd been anywhere near someone else's sperm.

Anna took long, slow breaths, but couldn't relax.

She shifted on the bed. "Sod it."

Her arm reached up and out, and instead of grasping her book, it picked up her thick green file on Doyle.

Anna knew it wasn't appropriate at that exact moment, but with Doyle's sperm inside her, she flicked open the file.

It contained all of the details Anna had gathered on Doyle Kennedy. Not just the files he had sent to them, files such as his medical checks, but also things she had discovered about him on social media after weeks of research.

The first page was Doyle's online profile picture. The picture gave her a warming sense of happiness, not because he looked like the model for a men's *eau de toilette* brand, but because it had been such a long journey to get a sperm donor that she was truly satisfied with.

The year before, Anna and John had received the devastating news that they couldn't conceive together because John's sperm count was too low. Instantly, Anna had done what she always did, she jumped into action and took control of the situation. Since she was fifteen years old, Anna had always needed to be in control.

Initially, they had registered with the local hospital to receive sperm donations, but their hopes were again dashed on hearing that there was a long waiting list. It was also disheartening to learn that they couldn't request any particular traits of their donor and were told to 'take what you can get', as there was such a shortage of available sperm for prospective parents. This lack of control had made Anna nauseous, and it wasn't long before she found herself online, looking for a private donor.

It was an exciting process, and Anna wondered if it was like using a dating website. She had always felt like a lot of her generation of married women had missed the online dating wave, and she marvelled at how satisfying it was to get online and pick a man.

After weeks of searching and emailing questions, Anna had finally settled on Doyle Kennedy, who had instantly given her a good feeling.

Anna had printed off several emails between them, and her eyes scanned a paragraph she had highlighted. '...the most important thing to me is family,' he had written. 'That is why I choose to be a sperm donor.'

Doyle was twenty-eight years old. He'd been to Bath University to get his degree in architecture, which is where

Anna had gained her degree in psychology. That alone made her feel like they had something in common. He was born and raised in Dublin, but had moved to the city of Bath to follow his career. From what she could see, he was single, although his online profile showed that he was connected to a lot of women. Anna also knew he had a holiday home in Cornwall. Was that too much information to know about a stranger? Probably. But it was important that her son or daughter came from a strong donor. He would be their biological father, after all.

Finally, her watch showed that ten minutes had passed since the insemination. She closed the file on Doyle, gently sat up on the bed and tilted her head towards the bedroom door, but the house was silent. Anna pulled her knickers back on and threw the used syringe and gloves in the bedroom bin.

She had done it.

Her first sperm donation had been used. She couldn't help but smile with pride. Her skin tingled with the sense of a job well done. There would be more donations from Doyle, but it felt so good to have completed the first one. She carefully packed the other nine syringes back into the box and replaced the box under the long bed.

Anna walked downstairs.

Her first action was going to be bleaching the downstairs bathroom. The second was going to be contacting Doyle to tell him they wanted the sperm donations produced before he arrived at their house next time. They couldn't have him turning up each time to masturbate in their bathroom.

She called down to John from the stairs.

"John, we need to email Doyle..."

Anna walked into the lounge and froze.

John and Doyle were both standing there, holding a bottle of beer each.

Doyle smiled at her. John's cold face glared at her.

Anna didn't know what to say; she was rooted to the spot. She felt her face blazing red.

"Hey, sorry, we got chatting." Doyle drained his beer bottle and set it down on the coffee table.

"Let me leave you guys in peace." He breezed out of the lounge towards the front door.

Slowly, Anna followed him out.

"I'll email you some further dates when I'm free," Doyle said.

"Alright."

And with that, he was gone. Out of the front door and back into his sports car parked on their drive.

Anna closed the front door and headed back into the lounge.

"We definitely need to ask him to do his donations before he arrives next time," Anna said as she entered the lounge.

The room was empty. John had already left.

She looked down at the coffee table where John's and Doyle's beer bottles stood.

One was empty.

One was full.

## 2

"What the fuck do you mean, you want a baby?!" Lara demanded.

Before Anna could reply, a waiter arrived at their table, carrying a tray. He gently set down a green tea for Anna and a large latte for Lara.

"Who's having the cake?"

Lara beamed up at the young waiter and gave her curly hair a little flick.

"Oh, that's mine, thanks."

The waiter blushed and put the plate down and headed back to the counter of the café. Anna and Lara watched him walk away, and Lara playfully wiggled her freshly laminated eyebrows up and down at Anna, who laughed at her friend.

Lara's phone vibrated, and she peered down at it lying on the table. She ignored the incoming call and instead turned her focus to Anna. The brown of Lara's eyes was a shade darker than her mass of thick, curly hair. She was the head of product design for a leading make-up brand, and that morning she was wearing shimmering lip gloss and bronze eyeliner. By chance, both Anna and Lara were wearing trouser suits, although Anna's was a grey slim fit and Lara's was gingham yellow.

"A baby?"

"I know it's out of the blue."

"Bloody right."

"But for a while now I've been thinking..."

Lara waved a hand at her, dismissing the forthcoming explanation.

"How many holidays have you had this year?"

"Three?"

"Including skiing?"

"Well, four, but that was only a weekend."

"It's only September, and you've already been away four times. What did we do last weekend?"

"Umm?"

"We were at the Hippodrome. Remember? Watching that bloody brilliant play about the crazy lady. Then we went to that restaurant and had those amazing cocktails."

"Ah yes."

"Aren't we in London in two weeks? Ballet and shopping?"

"So?"

"So how are you going to do all of this with a frigging baby in tow?"

"You know, your language is terrible."

Lara took a gulp of her latte. She flipped open a small pocket mirror and checked her lip gloss. Her phone buzzed on the table for a second time.

Lara peered at the mobile phone screen again and muttered, "Well, he can piss off."

"Look, I know I'm the last person you'd ever imagine having a baby. Or a family. But these past twelve months I've changed, and I've been thinking about family more and more since Mum died."

Lara tilted her head in sympathy. She gave Anna's hand a squeeze.

"That was tough. Bloody cancer."

"I've not mentioned this to anyone, but before she died, we were talking a lot. So many things were said. One of the conversations I keep replaying in my head is Mum saying I wouldn't be really happy unless I had a family of my own. At the time, I didn't give it much thought. But this last year I've done a lot of thinking about Mum and kids and what it means to be a family."

Anna sipped her green tea and looked towards the back of the café, where the young waiter was making a fresh coffee for a waiting customer. They were in the Porto Lounge café in Fishponds, which was conveniently situated halfway between Bristol University and Lara's office. The café was small and had a garish, eclectic décor that gave it a charm above what was usually found in the neighbourhood.

"I mean, I'm thirty-eight."

"You don't look a day over thirty."

Anna smiled at the compliment.

"This last year..." She paused. "After finally getting the promotion at work –"

"You did well to get it," Lara said.

"– I thought I would be happy being promoted, but when it was actually confirmed, I wasn't that bothered."

"You should be proud, darling. Head of Faculty at your age is a great achievement."

"I know." Anna struggled to find the words to explain how desperate she had become to have a baby. "It is good, but right now it just feels like a job. What I really want is a family to share these things with."

"You've got John."

"Yes."

"So you're keeping him busy, then?" Lara asked with a cheeky smile.

Anna snorted and then hesitated. Lara was her closest friend, and they had known each other since they had been at Bath University together. Lara was from a wealthy family and had clearly been spoilt as a child, but in a way that had made her fun as a young adult. On her first day at university, Anna had been so nervous, but the ditzy and confident Lara had drawn her in like a moth to a house fire. Lara studied hard and partied hard, and she had opened Anna's eyes to a whole new world beyond that which Anna had experienced before. Despite their closeness, Anna still couldn't admit that John wasn't able to conceive and they were using a private sperm donor. Also, Lara might ask how John was feeling, and the honest answer was, Anna didn't know.

Anna and John had used to joke about Anna being a workaholic, about her being always overly focused on a task, but in recent years they didn't laugh about it anymore. Now they both lived their lives knowing that whatever Anna wanted, she would push herself to the limit to get.

"Yes, we're keeping busy," Anna replied.

"Well, don't sound too down about it. I thought you said he was dynamite in the bedroom."

Anna rolled her eyes. "I tell you too much."

Lara laughed and bit into her chocolate cake.

"Oh, that's so tasty. Try some of this cake."

"No, thanks."

"No good watching your weight now. You're going to be a fat cow soon."

Anna laughed.

"I can't believe I'm going to lose my best friend. I thought we'd be partying together and living it up till we were old ladies."

"Oh, bless you, you're not losing me. We'll still go out, still go away."

Anna could see that Lara looked genuinely upset, and she did feel for her friend. But since her mum had died, Anna had done a lot of thinking. The career, big house and indulgent lifestyle were still important to her, but they had been superseded by the overwhelming need for a baby. For a family of her own. Even her friend's sadness was not enough to change her mind.

Anna checked her watch.

"Oh god, I'm late. I'm supposed to be teaching in twenty minutes."

Lara looked at her in surprise.

"You're late? You're never late."

Anna picked up her handbag and stood up.

"I can't believe I forgot."

Lara couldn't help but laugh through a mouthful of cake.

"It's finally happened; little Ms Organised is actually late for something."

Anna leaned in and quickly hugged Lara.

"Call you soon," she said as she put on her coat, tucked in her chair and left the café.

Walking back to the car, Anna dug out her phone and dialled John's number. As a sales director, he was often in meetings, but he was usually free at lunchtimes. The call went to voicemail.

She didn't leave a message.

---

THE AMPHITHEATRE at Bristol University was full of students and lecturers chatting noisily as they waited for her. As soon as Anna walked through the double doors, the talking subsided to a low murmur. There were three hundred of them sat watching her. The familiar smell hit her as she entered the hall; it was a heady mix of last night's alcohol and overscented perfume and shower gel.

Anna walked to the podium at the front of the hall and tried to control the rising anger she felt with herself as everyone's eyes followed her. She was never late, and it was galling that she had missed the start of her first lecture as Head of Faculty.

It was the beginning of a new university term. The first-year students would have spent the morning getting oriented around the main campus before coming to the amphitheatre for their first introductory lecture. Anna could sense the excitement in the air. This was the session where she would outline the course plans for the next three years. Not only that, but she would also introduce the lecturing team who would be teaching them.

The front row was lined with the faculty's academic staff, all sat with folded arms and furrowed brows. Since Anna's recent promotion, they were her lecturers, and she was now their superior.

And she was late for her first class of term.

Anna stood behind the large lectern and spoke into the thin black microphone.

"Welcome to the School of Psychological Science."

Her voice boomed through the speakers, and the hall became silent. On the lectern in front of her was a small monitor reflecting what was projected on a large screen behind her. The students could all see the large screen, which should have Anna's lesson plan on, only it was blank because she was late and hadn't yet had time to plug her memory stick into the monitor and set up her PowerPoint presentation. With a sinking feeling, Anna realised her memory stick was somewhere at the bottom of her handbag.

Panic pounded through her chest, and it occurred to

Anna that she was going to have to work hard so as not to seem utterly incompetent in front of both the new student intake and her new team of lecturers.

"In this first session, I will explain the key areas of study for the coming year."

At this point she was planning to put up a list of modules on the screen and talk through them.

Anna's skin felt clammy.

On the front row the line of academic staff watched her. There were a few looks of sympathy, but mostly she saw delight. Delight that she was floundering. 'I knew she was too young,' she could hear them thinking.

The staffroom would be alive with gossip later. No doubt the university's Dean, Dr Lyn Coldfield, would hear about her lateness and lack of preparation, and she would want to speak to Anna about it. Anna had a reputation for being organised and getting things done, and that reputation had earned her the position of faculty head.

She didn't have a baby yet, and already she had lost focus on her work. Maybe they were right. Maybe she was too young.

Anna stood before them. The tension in the hall was like a weight of black water pouring onto her shoulders and head. Her chest felt compressed, and she felt like she was drowning.

The silence stretched.

The students looked like they were enjoying the rising tension. Some were even leaning forwards in their seats, like Roman spectators watching to see if the gladiator would be slaughtered.

Anna swallowed.

She needed to take control. Her mind scrambled for inspiration.

"Let's start with a little exercise, shall we?"

Her voice quivered like a student teacher.

"There are many aspects to psychology that we will be teaching you over the next three years. Many areas within life sciences that we will study and review. I remember a few years ago, we had a student who wasn't attending lectures. A bright young man. When I confronted him, he said, 'Well, it's all been worked out anyway.' I asked him, 'What do you mean?' and he told me, 'All the theories have been written, so I just need to read the right books.' "

Her voice steadied. The hall stayed silent and attentive.

"So let me tell you what I told that –" she paused "– confident young man."

A titter rippled through her audience.

"When it comes to psychology, we have only just started to unravel and understand the human psyche. There is still so much to discover. What this means is that you are entering a world that is unexplored. You're all landing on Mars, ready to seek out new discoveries. Each one of you has the chance to theorise and quantify a new concept about the human mind."

Anna risked a look at the front row and was relieved to see that the disappointed looks of the staff had been replaced by indifferent faces.

"So, let us start with a little exercise." She took a deep breath, giving herself half a second to think. "Now, Charles Darwin had a half cousin called Francis Galton. Galton was involved in many fields of study. One of the areas he worked in was psychology, and in 1869 Francis Galton coined a new phrase: 'nature versus nurture'. I'm sure you have all heard this phrase."

The students slowly nodded and murmured agreement.

"It's an easy question to start with, then. Nature? Or nurture?"

Actually, it was one of the hardest questions they would

be asked over the next three years, but they didn't need to know that at this stage.

"Okay, everyone up on your feet. Come on, all of you stand up."

The students slowly followed her instruction, creating a wave of clattering and thuds as they dropped bags and notebooks that had been resting on their laps. The front row of lecturers stayed seated, and she could see a few smiles being cracked.

"Now, please be sensible with this, no pushing or shoving, but if you agree that we are products of nature, sit on the right side of the hall. And if you think it's nurture, please sit on the left side of the hall."

The mass of students sprang into life, full of fun and vigour. This was more entertaining than they had been expecting.

With the room distracted, Anna quickly grabbed her handbag from the floor and started pulling everything out: folders, a bottle of water, make-up, notepads. Her arm moved frantically until, at the bottom of the bag, she found her memory stick. For a moment, she clutched it to her chest as she exhaled with relief.

"No pushing," Anna called out, not bothering to look up at the mass of bodies shuffling around the hall.

The memory stick went into the USB port, and Anna watched the small screen in front of her come alive with her files. She clicked on the correct file with her class slides in just as the volume in the room subsided with expectation. Anna's sickening dread at being late and disorganised fell away.

"Okay," she addressed the students, causing them to fall silent again.

As Anna had predicted, the room was roughly split into

two groups with half of the students sat on the right and half sat on the left.

"So, you guys sat on the left believe we are made by nurture, by learned influences. You are environmentalists. You believe that we are not born to greatness or intelligence. That we are not born with an inbuilt knowledge. For you, it's all about experience, about a person's upbringing and parental guidance and how the world is perceived. You are in very good company here, with Albert Bandura and B. F. Skinner offering experiments and theories to support the idea of nurture being the main influence of behaviour."

The students on the left of the room looked pleased with themselves.

"And on the right of the room. You believe in the theory of nature. It's all about our DNA and genetics, and you think we are born as ready formed personalities. Right now, there are some persuasive new experiments being conducted in genetics that support a nativism view. There are many scientists and thinkers who believe the nature theory, from Plato in ancient Greece to Galton himself."

Anna could see the students processing what she was saying.

"The good news for all of you is that there is no right or wrong answer. The theory is over one hundred years old, and the question still has the power to divide a room. So, like I said, the field is still wide open for experiments and new theories. At the end of this year, we shall do the same exercise and see if you have changed your minds."

Anna could see the front row of lecturers looking amused. They knew as well as she did that it had all been a trick. That by the end of the year the students would realise it was both nature and nurture that determined how a person behaved. It had been a cheap trick, but it had bought her a few minutes.

Anna turned to her screen, feeling relaxed and confident now that she was back in control.

Before clicking onto the first slide, she looked over to the front row of lecturers with a cold face and met their stares. Anna was the Head of Faculty now, whether they liked it or not. And she wasn't going to fail.

"Right," her voice boomed, "let's go through the module plan for this semester."

## 3

I t had been a long day at the office, and John was happy
to get home. As he walked through the front door, the
dark house told him that Anna was still at work. He
went upstairs, and in the bedroom, it felt good to get changed
out of his suit and put on a pair of jeans and an old jumper.
Down in the kitchen, he resisted the urge to have a beer from
the fridge and instead made a cup of tea. Armed with his
steaming mug, he wandered around the house, restless and
wired.

He was looking for something to occupy his mind. John
knew he wouldn't be able to sit and watch the television, so
he didn't bother picking up the remote. Unread books
seemed uninviting. He considered cooking dinner, but
couldn't find anything to inspire him in the kitchen
cupboards. John drank his tea as he moved from room to
room in the huge house. It had been a stressful day.

As well as the stress of work, there was the other thing
occupying his mind, the knowledge that he was infertile. The
thought of it was like a burn on his skin, a pain that alternated between being distantly dull and deeply distressing. It

was a niggling thought he couldn't get rid of. He was still John, still working and playing golf, still going to the pub with friends and being a husband to Anna. But somehow everything was different now. It was like he was going through the motions, because the burning pain he was carrying was distracting him from enjoying his life.

He walked into the garage and flicked on the lights. Should he mow the lawn? The day's dying sun still offered enough light to work off some of his restless energy in the garden. He started to pick up the gardening gloves from a shelf and paused. Lying in a thick layer of dust were his old boxing gloves. He picked them up and turned to look at the boxing bag hanging at the back of the garage. Ever since he was a kid growing up in Plymouth, he had loved to box. John wondered why he had ever stopped.

He picked up an old cloth from the shelf and wiped down the black gloves and boxing bag. John then stripped off his jumper to reveal strong arms and a trim torso before he pulled on the leather gloves and stepped towards the boxing bag.

He gave it a jab. And another. And another.

His body fell into an old rhythm of stepping and punching. His muscles remembered the routine, and as the blood started to pump through his arms, he grinned. Dust filled his nose, but he didn't care.

John stopped and started, moving and tap-tapping his way around the heavy bag. He liked to win, to hit targets and achieve his goals. He was the youngest sales director in the history of his company because he always delivered, but being told he was infertile felt like the ultimate failure. He wasn't even sure that he wanted a baby, and he knew that he definitely didn't want Anna to use a sperm donor. Even as these thoughts came to him, he brushed them aside, unable to deal with them.

The stress of the past few weeks flowed through his arms as he smashed his fists into the old bag. The garage echoed with the sounds of the leather strikes and his heavy breathing. He thought about Anna being so determined to have a baby and his low sperm count, and then he thought about Doyle.

The goddamn Irishman, breezing into John's house and offering his healthy sperm to his wife. John's arms ached, and sweat poured down his chest as he pounded at the bag. The bastard, blue-eyed sperm donor. Giving his wife something he couldn't. The bag swung as he hit it. He changed from jabs to cross punches, to right hooks and back to jabbing.

He felt good as the stress poured from his neck and shoulders, through his arms and into the boxing bag. John had always had a quick right hook and he still felt the thrill of a clean strike.

His mind was suddenly torn away from his boxing as the metal garage door started to roll up.

It was loud and startling, causing John to stop his dance around the bag and spin towards the door as sunlight poured into the garage.

He thought Anna must be home, but as the garage door fully rolled up, he squinted into the sunlight to see Doyle standing there. John's evaporating stress poured right back into him at the sight of the Irishman.

"Hey, John, how are you? I was knocking on the front door, but there was no answer."

John was lost for words at the sudden appearance of their sperm donor. He stood there, dumbly staring at Doyle, who cast a long shadow into the garage.

"Sorry to interrupt you. Looks like you're having a good workout," Doyle said. He stepped into the garage.

John's first instinct was to tell him to sod off, but he thought better of it. Doyle was wearing black jeans and a navy polo top that was stretched over his thick arms, and John was suddenly aware that he was half naked. He wanted to pull his jumper back on.

John gathered himself and fought to keep an even tone in his voice.

"Anna's still at work. Do we have an appointment with you tonight?"

"Six o'clock on the twenty-fourth of September. Been in the diary for a few weeks."

"Oh, right."

"Guess you guys forgot, hey?"

"Umm, she didn't mention it."

"No worries. I'm happy to wait a little while."

Doyle casually stepped further into the garage, and John visibly flinched.

"Don't let me stop you, though." Doyle walked over to John. "Let me hold the bag for you. I did a little boxing myself when I was younger."

Doyle held onto the bag with a smile and nodded to John.

John pressed the gloves up to his mouth to stop himself from swinging a fist at Doyle. His body pulsed with the need to strike the arrogant arsehole. Instead, he stood still, breathing and blinking. *How dare he come in here?* John's mind bellowed. *Who does he think he is?* The only thing he could do to stop himself from swearing was hit the punching bag that Doyle was now holding. John gave it a little jab.

"Give it some force if you want," Doyle said, as if they were friends, which they weren't.

John struck it harder. When a boxing bag hangs down on its own, it has less resistance, so with Doyle holding the bag in place, John felt the strikes more as shock waves painfully rippled up his arms. His gloves sprang out and hit the old leather hanging in front of him.

"Nice speed on the jab," Doyle said.

John changed to throwing right and left hooks. Doyle shifted his feet at the change in force, and John hit the bag harder. As he added more power to his strikes, he could see Doyle having to strain to hold onto the boxing bag.

"Good power in them hooks."

John leaned in lower, dropped his right shoulder and started hammering kidney punches into the leather boxing bag. He heard Doyle gasp as he tried to hold onto the bag, and John swung his shoulders so that his whole body weight was focused in the strikes. The bag still didn't move as Doyle shifted to hold onto it. The sound of the punches filled the double garage. John's hits threw out more dust that swirled around the two men.

"That's a proper..."

Before Doyle could finish what he was saying, John moved his weight from his knees to his feet, stood taller and reverted back to a one-two jab that cut Doyle off as he reacted to the directional shift of power.

John's throat and lungs burned. His arms were screaming for a break, but he didn't stop; he kept the intense barrage going. What he really wanted to do was pummel the strikes into Doyle's face and body, but John kept his gloves focused on the bag. He hit harder and faster. He wanted Doyle to know, he wanted Doyle to understand that he was still worthy to be Anna's husband. That he was still a man.

The sudden roar of a car engine snapped John out of his violent trance. He dropped his hands and looked over his shoulder to see Anna's Mercedes pulling up on the driveway.

John's sweaty body heaved as he struggled getting air into his lungs, and he felt a pang of annoyance that Doyle seemed relaxed and unfazed by the force of the workout against the bag. Anna got out of the car and walked into the garage. She was wearing a cream blouse and smart black trousers that showed the slim curve of her long legs.

"Doyle, I'm so glad you are here. Did you get my message? I was caught up in work."

"No, but it's no bother. I thought you'd be home soon enough. I was just helping John with his workout." Doyle looked at John. "You've a good punch on you there, John."

John still didn't trust himself so kept his mouth shut.

Anna looked at her husband.

"Are you okay, John?" she asked, her face failing to hide her concern.

He nodded. "Just catching my breath."

"Shall we get to it?" Doyle suggested.

Anna smiled at Doyle. John noticed that even in the gloomy garage, Doyle's eyes were bright blue like a spring sky, as if there was so much life in him that it flowed from his eyes.

"You two carry on. I'll be there in a minute," John said.

As Anna and Doyle walked through the garage and into the house, a lump came to John's throat at the sight of the two of them together. It was a heartbreaking picture.

He could suddenly hear his father's voice in his head, telling him, 'Real men don't cry, John.' His father's words bounced around his mind as his eyes filled with tears.

John turned back to the boxing bag, and feeling swamped with shame, he pushed his face into it. Hot tears streamed down his cheeks, and he wiped them on the old leather bag, willing the burning pain to leave him in peace.

# 4

Anna pulled into Orchard Close and gently parked on the driveway. Opening the front door, she hung up her coat and handbag, kicked off her flat shoes and went into the kitchen. She was wearing a purple flowery dress with no sleeves over a pair of black tights. Her long hair was tied up in a twisted bun.

"John?" she called out.

There was no answer, but Anna could hear a faint banging coming from the garage. Walking through the kitchen and utility room, she opened the internal door to the double garage.

John was in the middle of the garage, bare-chested and dripping with sweat. As she stepped into the musty-smelling garage, she could see that he was wearing his boxing gloves and was pounding the bag. It was the third night this week that she had found him boxing in the garage.

As Anna watched him, she admired how toned and strong John was, but she also assumed the reason he had won so many boxing medals as a teenager was because of his speed. John's hands were just blurs of colour as he punched the bag.

"Hey."

He didn't turn around.

"How was work?" she asked him.

"Busy."

John continued to walk around the bag, jabbing with both his left and right fists. There was no rhythm to what he did. It was just mindless energy battered into the bag.

"Do you want to go out for dinner? The White Horse, maybe?" she asked.

"I've got to go out later."

Anna saw sweat drip from his nose as he panted around the boxing bag. She watched the taut muscles along his back and shoulders as he moved. He still had a tan from their recent holiday to the Maldives.

"Out?"

"Some directors are over from our head office in Italy. I need to take them out for dinner. I told you a while ago?"

Anna was certain he hadn't told her, but she didn't want to start an argument.

"Doyle is supposed to be coming over later. I'm still ovulating."

John stopped suddenly, his back to Anna. His head was facing the floor as he grabbed the bag to stop it swinging.

"I can cancel him though, tell him to come another time?" she asked.

"Okay."

It was a gruff reply, although Anna could sense that John was thankful.

"I'll text him now," she said.

John started to punch the boxing bag again, still unwilling to look her in the eye. It was the last day of her ovulating cycle, and it seemed like a wasted opportunity, however, she thought it was better to be tactful.

Anna retreated to the kitchen and unlocked her phone. She found Doyle's number and typed out her text:

*Sorry for the short notice, we can't do tonight. Will see you in a few weeks instead. Anna and John.*

She clicked *send* and then put the kettle on. What she really wanted was a glass of wine, but she knew it wasn't good for her body, as it could reduce the chance of getting pregnant, so she made a fruit tea instead.

John emerged from the garage.

"Nice guns," Anna said as she admired his naked torso from the breakfast bar.

"Thanks," he replied without stopping.

John headed upstairs and into the shower.

Anna wondered whether she should follow him up and playfully jump on him. Normally after a workout, John would be all over her; pumped up and half naked, he would grab her, and she loved it. But it had been weeks since they'd had sex, and Anna was worried about John. They still hadn't really talked about his infertility. As soon as the nurse had told them they couldn't have children together, Anna had gone into overdrive on the search for a sperm donor. Looking back, it hadn't been the most sensitive response from her. The problem she had now was that every time she tried to talk to John about his infertility, he would shut down. Had she left it too late?

Anna opened the large silver freezer and found some lasagne left over from the previous week in one of the drawers. She put the frozen food into the microwave, slammed the door and stabbed at the buttons to turn it on.

As she sat at the breakfast bar eating her dinner, John

reappeared. He looked smart and authoritative in dark trousers and a blue shirt. He had shaved, and his tanned skin glowed from the workout.

"This lasagne is better than I remember."

"Did you text the freak?" John asked her as he picked up his car keys from the kitchen counter.

"Doyle? Yes, I cancelled tonight. Why is he a freak?"

"I'll be home about eleven," John called from the hallway on his way out of the front door.

"No kiss goodbye?" she called back to him.

The only reply she got was the sound of the front door closing.

Anna sat in silence, eating her lasagne and drinking her fruit tea. Slowly, she stood up and put her empty plate and cup in the sink. She picked up her phone and thought about calling John. Thought about yelling at him, or pleading with him, asking him to come back so they could talk. Anything to get a reaction out of him.

The doorbell chimed, the sound of it reverberating around the silent kitchen.

Anna flew out of the kitchen towards the front door. She expected to see John there, sheepish because he had forgotten something. It would give her a chance to talk to him.

Anna opened the front door and squinted into the low September sun streaming into the house.

Doyle was standing on her doorstep. His wavy dark hair cast a shadow over his eyes, and he wore a smile so wide and friendly and absorbing that for a second Anna forgot to breathe.

"Here I am, right on time."

DOYLE STOOD IN THE LOUNGE, holding a cup of tea. Anna had panicked and let him into the house and made him a drink without thinking about what she was doing.

"You didn't get my text, then?" Anna said as she walked into the lounge, holding her own tea.

"No, sorry. I lost my phone last night."

"Oh, right."

"It's crazy how much we use them now, isn't it? I've been lost all day without it." He smiled at Anna.

*Why do Irish accents sound so charming?* she wondered.

"I know, I'm the same," she replied.

"How's work? Busy for you, too?"

Anna sat down on the corner sofa, and Doyle followed her lead and sat on the armchair opposite. He was wearing a white polo shirt and grey trousers that stretched tightly over his muscular thighs as he sat down.

"Yes, it's the start of term, so it's all a bit crazy at the moment."

"When you're a student, you don't realise how much work your lecturers put into those lessons. Half the time you're asleep anyway," he said as he ran a hand through his thick hair.

"I know. It's so annoying. But all part of the job, unfortunately. You would think with the amount we charge in fees that more students would try harder rather than just coast through the course."

Doyle laughed, flashing his white teeth. "So, anyway, what was the message about?"

Anna sat up straighter on the sofa. "Well, actually, I texted you to cancel this evening."

"Do you guys have plans? Should I go?" Doyle's smile faded, and he looked a little embarrassed.

Anna hesitated, unsure what to do. "Umm, well..."

Doyle stood up. Anna's eyes flickered to his thighs where the outline of solid muscle was showing through his trousers.

"No need to explain." He smiled patiently. "Let me get out of your way."

Anna thought about her pregnancy plan spreadsheet that listed all of her ovulating dates. Today was the last day she would be fertile for weeks. Her window to get pregnant was five days each month, and it was day five. She would need to wait another month now.

"No, it's okay. We had a last-minute change of plan. Now's good."

Doyle set his teacup down on the coffee table and took a small, empty pot out of his trouser pocket. Some hot tea spilt onto Anna's fingers from her own cup, but she hardly noticed.

"Is it alright to use the downstairs bathroom again?"

Anna nodded, and Doyle left the room.

She knew she should ask him to leave, and explain that they wanted the sperm produced before he arrived at the house, but at that moment, she didn't say anything.

Anna heard Doyle lock the bathroom door.

Within a minute, she could hear a faint squeaking sound as Doyle sat on the toilet seat, masturbating. Anna's face flushed red, and she quickly stood up to leave the lounge when an image of Doyle came to her mind. She thought about him in her bathroom, with trousers and underwear around his ankles and his cock in his hand. She pictured Doyle's bulging, naked thighs and his biceps bursting through the thin polo top. Slowly, Anna sat down and listened to the noise of Doyle masturbating. She could feel her heart pumping. Her breathing felt loud in her own ears.

After a moment the noise stopped, and Doyle reappeared from the bathroom. Anna felt her whole body tense and tingle as he walked back into the lounge, and she stood up to face him. He still seemed relaxed, although now his cheeks were pink.

"Here you go, just for you."

He handed her the pot of sperm. It felt molten hot in her hand.

"Thanks," she whispered, wondering where her voice had gone.

Doyle and Anna stood facing each other, close and silent. Anna marvelled at how blue his eyes were. They were like pools of water inviting her to splash in them. She tried to focus on something else.

"Money," she blurted.

"Sorry?"

"Let me pay you."

Anna almost ran to the kitchen and dug out her chequebook from the drawer. With the pot of sperm in her left hand, she scrawled out the amount and signed the cheque. She tore the cheque out of the book so fiercely that a corner of the paper ripped.

Doyle strolled into the kitchen.

"Here you go," she said, handing over the ripped cheque.

"Thanks."

"I'll email you soon."

"Sure." He smiled at her. "I'll leave you in peace. I need to get back to Ellie anyway."

Anna felt a little tug of jealousy, like a child pulling at her hair.

"Ellie?"

"My dog. Don't let the grown-up name fool you, though; she's a tiny little thing." Doyle's face lit up with warmth as he spoke. "I got her last year for company, and I feel bad if I leave her for too long. She'll be waiting for her dinner."

"Sounds cute." Anna couldn't help but smile along with

Doyle; his face was so alive with affection. "Thanks again for this evening."

"My pleasure," he replied before he turned and left the kitchen.

She watched from the kitchen as he walked down the hallway to the front door. He turned and gave her a little wave and a smile. In an instant, he was gone. Somehow, the house felt empty in a disappointing way.

Anna exhaled loudly.

She put the chequebook and pen away in the drawer and walked up to the bedroom with the pot of sperm held tightly in her hand. Her skin felt clammy with sweat, so she unzipped her dress and let it fall to the bedroom floor. She then rolled down her tights and knickers and unclipped her bra, so that she stood in the middle of the bedroom naked. Anna strained her ears in the silence, listening for a knock at the front door, wondering if he would reappear. As she stood there, her naked skin hungered to be touched.

After a dizzying moment, Anna forgot about Doyle and started to follow her routine. The pot of sperm went onto the bedside table. The insemination kit was pulled out from under the bed. She opened a new syringe packet. This time, she didn't bother with the surgical gloves as she opened the small pot and put the syringe into the liquid. Once again, the smell of the sperm wafted into her nose.

Carefully she sucked the sperm up into the tube.

Anna lay back on the bed and inserted the syringe.

It slid in easily.

She planned to push the liquid in slowly, but she couldn't help herself; with a sweaty hand she pushed the full load into her in one go.

Anna removed the syringe and rolled onto her back on the bed, her bare arse pushed up to the ceiling. As she lay there, she thought about blue eyes and big thighs.

# 5

It was a bright and cold day at the end of January. Clumps of dead leaves blustered across the car park as Anna got out of her Mercedes and took a small bunch of flowers from the boot of the car. Without hesitating, she set off up the hill amongst the graves, confident in her route after so many visits. Greenbank Cemetery in Fishponds was hidden behind a long street of terraced town houses. Ancient stone pillars and black metal railings surrounded the site, cutting it off from the modern world.

On the distant horizon there were dark winter clouds, but above the graveyard that morning was a patch of pale blue sky. Despite the dry weather, a biting wind whipped through the graves, and Anna dug her hands further into the pockets of her thick black coat, keeping the flowers tucked under her arm. She was glad that she had put on her big coat and woollen scarf, but her body still shivered from the bitter winter chill.

Amongst a line of grave plaques, Anna stopped and looked down. The stone in front of her was large and clean. It read, 'Lily-May Wilson. Beloved Mother to Anna. Always in our thoughts.'

It was strange how true that was, that her mum was always in Anna's thoughts. It had been just over a year since her mum had died, and the pain and loss was still a gaping slash on her heart. Over the previous year, she had slowly felt it heal and the pain subside, but Anna sensed the agony would never truly leave her.

Besides the plaque, there was a square pot of wilting flowers. Anna pulled them out and replaced them with the fresh flowers she had brought. From her coat pocket, she took out a small packet of cleaning wipes, dug a fresh wipe out of the packet, and cleaned the black stone plaque, carefully following the gold lettering. As she wiped off bird droppings splattered on the stone, Anna felt a nudge of guilt that she hadn't visited in a while.

Anna missed her mum every day. Looking back, it was strange, but perhaps understandable, that they'd never really connected until her father had left.

As a child, Anna had found it hard to watch her father beat her mum. He had been a traffic policeman and a drunk. She could still picture his fat fists raining down punches. She could still remember the lumbering giant looming over her frail mum, swinging his legs back to kick her. Anna was so young when she'd watched the abuse that she hadn't known any different. It was just part of her life growing up.

By the age of nine, Anna had worked hard at being out of the house, away from the screaming and the tears and the blood. They lived on the edge of Fishponds, which, she had worked out, was within walking distance to Bristol city centre. Anna took to wandering around the shops for something to do. She couldn't stay long in each shop before a security guard or member of staff began to watch her suspiciously. Anna would only spend a few minutes in each shop to get warm before moving on to the next one. Most days, she would walk the whole length of the shopping arcades and visit every store in turn.

One day, after about six months, a group of older girls noticed Anna and followed her into the shops, calling her names. "Weirdo," they had shouted from behind her. "Tramp! Got any money, weirdo?"

Anna had been terrified and left the shop she had been in, although the gang of girls followed her. Her little nine-year-old heart thumped in terror. She had been so scared she had started running, with tears of fear blurring her vision, so that she went the wrong way and arrived at College Green, which was the wrong side of the city.

Anna had stopped to catch her breath and get her bearings when she noticed the gang of girls in the distance, looking into each shop along Park Street, obviously searching for her so they could continue their torment.

She looked around, desperate for an escape, and saw that she was standing outside the Bristol Library. The building looked like an old church, and Anna went in through the double doors, hoping to spend five minutes hidden amongst the books before she made her escape home.

Inside the library, there were two old ladies behind the counter, and thankfully, they ignored her. Unlike the shops, it was quiet and serene at the library. Feeling like a thief, Anna took a small, colourful book off the shelf and curled up on a cushion in the kids' corner. Occasionally, an old person would shuffle past and smile at her, but otherwise, she was left alone. The book was about a cat in a rocket that went to the moon, and as Anna read it in the comforting silence, she felt like she had washed up on a beautiful island after being out on a stormy sea. She felt safe.

The library became a second home to her. After school each day, and most weekends, Anna still couldn't face being at home and instead would be at the library. It was a big, old building, and it was only after a year of visiting that one day Anna put down her book and looked up at the ceiling to admire the great, curved archways and opulent patterns carved into the high ceilings. By luck, she happened to be hiding away in one of the most beautiful buildings in the city.

Anna was a young girl on her own, but she was never questioned. The staff left her alone, and the other visitors must have assumed she was with a parent who was some-where else in the building. It was a place where no money changed hands, nothing was for sale, so it had a much more relaxed feel compared to the busy shops in the city centre. She would sit for hours and enjoy the peace, away from the screaming at her home, away from the smashed crockery and ambulance visits. Anna's childhood revolved around either being in school or at the old library. She wouldn't get home until it was dark, and then she would go straight to bed. For the most part, she avoided the violence in her house.

Like an ancient, medieval church, the building with its high ceilings and endless books became her sanctuary. Nobody knew she was there; nobody cared she was there. Over time, she felt her young mind expand and develop in a pleasing way.

The library visits continued, and the years passed. It wasn't until Anna was fifteen years old that things really changed, and she stopped hiding in the library. After one terrible weekend, everything was suddenly different.

It had started on a Friday evening when it was the end-of-year school ball. A few months before, Anna had managed to get a weekend job at a clothes shop. There were a few girls from her school who also worked in the shop, and to her surprise she actually made friends with them. Anna worked every weekend and spent the entire time saving her wages to buy a dress for the ball. The week before the ball, she had picked up a blue satin dress with a Chinese pattern on it. It hugged her long legs and curved body, and she felt like a millionaire in it.

Josh Barker had asked her to the ball, and she was thrilled to accept, not only because he was the best-looking boy in her year, but also because they got on so well. Anna and her friends had put their money together and paid for a limousine to pick them up and deliver them to the venue. They were a group of four boys and four girls, and all of them looked smart and were excited for the night ahead. They sang and drank and laughed. The ball had started at seven o'clock.

On the way into the hotel hall, Josh had taken her by the hand.

"Let's have a photo together."

They stepped into the booth, and Anna felt a jolt of pleasure as Josh wrapped his arm around her waist for the photo. She could see what the camera could see on a screen behind the photographer, and Anna marvelled at how attractive Josh was in his black tuxedo. They looked good together.

Josh led her by the hand into the main hall, and they were both impressed with the décor and the band that was playing on the stage. It all looked grown up and classy, especially to a few hundred fifteen- and sixteen-year-olds.

He led her onto the dance floor, and they danced together, their bodies thrust against each other.

"You look amazing," Josh said.

"Thanks. You look good in a tux; it really suits you."

He grinned in reply and kissed her. Anna had spent most of her spare time in the library, so she had never kissed a boy before. It was as electrifying as she had hoped it would be.

That night they kissed and danced, and for Anna it was the best night of her life. There were a few teachers around the hall, but they mostly left them alone.

The Friday night went by in a happy blur, and before she

knew it, the band finished playing and left the stage. The main lights were switched on, and she blinked and grinned in the bright lights. Anna caught her friends' eyes, and she could tell by their happy faces that they were feeling the same as her, that it had been a night they would never forget. The main doors opened to reveal a long line of parents waiting to collect their kids. Before they left for the night, Josh gave Anna another long, hot kiss. In the bright lights, it somehow felt more sensual.

Slowly the teens filtered out of the hall, the entrance becoming busy with a mixture of tired-looking parents and flushed teenagers. The hall was halfway empty when she spotted her mum step into the lights of the hall.

Lurking behind her mum was the imposing outline of her father.

It seemed like everyone in the hall had spotted them at the same time as Anna, and the noise dropped to a low murmur. Her mum was five foot two, and she looked cold, even with her coat buttoned up. Her face was covered in bruises. Her nose was freshly broken, and her neck was littered with bloody scratches.

As her father stepped into the hall light, Anna could see his red hands. They were covered in blood, and he didn't try to hide them. He seemed oblivious to the stares.

Time slowed for Anna. She could see everyone looking at her parents, and suddenly it all seemed so obvious to Anna. As a child she had stayed out of the house to avoid her father, but her mum didn't have that choice. To protect her sanity, Anna had blocked out any thoughts of what was happening. But at fifteen she wasn't a child anymore, and the full realisation of how wrong the situation was came crashing into her thoughts. The look of horror on the faces of the other parents felt like a whip cracking across her chest.

"Oh, shit..." Josh said.

Anna left him and walked across the hall to her parents. With each step, she felt more and more eyes on her. Before she reached the doorway, Mr Peel, the Deputy Head teacher, approached her. He was young and thin and bookish; he had always been one of the nice ones. His face was still, but concern was evident in his eyes.

"Hey, Anna," he murmured, "you don't need to go back with them."

His voice was low enough so that only she heard him. Anna smiled weakly at the teacher.

"It's okay, sir. Thanks anyway," she replied.

She continued to the doorway and her waiting parents. The hallway was busy, but the other parents parted before them, and the three of them left the light of the hall and stepped into the shadows outside.

As they got into the car, her father turned around from the front seat and glared at Anna, who was seated in the back.

"Who was that boy you were with?"

She stared at him in silence. A street light cast a muddy orange glow into the dark car, and it made him seem even more grotesque than usual. The wounds on his hands looked blue and purple in the light. The wounds from beating her mum.

"None of your business," she told him.

For a moment, he froze in shock. Anna had never spoken to him like that. The shock quickly turned to anger, and he raised a clenched fist at her.

"You cheeky little bitch, don't talk to me like that."

"Please don't," her mum begged. "She didn't mean it."

He turned on her mum. His look was enough to make her shrink back into her seat.

Anna remained still, a look of indifference on her face. She wouldn't be cowed by this thug anymore. Her father met her eye and seemed to sense that, for once, he would be better off leaving the argument or beating to another time.

He turned back to face the front. "Watch your mouth."

Anna clenched her jaw and folded her arms.

That Friday night, Anna had hardly slept. The guilt of leaving her mum to suffer and the realisation of how wrong it all was hit her in tremulous waves. She cried silently into her pillow. The moonlight stretched across the bedroom ceiling as she lay there processing her life.

When the morning came, Anna was a different girl to the one who danced at the ball the night before.

Anna got out of bed and dressed. She tied her hair back. She threw her library cards in the bin. With a quick phone call, Anna called in sick to her job at the shop. Using the last of her money, she took a bus to the city centre and went into the police station.

At first, they didn't listen. But then she screamed and shouted and threw a bin at the counter, so they took her into a small room to calm her down. Social services were called, and she was offered temporary accommodation.

"No. I'm not leaving my mum. You need to get him out of the house," she told them.

"It's not that easy, Anna..." they had said.

She screamed.

Anna ran out of the room and burst into the main office of the police station. "My dad is beating my mum up, and you lot won't stop him!" Her shrill call shattered the placid station, and a dozen police officers jumped in shock at the noise.

They had calmed her down again and took her back into the room.

This time, Anna threatened them. She threatened to run into other police stations all over the city until someone did something. She told them she would phone the newspapers and let them know nothing was being done. She was going to get a solicitor on a *no-win-no-fee* basis and sue the social services officer. She wasn't going to stop until her dad was out of the house for ever.

That day, luck was on Anna's side. One of the police officers she had startled with her outburst happened to be the chief constable of the whole South West. He had been visiting the station when Anna made her outburst.

As Anna continued to threaten his officers, the chief constable stepped into the room. He was a big man with a friendly face. He listened to Anna in silence before asking for her address and parents' names.

He turned to the others gathered in the room and spoke firmly to them all.

"Go to Ms Wilson's house and talk to her parents. Make sure you interview the mum on her own. And give the father a good grilling. If what she says is true, then we need to have them separated."

With that, things moved quickly.

Anna, accompanied by a social worker, was taken home in the back of a police car. She was told that the first step would be to interview both her parents to make sure that what Anna had told them was true. However, when they pulled up at the house, they were greeted by the sight of her father rolling and fighting on the front lawn with another police officer. Clearly, he hadn't responded well to being asked for an interview.

Anna stepped out of the car and watched in silence as a police officer tried to arrest her father. They had a small garden at the front of the house, and her father tried to strangle the officer in the flower beds.

As he throttled the officer, her father looked up to see Anna standing with the social services lady. His eyes were wild, and he looked drunk.

"This is your doing, you bitch," he slurred loudly at Anna. "I'm going to get you for this."

He stood up and stumbled towards Anna. The social services lady gasped and moved back, but Anna stood like a statue watching him. Thankfully, more officers arrived, and they jumped on the screaming madman. Eventually, the three officers managed to get a set of handcuffs on her father. They heaved him up from the muddy lawn and dragged him over to the waiting police car. Anna watched as her father kicked out and put his foot through the car window. Shattered glass was scattered across the pavement as he turned to bite one of the officers holding him. By then, they'd had enough and shot him in the face with a bottle of mace. He cried out in pain as he fell, and this time, when they dragged him to the car, he didn't resist.

For the rest of the day, Anna had coached her mum on what to say to the police and social services. She must have said, 'Tell them what's been happening; tell them the truth,' over a hundred times. Her efforts were rewarded, because by the time the police interviewed Anna's mum, she was ready to tell them everything; it was an outpouring of terror and abuse stretching back years.

After that weekend, they had never seen the violent thug again.

Once the police told them her father would never return, Anna felt a cold, hard sense of satisfaction at a job well done. It also gave her the idea that taking control of something was always better than being a passive observer of events. From that day onwards, Anna had developed an unshakeable need to be in control.

Suddenly it had just been the two of them, just Anna and her mum.

Anna had started to stay in the house and spend more time with her mum. Within days of her father leaving, Anna and her mum had slowly come out of their shells, like two children meeting for the first time. Over the following months, they became best friends, and nothing ever came between them again.

When her mum had died the year before, it had brought Anna so much pain and a sense of choking loss.

"Hey, Mum," Anna whispered to the grave.

She finished her cleaning; the black stone and gold letters gleamed in the dull winter sun. The new flowers were yellow, red and pink, and they offered a splash of colour against a sea of black stones and green grass. She knew her mum would love the flowers. Anna wasn't religious, but she had found talking to the grave helped with the feeling of loss. It still gave her a sense of closeness to her mother.

"I did it, Mum."

Anna pulled out a small photo from her coat pocket. It was black and white and showed the outline of a tiny figure. She gently laid it on the gravestone for a moment, and her eyes glistened.

"The donations worked. I'm pregnant."

She couldn't help but smile as tears of joy trickled down her face to be whipped away by the wind.

## 6

The house was filled with the smell of roast lamb.

"Hi," Anna called out as she walked through the front door.

"How was it?" John's muffled voice asked from the kitchen.

Anna entered the kitchen to see John peeling potatoes in a bowl of water placed in the sink, a glass of red wine beside him. The oven was on, and the windows were steamed up from the boiling pots on the hob. In the far corner of the kitchen, the radio was quietly playing old pop songs.

She walked up to John and hugged him from behind. Her long, thin arms wrapped all the way around him, and his back felt warm against her cold cheek.

"Emotional as always, but nice to put some flowers down."

"How is it out there? Looks cold."

"Yes, typical freezing January weather."

"Well, the lamb is looking great; that will warm you up. What time are Lara and her new boyfriend getting here?" John asked.

"I said about seven. That wine looks good."

John turned to face her from over his shoulder with one eyebrow raised.

"It's only another four and a half months. I can wait," Anna told him.

John continued to peel the potatoes. "Christ, that doesn't sound long."

"Yeah, before you know it, there will be three of us. It's going to be amazing." Anna rested her head on John's back and squeezed him tighter.

John sighed, and his body tensed in Anna's arms. He picked up another potato from the bowl of water and scraped it using his peeler.

"What?"

"What?" he replied.

"What's with the huff?"

For a moment, Anna listened to the thin blade scraping the brown skins off the potatoes. They had been married long enough for Anna to know when he was building up to saying something, so she kept quiet.

"You know I'm not sure about all of this." He dropped the vegetable back into the water and picked up another. "Having a baby? It still doesn't sound right to me. Why can't things just stay the same?"

Anna stepped back, feeling like she had been slapped.

"John," she groaned, "we've been over this. I said if you didn't want to, then we wouldn't do it. That was a year ago. A fucking year, John."

"I said we should think about it. Before I knew it, you had some sperm donor round here."

"You looked at his details, too. You helped pick him too."

"It's not even about that guy, what's-his-face," John said.

Anna knew he could remember Doyle's name, and she thought it was childish that he always acted otherwise.

"Doyle." The word was squeezed out of her clenched teeth.

"Yeah, Doyle. It's not about him. It's about us having a baby. Us being parents. I told you I'm not ready to be a dad. Our life is great. We can do what we want, when we want. Having a baby is going to be so much work and will really restrict us."

"Not ready? We're both nearly forty! We'll never be ready. John, I told you how important this was to me. How much I want us to have our own family, and only now you tell me you're not sure?" Anna stepped away from him with her arms folded. "Now?"

This felt like an ambush, after months of trying to get John to talk to her, he had caught her off guard, and she wasn't in the right mindset to have this conversation with him now. His timing was awful.

"Is this about you not being able to get me pregnant?"

"It's nothing to do with that!" John exploded.

He threw the potato he had been peeling into the bowl, splashing them both with dirty water.

"I said I wasn't sure. I said I needed time. We've got a good life, and now it's all down the pan because we're going to be tied down with a bloody baby."

"You've been avoiding talking about the baby. Every time I've mentioned it, you've pushed me away." Anna's voice grew louder as she struggled to control her bubbling anger. "I've been trying for months to talk to you. Why are you suddenly bringing this up now?"

He ignored the question. "One minute we're all happy; the next you want a baby. Then we find out we can't get pregnant and we've got to use some sperm donor."

John had turned to face her, clutching the peeling knife. His wet apron dripped onto the tiled floor. Without thinking about it, Anna stepped towards him like a street brawler, hands clenched and face turning red with rage.

"Well, it's a bit late now, isn't it? Now we've spent thousands of pounds, and I'm four months pregnant." She wanted to add a few insults but held back.

John's face twisted under a deep frown. "Your problem is you're a control freak. You've always got to be in control, taking charge, running ahead with things. You never stop to think about other people."

"Come on, then, let's talk about it now. I don't care that you're infertile."

John took a step towards Anna, their noses almost touching.

"Fuck you!" he screamed at her.

"Fuck you!" she screamed back at him.

---

Two hours later, Anna and John opened the front door to greet their guests. Lara stepped into the hallway, armed with a bottle of wine.

"Hiya," Lara sang, filling the hallway with her big voice, bigger hair, and huge personality. "This is Dave."

A squat man stepped into the hallway, holding another bottle of wine. He had a rugged face, as if he always spent his days outside.

"Nice to meet you," he said with a broad Northern accent.

Dave had a friendly face, but looked nothing like Lara's usual type of partner, especially with his plain green jumper, cream chinos and sensible shoes. Anna never thought she would see her best friend with a man who wore chinos. She looked at her Lara with an amused twinkle.

"Nice to meet you, Dave. Please come in," Anna said.

"Something smells good," Dave said.

"I'm doing a leg of lamb. It's been marinating all morning. Can I get you a beer, Dave?" John asked.

"Aye, beer sounds great, thanks."

John led them through to the kitchen. He opened a fresh bottle of red wine, and Lara gratefully accepted a large glass, leaving a smudge of glittering pink lipstick on the rim. John poured Dave a beer as both men peered into the oven to admire the roasting lamb.

"John's been busy all afternoon, bless him." Anna smiled towards John, who smiled back towards her although they wouldn't look each other in the eye.

Their earlier argument was unresolved and would still be going if it weren't for their dinner guests. Like most husbands and wives, politeness in front of guests had stilled their screaming. Anna and Lara walked through to the lounge and left the men with the meat.

"Cheers," Lara said as she sat on the grey corner sofa and tilted her glass to Anna.

The lounge smelt clean and fresh. The plush grey carpet was freshly vacuumed, the flowery curtains were neatly tied back, and the flat-screen television glistened in the lamplight. Not a speck of dust was visible.

Anna sipped her lemonade and hoped that, with the ice and slice of lemon, it looked like a gin and tonic to Lara. *God, I want a real gin*, Anna thought.

"Cheers," Anna replied.

"How's the new term going?"

"Really busy, but I know it will get better. The students are still as dozy as ever."

Lara laughed.

"Oh, it's nice to have a drink. This week has been crazy."

"Dave seems nice," Anna said, a huge grin on her face.

Lara returned the grin. "Go on then, say it."

"What?"

"He's not my usual type?"

"Isn't he?" Anna asked, pulling an innocent face.

Lara laughed and flicked the curly hair from her face.

"He's a builder, and he's from up North."

It was Anna's turn to laugh.

"Yeah, I noticed."

"He's from Penrith. Or the Pennines. Somewhere north of Manchester. Where the hell is that?"

Anna smiled and shook her head.

"And he's a builder." Lara lowered her voice. "He's always got dirt under his fingernails. You know, from working outside all the time."

Anna laughed again.

"Little Ms Cosmopolitan has got herself a bit of rough?"

Lara snorted and playfully dropped her head in her hands.

"What am I doing?"

"Hey, I'm teasing. He seems really nice," Anna said.

"Really?" Lara asked hopefully.

"Really."

"It's just that I'm so bored of the usual men and the usual dates. I just want something like you have with John."

Anna sipped her drink as her eyes fell to her feet.

"I always remember that night you met John. We were in the student union bar. We were so pissed. You had just split up with that older bloke..."

"Phil."

"Yes, Phil. You spent all night moaning about men and how you were going to be single forever. What was the thing you kept repeating?"

"I hated arrogance. Arrogant men were the worst."

"Ha, yes, that's it. You hated all men, but the arrogant ones were the worst," Lara said.

Anna thought back to that night and how drunk she had

been. The place had been packed with students, the music blaring out from the DJ booth. John had walked in on his own, but had been treated like a celebrity: Everyone was saying hello to him, giving him hugs and high fives...even the DJ gave him a shout-out on the microphone. Anna had watched as the barman had a drink ready for John by the time he reached the bar. It was like he owned the place, although Anna later found out he was just really popular around the university.

Lara and Anna had been watching from a table.

"What an arsehole," Lara had called over the music to her friend.

"Yes, complete knobhead," Anna had replied without conviction.

She felt Lara watching her watch John.

"What?"

"I thought you were off men?" Lara called out.

"I was. I mean I am."

Lara had laughed so hard she had spilt the drinks on their table.

Anna had made her way through the busy bar to John and introduced herself. Despite his bold entrance, John had a humble demeanour that drew Anna in. They had spent the night talking and dancing together.

Anna smiled at the memory. It was strange to think back now at how in love her and John once were. The love was still there now, but it had mellowed with time. Perhaps age mellows every emotion, even love. For a second, Anna could remember that feeling and felt a stab of loss for it. Is that why people had affairs, she wondered, to try to capture that feeling of a new, all-consuming love?

"It's like, since that night at university you two have been so close. Being single is starting to get boring," Lara said.

"Well, like I said, Dave seems like a decent guy. I'm sure you'll have some fun together."

Anna sipped her fake gin and tonic and thought about her earlier argument with John. They still had a lot to talk about.

"Dinner is served," John called to them.

Anna and Lara entered the dining room to see Dave already sat at the table, eyeing the huge bowl of roast potatoes. As the women sat down, John arrived carrying a platter with a huge leg of lamb glistening on top of it. The smell of roast meat instantly hit them. Lamb was her favourite, and John often made it for her. She looked at the meat. He was always trying to make her happy.

"Well done, chef," Lara said.

"That looks amazing," Dave said.

"I'll carve," John told them. "Lara, pass me your plate."

The food was served, and the room became quiet as they ate.

"These roast potatoes are incredible, John, although it looks like you've done enough for ten people."

John and Anna looked at each other.

"Thanks."

They ate and drank and talked. Dave proved to be good company, happy to listen to the three friends telling old stories and new anecdotes. At the end of the meal, Anna once again caught John's eye and gave him a small, expectant nod. At first he ignored his wife and sipped his beer. Anna stared pointedly at him, and eventually he acknowledged her and looked at Lara.

Forcing a smile, John cleared his throat.

"We've got some news."

Lara and Dave looked up, attentive and curious.

"Well." John paused, clearly trying to find the words. He shifted in his seat and took another sip of his beer.

Anna couldn't wait: "I'm pregnant."

Lara's mouth fell open.

"Wow! That's amazing. Congratulations," Lara said as she leaned over and hugged Anna.

Dave shook John's hand.

"Brilliant news, mate. Well done."

"Honestly, of all the people I know, I thought you would be the last to have a baby. I can't believe it's actually happened," Lara said.

Anna beamed. She could see the surprise on her friend's face, but she could also see real happiness at the news. Anna thought back to John's response to the news a few months ago, about how underwhelmed he had been. It was great to finally get such a positive response.

"I'm so excited," Anna burst out.

"I thought it was just something you were thinking about?" Lara asked.

"Well, things have progressed. We've been trying for a while, and now, I'm four months pregnant." Anna looked at John, who seemed focused on his plate. "We're both really pleased."

"Well, I think it's brilliant. You are going to be an amazing mum."

Anna couldn't keep the huge smile from her face. "Thank you."

"I suppose that explains why you didn't come out for our Christmas drinks this year?" Lara asked with a big smile.

Anna laughed. "Yes, sorry about that, I've been trying to avoid any temptation of a drink." She waved her drink at Lara. "I'm purely on the lemonade for a while."

"I've got my niece's old pushchair in the attic if you want it; it's hardly been used," Dave said. "It's a good one, too. Solid wheels on it. A real good runner."

"Bit of a petrolhead, eh, Dave?" John asked.

"It's top of the range that, but yes, I love me cars," Dave replied.

"Oh, I'm just so pleased for you. We'll babysit too, won't we, Dave?" Lara said.

"Oh, aye. Lara can watch the baby while I look after your beer fridge."

They all laughed, even John, who seemed to be finding the sense of goodwill intoxicating.

"Let's have a toast," Lara said, raising her glass of red wine. "To the new Wilson baby. Cheers."

They all raised their glasses.

"Cheers," they called in unison.

As they drank their toast to the new baby, the doorbell rang. The chime was loud and seemed to cut through the room.

Anna looked to the clock on the wall, which told her it was nine o'clock. She then looked to John, seeing if he knew who could be at the front door. John looked back at her blankly and gave a small shrug. They weren't expecting anyone.

"It's probably the old lady at number four looking for her cat again," John said.

"I'll get it," Anna said, standing up from the table.

John stood up also. "I'll get the desserts. Won't be a moment."

Anna left the dining room. John followed her out.

She spoke to John over her shoulder as she walked through the kitchen. "I think we need another bottle of wine."

"No problem. I'll get Dave another beer, too."

He smiled at her, and she noticed that his head was up and his shoulders were dropped; the tension he had been carrying around with him had gone. It was the most relaxed she had seen him in weeks. The evening meal and sharing their news had obviously been good for him.

Anna walked through the kitchen and out to the hallway. Behind the glass of the front door, she could see two figures stood out in the darkness.

She hesitated. Who could be calling on them at this time of night?

From the kitchen, John could see she had stopped. "Everything alright?" he called to her.

"Yes," she replied. "Just wondering who it is."

The uncertain tone in her voice summoned John from the kitchen, and he walked down the hallway towards her. He was carrying a fresh bottle of red wine and a bottle opener.

"Open it," John said, his tone reassuring.

Anna opened the front door.

A man and woman were standing there. They both wore suits and long coats. The man looked to be in his early sixties. He was tall, and his face had too much skin on it, as if he had recently lost a lot of weight. The woman was tall, broad-shouldered and black. She had a warm smile and cold eyes.

"Mr and Mrs Wilson?" the man asked gruffly.

He looked like he knew the answer, but was obliged to ask anyway.

Anna didn't say anything.

"Yes?" John replied from behind his wife.

"We're detectives with Avon and Somerset Constabulary," the woman informed them. "I'm Detective Wright, and this" – she nodded to the old man beside her – "is Detective Gleadless."

"I know who he is," Anna said.

Anna couldn't take her eyes off the man.

The old man stared back at her, their eyes locked onto each other.

"We need to speak with you. Do you have a few moments?" Detective Wright asked politely.

The cold winter air felt biting to Anna. The sense of happiness and warmth from the evening was ripped away in the wind.

"What's this about?" John asked.

"It would be better to talk inside," Detective Wright replied.

John seemed to sense his wife's discomfort, and he laid a hand on her shoulder.

"Anna?"

"John," Anna said, "meet my father."

## 7

John and Anna were standing close to each other in the kitchen. The detectives stood opposite them, near the kitchen door. Detective Wright watched them while Detective Gleadless looked around the large space. His eyes lingered on the old holiday photos stuck on the fridge. Anna thought they made an odd pair: an old man and a tough-looking black woman, both wearing long coats and suits.

"You have guests?" Detective Wright asked them, her voice quiet and even.

Anna studied her. She was tall and masculine except for the bright red lipstick. Despite having the build of a man, she was strikingly beautiful, with high cheekbones and full lips. She wore a friendly smile, but her eyes were cold and lifeless, like they were stuck on. Beneath her cream trench coat, she was wearing a smart navy suit and blouse.

"Some friends over for dinner," John replied.

"Maybe you should ask them to leave?" Detective Wright suggested softly.

"Why?" John asked.

"So we can talk."

"What are you looking at?" Anna snapped at her father.

He glared at her with his sour, gnarled face.

"Just looking," he growled, like a rabid dog.

He had lost weight since she had last seen him, but he was still bulky, like an old bull. His bald head was mottled, and his nose had grown too big for his saggy face. Even though his dark coat hid most of his black suit, Anna could still see that it was a bad fit and crumpled out of shape. She suspected that despite his old age, he could still throw a punch. That he could still kick a defenceless woman as she lay screaming in terror.

His face held a thousand memories for her, and none of them were good.

"What do you want? You're not welcome here," Anna said.

She realised it was a mistake to invite them into the house, and she wanted to throw them both out. Anna's breath became short as memories of her childhood came back to her. She had images of him beating her mum. He would stumble and weave into their small two-bed house in Bristol, his balance gone due to the alcohol. Within an instant, the bawling would start. They had learnt not to rise to it, because if they did, he would steam in with his fists.

"We're here in an official capacity. We have some questions for you," he told her.

"Still a traffic copper? Want some information on a speeding car?" Anna sneered at him.

John looked sideways at his wife.

He seemed unnerved by her, as if he had never seen her acting in such a way. Anna had never talked to John about her father. Only in the briefest terms had she told him about her childhood and teen years. For his part, he had always understood she didn't want to talk about it, so he had never asked. Anna ignored John's look, trying desperately to control her rising anger before she did something that got her arrested.

"I'm not on traffic anymore," he told his daughter. "I'm a detective now."

"I bet you're still a bastard, though."

"Let's keep this civil, shall we?" Detective Wright interjected.

The door that led into the lounge opened, and Lara appeared.

"We're going to head off," Lara whispered loudly.

"You don't need to," John told her.

Anna looked at her friend in the doorway without really seeing her, and nodded. Beside her, Anna could sense that John felt confused, that he was unsure what was happening.

"I'll call you tomorrow," Anna told Lara.

Within a few seconds, they heard the sound of the front door opening and closing. Anna felt grateful that Lara was discreet enough to leave, but it saddened her to think that the happy moment they had been sharing together had ended so abruptly.

John moved towards the kettle. "Would you like a drink?"

"No," Anna's voice boomed out, "not for them. I'm not making him a coffee."

Anna glared at her father. He glared back at her.

Like an old bull, she knew he would charge at her if she pushed him too much. Detective Wright seemed to be ignoring the tension between father and daughter.

"Forget the coffee. We need information," he growled.

Anna huffed and walked into the dining room to clear away the dinner plates. The serving bowls of food were all empty apart from the large bowl of roast potatoes. There was still a mound of them left because John had peeled and roasted too many.

Her hands were shaking.

Anna grabbed the back of a chair to steady herself as a wave of dizziness washed over her head. A scream was threatening to explode from her, but she bit her cheek to stop it.

She couldn't believe he was here. The horrible, abusive man who had conceived her. Her only living parent. She didn't want him in her house, especially not near her tiny, unborn baby. The last time Anna had seen her father had been the awful weekend when she was fifteen years old and she'd had him arrested.

Anna's mind drifted back to that weekend in April.

It had taken so long for her and her mum to put their lives back together after he had been dragged away by the police.

Once her father had gone, that first night at home together her mum had made her fish and chips for dinner. The fish was dry, and the chips were burnt, but Anna had loved it. It was the first meal they'd had together, just her and her mum. They sat watching each other eat, smiling awkwardly, like they were on a first date. Occasionally, a flash of pain would come over her mum's bruised face as she tried to chew a chip.

"This tastes great, Mum."

"Think I've overdone the fish."

"Nah, adds to the flavour."

Her mum laughed at that before wincing and holding her jaw in her small hands. Tears of pain crept into the corners of her eyes. At fifteen years old, Anna was already taller than her mum, who was not only short but thin and wiry. She looked like she would blow away in a strong wind, and it broke Anna's heart to see how much pain and discomfort her mum was in.

Anna stood up and took their empty plates. "Well, you cooked, so I should wash up."

"I can do it," her mum said.

"No, let me. Maybe you could dry them?"

"Alright."

Anna had run the hot water and squirted some washing-up liquid into the small sink. There was a radio on the kitchen windowsill, and she turned it on.

Her mum tensed. "We shouldn't have the radio on."

"Why not, Mum?"

"Well..." Her mum looked terrified. "The music is too loud..."

Anna wrapped her arms around her mum in a gentle hug. Her mum felt so frail, like a poor wounded animal. Anna willed herself not to cry, to be brave for her.

"We need to make sure he never comes back, Mum. You need to get an injunction on him," Anna said.

Her mum stirred in her arms. "I don't want to make a fuss..."

"I'll help you. We can do it together," Anna said.

Her mum didn't reply, and Anna realised she would need time to think about it. Anna didn't push her, feeling sure that her mum would do the right thing.

"Come on, let's wash these dishes."

Anna turned to the sink and started scrubbing a pot. Her mum picked up a tea towel and began drying the cleaned pots and crockery.

A Spice Girls song came on the radio.

"I love this new band. Everyone was singing this song at school today."

"Is this those girls always wearing them skimpy outfits?"

Anna laughed and started to sing along with the radio. Out of the corner of her eye, she could see her mum looking around nervously as if their dad would burst through the door at any second. Anna ignored it and started dancing as she sang and washed up.

Towards the end of the song, her mum had started to hum along too. It made Anna so happy.

The following day Anna helped her mum fill out the paperwork and apply for an injunction. Anna knew it would enrage her dad, but she hoped he would stick to it. An emergency injunction was granted that stopped her dad coming back to the house, or anywhere near them, and a few days later, a letter arrived in the post with their court date on it.

Every evening that week, they ate and washed up together. By the end of the first week, her mum was singing along with Anna and the radio.

Within a few weeks of her dad's arrest, they went down to the Bristol court together. Her mum's injuries had been so bad that she still had a purple face and the remains of a black eye. Anna had held her mum's hand through the court hearing, but it had all been easier than what they'd been expecting. Her dad didn't attend court, and the judge was sympathetic to them. Their case only lasted twenty minutes before they were granted a permanent Occupation Order. It meant that her dad was not allowed to come to the house or the surrounding area. It was a huge relief for them both.

Afterwards, they went to a café to celebrate and had drinks and cakes at a small table window. Her mum cried, and Anna hugged her.

"You did it, Mum. He won't be able to hurt you anymore."

Her mum had smiled. "Thanks for your help. I don't think I could have done it without you."

They hugged each other and cried, but for Anna they were tears of happiness; she finally had a mum and a home.

They were like two long-lost sisters. Like two survivors of a great storm, bonded by the suffering they had gone through and both happy just to be together. They discovered that they could wear what they wanted, talk to who they wanted, and chat and gossip together like two old friends. It was the late

'90s, the time of *Girl Power* and short skirts, and suddenly they were living their lives. The weeks turned to months, and the months to years. She never saw her father again.

She had not seen her father in twenty years.

And now he had returned.

Anna piled the plates up in the dining room and paused. She tried to catch her breath, tried to stop her mind from whirring. For so many years, Anna had worked hard to forget about her father. She had thrown herself into her studies and then her work, always pushing herself to keep her mind busy so that it never had a chance to dwell on old memories. Seeing him now was too much to process. She wanted to run into the kitchen and jump on him and scream at him.

Anna picked up the pile of dirty plates, took a deep breath, and walked back into the kitchen.

"You've got thirty seconds, then you need to leave," Anna said.

"Fine."

Her father dug into his coat pocket and produced a small colour photograph. He stepped forward, laid it on the marble worktop and slid it across to John and Anna with one stubby finger.

"Do you know this man?" he asked.

Anna refused to look at the photo.

She placed the dirty crockery in the sink, folded her arms and looked at the ceiling spotlights. Even his voice made her angry. Anna thought back to hearing him shout at her and her mum. Even though he had always been drunk, it was never enough alcohol to stop him from thinking up the most cutting insults.

"No. Now leave."

John leant down to look at the photo on the kitchen counter.

"Yes. We know this man."

The tone of her husband's voice caused Anna to falter, and despite herself, she looked down at the photo on the kitchen counter.

It was a photo of Doyle Kennedy.

The photo looked like a mug shot, with Doyle facing the camera. Even in the small picture, he still looked cool and relaxed.

"In what capacity do you know this man?" Detective Wright asked as she pulled a small notebook and pencil out of her coat pocket.

"Why?" Anna replied.

Her father snapped and pointed at Anna.

"You can answer our questions here or down at the station. But you need to answer them."

"What my partner means is," Detective Wright said, "once you've answered our questions, we'll leave. We found your details in amongst his things, and we need to understand how you know each other."

John looked to his wife, waiting to follow her lead.

Anna leant back on the counter and kept her arms folded. "We bought something from him. He came to the house a couple of times, but we haven't seen him in a few months, not since late September."

"What did you buy?" Wright asked.

Anna clenched her jaw. "That's none of your business."

"We need to know."

John turned to his wife. He gently laid a hand on her arm and gave it a squeeze, which was reassuring.

"We need to tell them," he said softly.

Anna looked at her husband, thankful that he was remaining calm. She was so angry, but it was the embarrassment that had turned her face red. It was such a happy evening; Anna had been looking forward to it for weeks. Why did her father have to suddenly appear on their doorstep and ruin it?

Anna controlled herself and studied her father's face in the bright kitchen light. He seemed a lot older, but she didn't think he had changed much. The man still seemed as callous and unrelenting as she remembered him.

Anna exhaled loudly.

"He was a sperm donor. We found him online and paid for several donations," Anna told them.

Anna could see both detectives digesting this news. Detective Wright wrote something in her small black notebook.

"He was a sperm donor?" Wright confirmed.

"Yes."

"Why did you stop using him?" she asked Anna.

"It worked."

"It worked?"

"I'm pregnant."

Wright and Gleadless looked at each other. The news seemed to throw them off balance. Their eyes communicated something to each other, but the message was lost on Anna.

"You're going to be a granddad, partner."

"By Doyle Kennedy?"

"I'm going to be the baby's father," John said quietly.

Gleadless looked at John, his dark eyes piercing and amused.

"Firing blanks, eh?"

"Leave him alone," Anna snapped.

John frowned at the detective, and his shoulders tensed. "We've told you what you wanted to know, so now you can leave."

Gleadless looked back at his daughter.

"How did you contact him? Did he give you a phone number or email address?"

Anna rummaged through the kitchen drawer and pulled out Doyle's business card. She slammed the drawer shut.

"Here. This is what we used to text and email him."

"We will need you to come to the station tomorrow and make a proper statement. We need all the details from you."

"I'll come down in the morning," John replied.

Wright nodded as she pocketed the business card. "Both of you will need to come."

Anna didn't reply. Instead, she turned to her father.

"What has he done? Why are you investigating him?"

He looked at her, his face still the battered lump of meat she remembered from her childhood.

"It's confidential," Wright said.

Gleadless caught his partner's eye.

"They should be told," Gleadless suggested.

Anna could see that her father would take delight in telling them why they were investigating Doyle. She knew it was bad news, and that was why he would share it with them. Anna had spent most of her life hating this man; seeing him then, she knew that she was right. That he deserved to be hated, especially by his only daughter.

"We are very interested in Doyle Kennedy. He is the main suspect in several murder cases that we are lead investigators on."

"Murder?"

"Three women have been murdered in Bristol over the past few years, and we believe it is the same killer for all three. Right now, Doyle Kennedy is the lead suspect."

Anna felt like she had been punched in the stomach.

Her legs felt weak, and it took all of her focus to walk to the breakfast bar and sit on a stool. Doyle was a murderer? He had been into their house. She had liked him and felt like there had been a connection between them.

Anna was carrying a murderer's baby?

"Proper piece of work this guy is," her father continued. "A real psycho."

Anna glanced up to see her father looking delighted at her shock.

"Get out."

# PART II

## 8

Anna wept. She paced the lounge as tears streamed down her face.

Her father and Detective Wright had left the house. She was glad they were gone, but she also wanted to ask them some questions. Anna's mind raced with the information they had given her.

"He's a killer? Three women. And they said there could be more?"

"We don't know that yet," John replied.

He was slumped on an armchair in the corner of the lounge.

"Doyle seemed so normal," she continued. "Just a normal guy. He said family was important to him. It couldn't be him, could it?"

"I don't know."

"I'm giving birth to a..." Anna couldn't finish the sentence, but screamed instead.

It was a scream of anguish that echoed out of the lounge and around their home.

The awful noise seemed to snap John out of his dark

reverie. He jumped up and wrapped his arms around Anna. She tried to push him away, but he held on tight. Anna's instinct was to keep pacing, but after a moment she stopped fighting him, and instead buried her face into his chest. Anna wept long, deep sobs as John held her.

"How could this happen? Our sperm donor is a murderer?"

Tears and mascara stained John's shirt.

"How about a drink?" he asked her gently.

"Not while I'm pregnant."

"I think one won't hurt. It will calm you after that bloody bombshell."

Anna sniffed. "Alright."

John stepped away from her, and she sat heavily onto the grey corner sofa, her head in her hands. She felt awful. Her mind felt like it was scrabbling up a vertical hill to try to comprehend the news. The fact that her father had been the messenger made it worse. Over twenty years of not seeing each other. Then he unexpectedly shows up, and she has to tell him that she is pregnant by a sperm donor who is now a suspected murderer. Anna had hoped to never speak to her father again, especially not to have such a heart-wrenching conversation.

John returned from the kitchen and handed her a gin and tonic in a long crystal glass. Anna gulped at it and gasped. It was bitterly strong, and the icy bubbles needled her lips, but it was just what she needed.

"What did they say again? Doyle is their main suspect? Does that mean nothing has been proven?" John asked.

"They made it sound like there was a lot of evidence."

"Jesus. Of all the things I thought they would tell us. A bloody murderer? Imagine if it's true. He's been in our house. He could have killed us, for Christ's sake."

"It's crazy. John, I can't be carrying..." Again, Anna couldn't finish the thought.

Instead, she jumped up from the sofa and lashed out with her foot, kicking a cushion that was on the floor. She started pacing again, and for a moment, the ice clinking in her glass was the only sound in the room. John returned to his armchair and knocked back the large whisky he had poured for himself.

"If it's true," John said after a while, "we would always be associated with a murderer. An actual serial killer. How would we even tell our child?"

Anna stopped her pacing and looked at him. She couldn't bring herself to answer and instead sat back down on the sofa and sipped her drink.

"And what if people found out? You know what social media is like. The stigma." John spoke in a trance of torrid thoughts. "They would be bullied, labelled a killer's kid, hounded. Can you imagine how hard it would be for them to live a normal life? How difficult it would be for the three of us?"

Tears rolled down Anna's cheeks and into her glass. She wanted to tell John to shut up, but he was only saying what she couldn't bring herself to think about. She caught an image of herself in years to come, sitting at the kitchen table with her child, trying to explain that their biological father was a serial killer. Someone who was twisted, who enjoyed causing extreme suffering to others. How would the child react? How would *she* react if someone told her that one of her parents was a psychotic murderer? It would almost be too much to comprehend, too much to process. If it was her, she knew she would always feel tainted in some way.

Of course, there was the option of not saying anything, but surely it would be even worse if they found out in some other way?

Anna felt sick and was torn between getting up for another gin or rushing to the bathroom to throw up.

Over the past few months, she had imagined a world full of only family love, but in reality, there would now be a dark cloud hanging over them. A terrible, dark cloud.

Was she carrying the seed of evil in her body?

"I need another gin."

John drained his glass and went to the kitchen.

"What if Doyle is the killer?" John asked when he returned with their drinks. "Will it affect the baby? Is that a thing?" He paused. "Is being a serial killer hereditary?"

John handed Anna her second gin and tonic and returned to his armchair.

"What if we have the baby and it starts acting weird?" John continued. "We're always going to be worried. Always watching and worrying about them too much. That can't be good for the kid. Can't be healthy."

"It would always be on my mind," Anna whispered.

She set her fresh glass down on the coffee table and held her stomach. When Anna was six years old, her parents had taken her to Weston-super-Mare beach, where she had accidentally stepped on a fishing hook that caught in the soft skin of her foot. The hook was still tied to some fishing line buried in the sand. Every time she'd tried to move away, the hook held her in place, pulling at her flesh, so that her blood and tears mixed in the sand. Anna had that same feeling of pain and helplessness now. Her maternal instinct was causing the same tugging agony; she wanted to run away from this nightmare, but she couldn't.

"Son of a bitch," John said. "I'd like to ask that Irish twat some questions myself. What the hell has he been up to? Should we have suspected him? I mean, he was too familiar around here, making himself at home." He sipped his drink and stared at Anna. "But then he's a good-looking sod; maybe we just fell for his Irish charms?"

Anna didn't look at John. Instead, she picked up her glass and gulped at it.

---

LATER, Anna lay on the sofa with her head on a small pink cushion and her hands covering her stomach. The gin had had the desired effect of calming her, but now she felt guilty for having alcohol while pregnant. John sat slouched over the corner armchair, holding his whisky and staring up at the ceiling. Only the small lamp on the windowsill had been switched on, so the room seemed gloomy. The coffee table between them was littered with used tissues covered in mascara.

"Don't you do this sort of thing at work?" John slurred.

"Huh?"

"Psychology. The human brain." He waved his whisky glass in front of him. "Can't you tell if someone is going to turn out like their biological father?"

It was a good question. Anna thought about it, but she didn't want to try to answer it. Her mind was filled with facts and theories about children inheriting a parent's traits and the impact on a person's biology. The gin she'd had was making her feel both lethargic and sick.

"It's all about genetics," she said.

"So?"

"Right now, the schools of thought are leaning towards nativism, I suppose."

John gave a little dismissive shake of his head. "What I'm asking is, what are the odds? Say Doyle is this bona fide psycho killer the police reckon he is. What are the odds that we have this baby and it grows up to be like that? That the kid starts bloody murdering people?"

Tears rolled down Anna's cheeks and into her ears as she held her stomach tighter.

"Like a million to one? Or are we talking less than that?"

"Less," Anna whispered.

John exhaled. "Less? What, one in a thousand?"

"Honestly, John, I don't know. No one knows really. There have been so many studies done, but there's nothing definitive everyone agrees on. There's a lot of information, but no real knowledge."

"It's the twenty-first century! How the hell don't scientists know this yet?"

Anna tapped her head. "People have a lot of stuff going on up here. You're talking about the molecular genetic architecture of personality."

"No, I'm not. I'm talking about odds. What are the odds that our baby inherits their biological father's bloodthirsty personality?"

Anna tried to clear her mind. She tried to think logically, like a university lecturer, with the facts she knew on genetic psychology, but she was too upset to think clearly. Dates, names and facts swam in her mind alongside flashes of blue eyes and broad shoulders. She took several shaky deep breaths.

"The chances of inheriting a parent's violent genes are around forty percent." Burning acid crawled up her throat.

John sat up. "Forty percent?!"

"There is one in particular called the MAOA enzyme. It's nicknamed the Warrior Gene. Violent people have a low activity of it in the brain."

"You can inherit this Warrior Gene?"

"Yes, but it's not all about your genes. It's only when people have a low MAOA activity that's then combined with a terrible childhood – being abused and stuff like that – which can lead them to become violent."

"So forty percent chance the child has this gene thing, and if we slap them about, they're going to turn nasty?"

"It's not that simple."

"But we won't be abusing our child anyway, so that shouldn't be an issue."

"Abuse can be from someone else. It could be a small fight in the playground with another child that could trigger them to switch personality."

John slumped back in the armchair.

"It's a bloody minefield." He drank some whisky. "And I don't like the sound of this Warrior Gene."

"Scientists have been trying to find a link between violent behaviour and genetics for years. Every year, a new study comes out. Some scientists support it. Some call it all crap. I think what has been proven for sure is that men with low-level MAOA who experience violence in their childhood are much more likely to grow up to be violent men."

"And in our case, by 'violent' you mean being a killer. Growing up to be a killer."

"There have been studies done where violent people have tended to have violent ancestors; they've traced it back to show it's all been in the family for generations. But then there are thousands, probably millions of people out there today with low MAOA activity who are normal, happy people."

"Which brings me back to my original question. What are the odds that, if Doyle is a murderer, the kid could turn out like that, too?"

Anna dabbed at her tears. That morning, she had been reading about the baby she was carrying. When she had read that its heart was already formed, she hadn't been able to stop grinning at the thought of that tiny heart beating inside her.

"Honestly, John, I just don't know. I don't think anyone would ever really know. From all the research I've seen, I think there is a link between a person's genetics and violent behaviour, but the odds of it being passed down from person to person are very low. It's just a risk we need to take."

Anna sat up and looked at John, who was now tapping away on his mobile phone.

"Did you hear what I said?"

John squinted at the screen of his phone. "Rostov Ripper," he muttered.

"What?"

"Russian guy who killed fifty people; years later, his son was arrested for stabbing someone."

"Jesus, John."

"Huh, I don't believe it. Fred West's son…"

"John."

"He was arrested for having sex with underage girls and…"

Anna screamed in frustration: "Turn that clickbait crap off."

He lowered the phone. "Sorry."

---

LATER, they lay in bed. A sliver of light from the street lamp outside the house pierced the curtains, and it was just enough for them to see each other. John had his head buried into the pillow. Anna lay on her back, staring at the ceiling.

"Your father is an arsehole, by the way," he said into the pillow.

"I know."

"Now I can see why you want nothing to do with him."

She didn't reply, and the silence drifted along. John's

breathing became heavier, and she thought he'd fallen asleep.

"What about an abortion?" John suddenly asked into the darkness.

The word was like a kick. Anna wanted to shout at John; she wanted to protest loudly and argue against it, but in that moment, she didn't move. Her eyes filled again, and she wondered if a person could run out of tears from crying too much.

Eventually she said, "No way. I'm not having an..." The word caught in her throat. "I'm not doing that. We've tried so hard to get pregnant, John. I want us to have a family so much."

"I know," he replied.

Since her mum had died, it felt like her eyes had been opened. She'd looked at her life, at the things she thought were important, and realised none of it mattered unless you had a family to share it with. When they had learned about John being infertile, it had come as a blow to them both, but Anna's controlling nature had taken over. She had sped ahead with getting a sperm donor. It had put a strain on her and John, but she'd felt like the means would justify the end. Having an abortion now would put them back to the start. Not only that, it would mean killing the baby growing inside her.

Beside her, she could hear John starting to gently snore into his pillow. The clock on the nightstand told her it was two thirty in the morning, but she couldn't sleep.

She rolled out of the bed, walked across the landing and into the office room.

There were two desks in the room, one each for her and John. Anna sat at her desk, which she used when working from home. She clicked on her small table lamp. Her laptop was still open from the previous day. She powered it on.

The white light from the screen hurt her eyes, and she realised she still felt a little drunk. It had only been two drinks, but she wasn't used to it. The gin had sunk down into her body, and already a hangover was creeping into her temples to join the guilt she felt at having a drink while pregnant.

Anna logged into the computer and typed 'Bristol murders' into the news search bar. The computer threw up a mass of historic stories, but there were also more recent ones, stories she wasn't even aware of. Anna always thought she kept up to date with the news, but she realised it was usually Brexit or who was going to be the next Prime Minister, and less about local news. Locally, girls had been getting murdered.

She flicked through various stories, after a while finding three murders that were linked. Could they be the ones Doyle was supposedly responsible for?

The first story was about a girl called Rachel White, aged twenty-four. She had gone missing after a night out with friends, nine months ago. Her body had been found in a shallow grave on the outskirts of Bristol. The story told of hundreds of bite marks over the dead body, as well as evidence of sexual assault. The bright computer screen showed her an image of a deep bite mark on pale skin. Anna's stomach threatened to be sick, but she still clicked on another link.

This article was about a girl called Abby. Abby had been a nineteen-year-old graphic designer who was murdered by strangulation and stabbing two years ago. Her body had been found by a dog walker in the village of Keynsham, which was situated between Bath and Bristol. Once again there were bite marks discovered on the corpse.

Anna spied half a bottle of water on the shelf beside her

desk and drank it in one long gulp. The light was still hurting her eyes, but she couldn't help but click on a third link.

It was a story about Ruth Collins. It didn't list her age, but in the photo, she looked older than the other girls. Maybe thirty? Her big brown eyes stared back at Anna from the screen. The story explained how no one had even known Ruth was missing; it was only by chance that her body had been discovered in a commercial bin behind a restaurant in the city. Once again, Anna read that she had been sexually assaulted, and there were deep teeth marks all over the body. The story of Ruth's murder was eight years old, which was when Doyle had been a student at Bath University.

Flicking through the stories, Anna saw the pattern that the police had reported on. All three girls had been attractive and murdered by suffocation or strangulation. They also had bite marks all over their bodies.

Anna thought about Doyle. He was handsome, and it was one of the reasons she had chosen him. Reluctantly, Anna opened one of the desk drawers and pulled out her thick file on Doyle. She laid it on top of the desk and slowly opened the folder.

The first page in there was Anna's tick sheet, a list of all the things she wanted from a sperm donor. It was so typical of her and her organisational habits. Without thinking about it, Anna had listed things she would want for her child, knowing that if the father had these things, then her son or daughter would likely inherit them, too. Her eyes flitted down the list, which included the donor being tall, having a full head of hair, having a good job, no history of medical conditions. Right at the bottom of the list, she had written 'nice teeth'.

Anna had been so impressed with Doyle's great smile, with his straight white teeth. Reading about the dead bodies covered in bite marks was awful. A surge of emotions hit her like being strung up and stoned: anger, guilt, disgust.

Had Doyle's straight white teeth bitten these girls? She had been so drawn to his smile. Could such a nice, handsome man be responsible for these terrible deaths? She couldn't imagine his warm smile turning nasty, clamping onto the innocent flesh of these girls.

Anna laid a hand on her stomach. Could she really give birth to a serial killer's baby? She turned the computer off and crushed the empty water bottle in her hands.

'Main suspect,' her father had said. What did that mean? Was Doyle one of several suspects, or the only one?

Sitting in the dark office, a sudden thought occurred to Anna; she had to know if Doyle was a murderer. Her scientific mind was kicking in, and the only thing science cared about was facts. Anna needed to know the facts.

Slowly, she left the office and slipped back into bed. John was asleep under the covers. In the dull light, Anna leaned against John's back in the bed.

"John?"

He groaned at her. Anna caught a whiff of whisky.

"I need to know."

"Huh?"

"If Doyle is a murderer. I need to know."

John peered up at her with one eye, unsure what to say. He seemed unsurprised. Eventually, his open eye closed, and he fell back to sleep.

The idea felt like the first clear thought she'd had all night. Sod her father and the police. Sod accusations. Anna wasn't going to spend the next fifty years worrying about her child if Doyle was innocent.

Of course she would never have an abortion, but even so, she did the maths in her head. Anna was eighteen weeks pregnant, and she knew you could have an abortion up until twenty-four weeks. It gave her maybe six weeks to find out the truth, just in case it was something they needed to think about. Just as a backup.

Anna was a psychologist, and she needed to know for herself the type of mind Doyle really had.

She was going to investigate Doyle.

## 9

Dr Cole had been a lecturer at Bath University for thirty years, but to look at his office, you would assume he had been there twice as long. For an office, it was relatively large, and Dr Cole had taken advantage of that fact by filling it with hundreds of books and papers; some were based on his specialist subject of psychology, but most were just random titles he had accumulated over the years.

Anna peered through the slim glass panel on the office door and could see that the room was unoccupied. Her long dark hair was tied back in a bun, and she wore a cream pencil skirt and a dark purple blouse.

She always avoided high heels because she was tall and the extra height made her feel self-conscious, however, she had a large collection of flat-heeled Kurt Geiger shoes, and that morning she was wearing her new bone-white flats with gold lobsters on the front.

She gave a tap on the office door, and when there was no response, Anna gently opened it and stepped into the room. A large window was on the far wall and overlooked the green fields surrounding the university campus. Despite the sunlight that the window let in, the room still felt dark from all of the clutter. In the middle of the office was Dr Cole's desk, and Anna stepped carefully over to it and sat down. The office smelt of old paper, which wasn't unpleasant.

She nudged the mouse, and the computer screen came to life.

Adrenaline and fear tingled down her arms.

Nobody knew she was there, especially Dr Cole, and if she was caught, it would be very difficult to explain herself. What was she doing? Anna pushed the thought from her mind.

With shaking hands, she pulled the keyboard towards her and turned it over. Stuck on the bottom of the keyboard was a slip of paper with the word THALAMUS99 scrawled on it.

It had been at least fifteen years since she had sat at the desk. Back then, she had been a student helping Dr Cole with a paper he was writing. It was on false memories and distorted recollections, which was also the subject of Anna's dissertation, so one summer she had volunteered to help him. It had been tedious work, but on reflection, she had learnt a lot from the old professor.

One thing she had learnt was Dr Cole always kept his latest computer password stuck underneath his keyboard. She turned the keyboard back to the correct position and typed in the password. It was accepted, and Anna couldn't help but stand up with the nervous energy. Good old reliable Dr Cole, she thought.

Anna sat back down, but her hands started shaking too much. She clenched her fists and took a deep breath to steady herself. After a moment, her hands stilled, and she searched for the archive files, which came up instantly.

Moving the computer's mouse quickly, Anna clicked into the university's archives on the screen. As a senior lecturer,

Dr Cole had access to all of the files, and Anna went into the file marked '2001' and then 'Students'. Thousands of files began to materialise as a list on the screen. Clicking on the search bar, she entered 'Doyle Kennedy'.

Several files came up on the screen.

"It's worked," she whispered triumphantly.

Anna suddenly heard voices outside the room and froze. Her stomach dropped, and she stood up in a panic.

A shadow hovered outside the office door, and for a second, it seemed like someone would enter the room. But the voices suddenly dissipated into the corridor and beyond.

She was so nervous that a little laugh escaped from her mouth, which sounded ridiculous and inappropriate in the silent office, but there was so much adrenaline pumping through her she wasn't entirely in control of her body.

If Anna was caught sifting through the old university records, it had the potential to be professionally very bad for her. It was also illegal, and she could face arrest. Even as these terrifying thoughts came to her, she sat back down at Dr Cole's desk and peered at the computer screen.

There were four files titled 'Application', 'Modules', 'Certificates' and 'Housing'.

Anna didn't have much time. What would give her the best information on Doyle?

She clicked on the 'Housing' file.

Within the file there were a dozen documents. Anna knew universities had separate departments for student accommodation, and these were the files she was looking at now. There were old, scanned copies of identification and signed tenant agreements spanning three years. Anna clicked on one of the documents. A scan of an old passport came up on the computer screen.

The old picture was black-and-white, but it was unmistakably Doyle. His handsome face stared back at her on the screen. She tried to imagine being at university with him. It was a distracting thought.

The document didn't tell her anything new, so she closed it.

The next one was an old tenant agreement for a student house that Doyle had rented with some other students. There were four names on the agreement, which seemed useful. She clicked 'print', and in a second, the printer beneath the desk spat out a copy of the agreement for her.

She closed the file and opened a second one, which was another form of identification. This one was an old water bill in the name of Mrs Kennedy, which Anna assumed was his mother. The address was in Dublin, which must have been where he had lived as a teenager before he left home for university. Anna again clicked 'print', and again, the printer buzzed efficiently by her feet.

She closed the document and opened another. It was a generic receipt for a house deposit. Anna closed the document and closed the file.

Next, she opened the file named 'Certificates'. There was only one file in there, which was Doyle's degree certificate. It showed he had passed with a two-two grade. Anna snorted as she remembered his company website biography mentioned he had a first grade from Bath University. He had lied. Did that tell her anything? Probably not. Everyone lied on their CV.

She closed the file and stared at the remaining two files: 'Application' and 'Modules.' Anna was deciding which to look at when another shadow fell over the glass of the office door.

She closed the files on the computer screen.

The office door began to open, and Anna spun around in the chair so it seemed like she was staring out of the window. Her legs began to shake.

"Hello?"

"Oh, Dr Cole, there you are."

"Can I help you?"

"It's me, Anna Wilson. You taught me psychology a few years ago. I'm lecturing at Bristol now." Anna tried to keep fear from her voice.

"Ah yes, Anna. It has been a while. Didn't you help me on a paper one summer?"

"That's right!" Anna almost shouted with relief. "It was on false memories."

Dr Cole waddled into the room and chuckled. He had thin grey hair and a huge stomach poking through a blue cardigan. Anna always thought he looked too old to be that fat, as if he should have been forced to lose weight or keeled over from a heart attack years ago.

"What a laborious trial that paper was," he said, dropping a set of keys onto the desk.

"Indeed. Anyway, I was in the university and thought I would pop my head around the door to say hello."

"Very kind of you, dear."

Anna stood up and moved away from the desk. She was unsteady, and she silently willed her legs to stop shaking.

"Sorry, it's been a long morning, and I couldn't help sitting down for a moment." She felt her face burning with the lie.

"No problem. You were probably reminiscing about typing up that old paper for me." He smiled.

Anna laughed. It was too loud. Too jolly.

She was just about to make her excuses and leave when her heart sank. The printouts were still sat on top of the printer beneath the desk.

"Are you alright?"

"Yes, just tired, I think. So, Dr Cole...I, umm...I'm a lecturer at Bristol now."

"You said."

He stared at her without expression. He was so over-weight, he was breathing heavily from just standing.

"Well, I'm actually the head of the faculty, and we are looking for some guest speakers. Some guest lecturers to come in to a few lessons." The lie felt like she was trying to get a bee out of her mouth; it was forced and frantic. "I was wondering if I could buy you a coffee and talk through some ideas for half an hour."

"Sounds interesting." He looked at his watch. "Maybe…"

"And we could get one of those custard slices they used to do here?"

His face picked up. "They still do them in the canteen."

"Great, shall we go, then?"

"Lead on, my dear."

Anna and Dr Cole stepped out of the room. Sweat trickled down her back, and she had to fight the urge to run away down the corridor.

"Oh, sorry, Dr Cole, I've left my bag in there. I won't be a moment."

He looked at her with suspicion now, with narrowed eyes and a frown. She kept her face even, but inside she was crying from the shame. *I'm such a terrible liar; there is no way he believes me,* her mind wailed.

Without hesitating, Anna walked back to the desk, picked up the papers from the printer under the desk, stuffed them into her handbag that lay on the floor, slung the bag on her shoulder and walked back out of the office.

Dr Cole made a point of locking the office door behind Anna, and she wanted the floor to swallow her up from the embarrassment. They set off to the canteen. Once there, they ordered drinks and cakes, and as they sat down, Anna could feel herself relax.

The canteen was full of students, and the sound of their chatter was relentlessly loud. The place reminded Anna of

Bristol University's canteen, but with more paintings on the walls, and nicer views. It also had the same smell of coffee and fried chips that the Bristol canteen had.

Anna and Dr Cole talked for a while, and she realised that, as a happy accident, it would actually be useful to get Dr Cole over for some guest lectures for her students, as they were short-staffed at Bristol. She had the budget to pay him, and he was an expert on the right subject areas.

Dr Cole lifted the custard slice to his mouth and took a gulping bite of it. The firm custard clung to his lips as he chewed, and he struggled to breathe through the mouthful of cake. To her left, Anna could see a table of young students watching the professor eat with big grins on their faces. From a distance, she could imagine it was amusing to watch him, but from up close, it made her stomach churn. The only thing worse than watching Dr Cole eat was the sound of him eating; it was like a horse chomping next to her face.

Anna sipped her decaffeinated coffee and tried to ignore the lump of custard that had landed on Dr Cole's blue cardigan. She studied the gold lobsters on her new shoes.

Despite the terrible table manners, Anna remembered how knowledgeable the old professor was. Something occurred to her.

"Dr Cole, did you ever do anything on genetic aggression?" She looked down at the table as she spoke. "It's not my field of expertise, but we may want a lesson covering some points on it. Specifically, around hereditary violence in the individual."

He swallowed loudly. "You mean MOAO enzyme, that sort of thing?"

"Actually, yes, that's exactly what I mean."

"Well, I've done a little on it over the years. As you know, aggression is a multidimensional concept, and we still have very limited information on it. Most studies have been done on animals."

"Have there ever been human trials done?"

"A few, but none with any firm conclusions."

"What do the animal trials say?"

"Mostly that you can breed aggression." He licked his lips. "There have been trials on mice, dogs, fish and birds, and they can all be bred for violence. I suppose with dogs, people have been breeding aggressive types for hundreds of years."

"Hmmm."

"Are your first-year students covering genetics this term? Seems a bit strong for first-year students."

"You're right, it's probably too much for them. No, I was just thinking ahead to next year."

He finished the final mouthful of cake and sucked the remaining custard off his fingers.

"I'd be quite happy to cover hereditary violent personality disorders too. I could whip up a lesson on it."

"That's very kind of you. I will check the schedule and let you know."

The cakes and coffees were finished, and Dr Cole's eyes started to drift around with boredom.

"Well, my dear, it has been lovely to see you. Now I must get back to marking some papers."

"Of course, it was lovely to see you again."

He strained his huge frame up from his seat and held his hand out for a goodbye handshake. Anna shook his hand and tried to keep the disgust from her face as the greasy fingers wrapped around her hand. His hand was wet with custard and saliva.

"And perhaps next time you could wait outside the office instead. There is some seating at the end of my corridor."

"Of course."

Anna blushed furiously, but Dr Cole had already turned

and left her, waddling away towards the main door. Anna felt riddled with shame. She was tempted to call him back and apologise, but she couldn't bring herself to get up and follow the obese professor. Instead, she found a tissue in her bag and wiped her hand.

*What am I doing?* Anna admonished herself. The night before she had learnt that her unborn baby could have a murderer as a father, and she was already doing something that risked her whole career. Even as she was thinking about her actions, Anna dug back into her bag and pulled out the printouts from Dr Cole's computer.

There was a home address in Dublin on the first sheet, and a list of names of other students Doyle had shared a house with on the second sheet. She wasn't sure what she was going to do with this information, but it made her feel better just having it in her hands.

The home address in Dublin was in a block of flats. Anna wondered if it was a council flat. Did it really matter if Doyle had grown up poor?

"What are you doing here?" a voice demanded.

Anna looked up to see her father glaring down at her. She stared at him, unable to keep the horror from her face. Detective Gleadless stood alone with his hands by his sides. He wore the same black long coat and navy suit as the previous night.

"Why didn't you come to the station this morning?"

She suddenly felt like a child again, with her angry father questioning her with his biting glare. His battered old face was sinister as he stood over her. Why was he here? Anna realised he was probably here to do the same thing she had done: to get some background information on Doyle. She became aware of the printouts in her hands with Doyle's name all over them. It felt as though she were holding a scalding baking tray that she wanted to throw down. For the second time that morning, she wanted to run away.

"I didn't think we had a set time?" was all she could manage. Her voice sounded small. She felt weak.

"We need to question you and your husband about an ongoing murder investigation. You should have been there first thing."

His voice sounded rougher than she remembered, and his impatient tone set a hundred horrible memories flooding to her mind.

"Still smoking?" she asked.

"Don't change the subject."

He stepped forward and sat down in front of her where Dr Cole had just been. His eyes never left her. *If he looks down at the papers I'm holding, I'm in serious trouble*, Anna thought.

"I can come down to the station later?"

"Let's do this now. We can't be wasting any more time."

Up close, she could see the veins and tiny tufts of hair on his bald head. He was half the size of Dr Cole, but somehow he seemed to fill the space where the professor had sat.

Anna tried to appear calm as she folded the papers she was holding and put them back in her handbag.

"I was just leaving..."

"Fuck that." He pointed at her. "Stay there and let's talk."

Anna wanted to swear back at him, but she couldn't muster the voice. She could only nod her compliance. *He won't strike you in front of two hundred witnesses,* she told herself.

He pulled out a notepad and pen from his coat pocket.

"Where's Detective Wright?"

He ignored the question and flipped open his notepad.

"From the beginning. How did you get in touch with Doyle Kennedy?"

Anna took a deep breath. She needed to do this interview,

and a student canteen was better than a police interview room. Despite her hatred of the man in front of her, she did genuinely want to help, so she focused on giving him all the information she could.

She talked about the past year, keeping it factual and thorough.

"We realised we couldn't have children together nine months ago, so I registered us with the local sperm donation clinic in Bristol. But we were waiting for months with no response. There's a shortage, you see, a lack of sperm donors. Even then, you can't get any details about the donor or see any photos of them."

He nodded.

"So we registered online. I registered us. There are websites where people offer sperm donations. There are thousands of people listed. They put all of their details on there; it's information about themselves that potential parents would want to know. It's all legal, you just can't pay them much. Just cover their expenses, petrol, that sort of thing. So, after months of searching and asking the people online a lot of questions, we settled on Doyle. He seemed to have the right balance of being a normal guy and having a good job and education."

Anna didn't mention the long list of requirements she'd had for a sperm donor.

"He came to the house twice. Both times, he gave us a donation. Like I said last night, we were planning for a lot of donations, but after a few attempts, I got pregnant."

She watched her father's face for a reaction, but he looked blankly at his notepad. Anna looked down at the small leather notepad he was writing in and could see that he had made a list of bullet points. It was the same way she made her own notes, and Anna suddenly wondered what other traits she shared with her father.

"When he came over, Doyle seemed normal enough. A bit too familiar, but it's all a very odd situation, so we didn't think much of it. He was only with us for fifteen minutes each time."

She talked for half an hour, and her father wrote his notes in silence. Anna told him all the details she could think of that were relevant, but she left out the arguments that it had caused between her and John. She also didn't mention her physical attraction to Doyle, especially her daydreams about his muscular body, friendly smile and blue eyes. Once she had finished speaking, he looked up.

"I will need a copy of his emails. And copies of the documents he gave you."

"I'll send them over this afternoon."

"Okay, that's it for now." He closed his notepad.

"That's it?"

He stood up, already looking around for the exit. Although she didn't want to be around him, Anna still felt like someone was walking out on her on a first date.

"Why didn't you come to the funeral?"

The question was out of her mouth before she could stop it.

He looked down at her, and she saw the pain and loss in his eyes. Anna felt surprised at the feeling of pity that crept into her. For a brief moment she wondered if it had really been all bad, her childhood. Were her memories really an accurate reflection of the man he was? After all, his wife and daughter had been taken away from him.

"What?" he asked.

"Last year. The funeral."

She could see a mixture of emotions playing out on his face.

He leant in, his hands placed palm down on the table. His

face was too close to hers. His breath stank of cigarettes and tea. She saw his eyes had no white in them, just grey.

"You drove her away from me, that's why. You, with your fucking whining about our marriage."

The pity for him vanished.

"I saved her..." Before she could finish, he strode away.

The groups of teens parted before him. Anna ignored the students staring at her, their looks both curious and wary.

On the table, she could see her father's huge, sweaty handprints glistening in the fluorescent light.

## 10

Anna sat in traffic on the A36 out of Bath city. She was heading back home to Bristol, but the twenty-minute drive was looking more like it would take an hour. It was only four o'clock, but already the Friday traffic was bumper-to-bumper in the dark, January afternoon.

The image of her father's miserable face was still seared onto her eyes. His bad breath still filled her nose.

Anna pounded the car's horn.

"Come on, move, you arsehole."

The driver in front looked in his rear-view mirror with raised eyebrows and caught her eye. The look said, *What do you want me to do? The road's blocked.* Anna glared at him in return.

Her hands gripped the steering wheel so tightly, her knuckles looked like they would burst through the skin.

The car started to close in on her, and Anna's right foot began to shake with a desperate need to stamp down on the accelerator pedal. She needed to get out of the car.

Looking out the window, Anna saw that she was opposite

a T-junction leading onto Westmoreland Street. The road was familiar to her, but she couldn't fathom why.

Westmoreland Street.

It was where Doyle's office was based. The realisation was like a drip of water on her neck. The hairs on her arms prickled.

In an instant, Anna flicked up the car's indicator and pulled out into the road. She had to quickly reverse and pull forward to get the Mercedes angled correctly to drive down onto Westmoreland Street.

The road was narrow with pale terraced houses on either side. Although they were small houses, they were made from Bath stone and would likely be expensive properties. As the car inched forward, the right-hand side of the street suddenly opened up, and nestling within the row of houses was a squat building with large glass windows. It looked like an office block.

Anna drove slowly past the building and found a parking space fifty meters down the road. She eased the car into the space and turned the engine off.

She could see the building in her rear-view mirror.

The lights were on, but there was no sign of any movement.

Anna got out of the car and locked it. Instantly, she felt the cold air on her cheeks and hands. Acting casual, she walked towards the building as her breath steamed in the dark. In the distance she could hear the traffic, but along the street, it was quiet.

Approaching the entrance, Anna could see a glass panel screwed to the front of the building with a list of four businesses that were based in the office block. There were four floors; each business had its own floor. There was an accountants' office, a gift company and a financial advisor's on the

first three levels. The fourth floor was listed as Doyle
Kennedy Architect Practice.

She stood back from the sign and looked to the top of the
office block. The building was lit up apart from the fourth
floor, which had no lights on. Anna looked up and down the
road. There was no sign of the police.

"Sod it."

She entered the building. It was warm and light inside,
and it felt good to be out of the cold. There was an unmanned
reception to her left and a staircase to her right. Noncha-
lantly, she went to the stairs and started to walk up them. As
she passed each floor, she saw corridors leading off to various
offices. Keeping her head down, Anna kept moving upwards
to Doyle's office.

Her footsteps echoed in the stairwell. As she reached
each floor, she could hear the sounds of people talking and
laughing and phones ringing. It was only as Anna reached
the top floor that it became quiet.

In front of her was a small corridor with one closed door.
Beyond it was only darkness. Anna hesitated. Hadn't she
done enough snooping for one day? But, even as she asked
herself that, the answer was there; she needed to know more
about Doyle. She wanted to know if he was capable of
murder. Was he the sort of man who killed innocent women?
Standing alone on the top floor of the building, Anna knew
she wouldn't learn anything about Doyle just from seeing his
office. But her hand still reached out and tried the handle.
She would just have a quick look around and then leave.

With a bubble of nervous excitement, Anna found the
door unlocked. She opened it, and with one hand on her
stomach, she silently stepped into the room. A weak, grey
evening light filtered through the windows, just enough for
her to make out a large office space with several desks and

chairs spread around the room. She closed the door behind her.

On the wall to her left there was a long row of light switches. She peered in the darkness at the little white switches, but they all looked the same. She picked a switch at random and flicked it on. Thankfully, only a small corner light came on. It was enough for her to see the room, but hopefully not bright enough to attract attention from outside. An air freshener had been placed on one of the desks, and it gave the office a sickly, floral smell.

Anna exhaled loudly and tried to relax.

She was far too jumpy, but then, this was the second time in one day that she was somewhere she shouldn't be.

Now that the light was on, Anna could clearly see four large desks covered in technical drawings and computers. It didn't seem like a very secure way to leave the office. But then, looking at the place, it seemed to have been closed in a hurry. Anna tried to imagine the police raiding the office, ushering the staff out and rooting through files and computers, looking for evidence that Doyle was a murderer. What was she hoping to find that the police hadn't? she asked herself.

At one end of the large office, there was a separate room. Anna wandered over. It had glass walls and a sturdy door that was ajar; on the door was a nameplate with *Doyle Kennedy* written in white lettering. In the stillness, she could hear the faint sounds of people talking from the office below.

Something didn't feel right to Anna. She looked into Doyle's darkened room, then back to the four desks in the main part of the office. It was Doyle's business, but if he had been arrested, why wouldn't the rest of the staff still be in to work? Just because their boss was out, surely they would still be coming in to the office every day?

She stepped into Doyle's room and flicked the light switch on the wall. The office lit up, and Anna paused, feeling like a cat that was exploring a room with wide, curious eyes. There was a large desk and a high-backed chair to her left, and oak-panelled filing cabinets to her right. Between them both, the far wall had a square window that looked down onto Westmoreland street.

Anna sat on Doyle's chair. When had he last sat in it? She wondered what he was doing right now. Was he all alone in a jail cell? Was Doyle terrified? She tried to imagine the cool Irishman looking scared, but couldn't. Anna could only imagine him with a humble look on his face, keeping his head down and trying to get through his ordeal.

There were unplugged leads lying on top of the desk where a computer had been. The police must have taken it. Above the desk, there was an empty shelf where she imagined files once stood. Dust was already gathering on the desk and shelf. Gently, Anna opened one of the desk drawers.

As she slid open the drawer, her mobile phone rang, the sound of it horrifyingly loud in the empty office.

Anna jumped and slammed the drawer shut on instinct. Her heart hammered in her chest.

She quickly pulled the phone out of her coat pocket.

It showed a withheld number.

"Hello?" her voice squeaked.

"Anna, it's Marianne."

Anna had left Marianne a voicemail that morning. She was a general practice doctor and a friend from university.

"Thanks for calling me back."

"Are you okay? You sound stressed," Marianne asked.

Anna tried to laugh but failed. She took a deep breath. "I'm fine," she lied.

"I've got a patient coming in to see me in around five minutes and can't be long, but your message sounded urgent, so I thought I would try you now. Is everything okay?"

Marianne and Lara had been housemates at university.

Lara had introduced them on a night out, and Anna had been impressed with the rugby-playing, trainee doctor. Marianne had played for the university women's rugby team, and by all accounts had been very good. It had been a while since Anna had seen Marianne, but she was still someone she trusted.

"This is a bit awkward, and it's probably a conversation to have face to face, but I really need some information." Anna paused. "And some advice."

"No problem," Marianne replied, now sounding more like the local GP that she was.

"I'm pregnant."

"Congratulations."

"Thank you." Anna paused again. "There is a small chance, well, a very small chance, that I may need to, possibly, think about having an abortion, although it really isn't likely that I would ever..."

To say it made the blood ring in Anna's ears and her stomach sink. She looked down at the office bin and wheeled the chair closer to it, in case she threw up, which was feeling very likely.

"You're right; this is probably best done face to face. I'm free next week, if you want to come in to the practice here?"

Anna chewed her cheek and rubbed her forehead with her free hand. A big part of her wanted to hang up the call and never think about having an abortion again, but she needed to have this conversation.

"I don't have much time. Maybe I could ask you a few questions now? Then come in next week if needed."

"What do you want to know?"

Anna gripped the phone in her hand so hard she thought it would break. *Has anyone ever crushed a phone in one hand?* she wondered.

"What is the..." She couldn't breathe. "When is the latest you will perform an abortion?"

"Terminations need to be performed within twenty-four weeks of pregnancy. But, to be honest, I know a lot of doctors won't even perform the surgery past twenty weeks, because the baby is so formed at that point."

Anna found she couldn't speak. She saw her reflection in the window. The tears in her eyes shimmered back at her.

Marianne's voice softened. "What term are you?"

Anna sniffed. "About eighteen weeks."

Marianne didn't reply.

They could both do the math. At best, there was a two-week window to have the abortion. Anna couldn't imagine anything worse than having the operation to remove the baby. She was so desperate for her baby to be born. On the other hand, she didn't want to raise a ticking time bomb, a child who would grow up to harm other people.

"This is all hypothetical, because I'm not having one."

Anna stood up and walked to the window. Outside, the afternoon was gloomy and uninviting. The sky was covered in dark clouds; they were purple and black and looked like bruising on pale skin. Anna could scarcely see her car parked on the street below. As she looked down to the street, she saw a man on the opposite side of the road walking along with a briefcase.

"Listen, you should really come in and talk to me. A termination is not something to take lightly. At eighteen weeks, the baby is five inches long, and it's not a simple procedure. It's very serious."

A tear dropped from Anna's nose onto the windowsill.

As she watched the man down on the pavement, he suddenly stopped and turned to look up at the fourth floor of the building, much like Anna had done minutes before.

Anna quickly blinked away her tears. Why was he looking up at the floor she was on? The man crossed the road to the building. He looked like he was heading straight for her.

The sight of the man striding towards the building snapped Anna out of her trance. She was trespassing. Was the man a friend of Doyle's, a member of staff, or a police officer? Whoever he was, Anna knew she didn't want to be caught snooping around Doyle's office like this.

"Marianne, I have to go."

"Why don't we meet up this week, have a proper catch-up?"

"Yes, maybe, I'll let you know. Thanks for the call."

"Take care, Anna."

She hung up the phone and looked around the office.

Quickly, Anna opened the drawers and rummaged through the papers and stationery contained in them. What was she looking for? A diary. A hidden memory stick. Something. Anything. But even as her hands flittered through the papers, she knew that anything useful would have been taken by the police. By her father.

She was running out of time, so she pushed the drawers shut and left Doyle's office. Back out in the main architect's office, Anna wiped her eyes dry and looked at the desks. They had nothing to tell her. It was time to leave. As Anna walked to the main door, a shadow appeared at the door's window.

She stopped.

'A termination is serious.' Marianne's words bounced around her head.

The door opened, and the man from the road appeared in the doorway, like some badly planned magic trick. He was short and blonde and wore a navy Mac and striped scarf. He was out of breath and smelt of sweat on cold skin. His face was young, but when he spoke, his deep voice made him seem older.

"Can I help you?" he asked her.

"Oh yes. Do you work here? I was looking to get a quote

on some work my husband and I are looking to do. It's an extension." She had never lied so much in one day in her life. "We live in Bristol, and you were recommended to us. It's a small extension, really. But we need some plans drawing up. By an architect." Her voice was gradually getting higher and faster. "I don't have any measurements, but thought we could get some pricing from you?"

He watched her babble with folded arms. She could see he looked unsure. She waited for him to respond, silently willing him to believe her lies.

"The office is closed at the moment. If you leave some details, we can contact you when we are open again," he finally said.

Anna tried to keep the relief from her face.

"That would be good, thank you."

The man stepped into the room and walked to one of the desks. He took a pen and a slip of paper and leant down on the desk, ready to write.

He looked up at Anna.

"What's the name?" he asked.

"Name?" She blinked. "Alison."

*Where did that name come from?*

"Phone number?"

Anna reeled off an old phone number she still remembered, and he wrote it down.

"Alright, someone will call you next week, Alison."

In the space of one day, she had become a trespassing liar who was going to get herself arrested.

"Thank you."

Anna walked out of the office and down the stairs. She left the building and stepped out into the darkness. The cold air felt good on her flushed face, and a sudden blanket of exhaustion wrapped itself around her. As she walked back to her car, she realised the man hadn't introduced himself or confirmed that he actually worked there. He could have been anybody. Anna couldn't help but look up to the fourth floor again. Standing in the window of Doyle's office was the young man. He stood there, looking down at the street and at Anna.

She wondered if her tears were still on the windowsill.

## 11

The clattering of golf clubs woke Anna. It must be a Saturday. John was packing the car to play golf, and no matter how many times she asked him to be quiet on the weekends, he always managed to disturb her sleep.

The clock read seven thirty am.

"Always with the bloody golf clubs," she mumbled into the pillow.

As usual, she couldn't get back to sleep, and her mind drifted to the baby. It was five inches long. Her hand went to her stomach, and she could feel a hardness along one side. She wondered if the baby was content inside her, happily sleeping and growing. Anna still couldn't imagine meeting her baby for the first time; it was too much of a hopeful dream to imagine. At eighteen weeks, some people had felt the baby kick, although she'd had nothing yet, which was quite common, apparently. Was it a boy or a girl? She didn't mind which, only that it was healthy.

With a stretch and a yawn, Anna got out of bed and went to the bathroom. On the way back, she passed the spare room and stopped. It had been emptied, ready to decorate that weekend. She suddenly remembered that John wasn't due to play golf today, as they were supposed to be painting the spare room for the baby.

Pots of yellow paint, brushes and paint rollers were neatly stacked in the corner of the empty room, ready to transform the walls from white to a baby-friendly yellow. Anna had also ordered a flat-packed cot that lay in the room, waiting to be assembled. It looked like John didn't want to spend the weekend getting the baby room ready.

Anna tried to picture the room painted and fully decorated. They had chosen 'Sunshine Yellow', and she thought it would look bright and cheery. She stood in the doorway with her hands on her stomach and stared into the room. At eighteen weeks of pregnancy, most mums-to-be started to feel their baby move, and she had taken to holding her stomach every day, waiting to feel the first kick. So far there had been nothing, but Anna knew it could only be a matter of days before the baby rolled or kicked in her womb.

---

Anna had a list of chores neatly written out. She knew it was going to be a busy day. She still felt worn out from the stress of the previous few days, but she was also looking forward to some normality over the weekend.

She showered and dressed. Breakfast was a bowl of fruit and oats with almond milk. The washing machine was filled and switched on. The dishwasher was emptied from the night before. Her arms pumped as she pushed and pulled the vacuum around the house. Then Anna grabbed her car keys and drove along the M32 and into the city, foot down on the accelerator all of the way.

She left her car at the Polish car wash and ordered the

deluxe clean. In the post office, she bought a birthday card, wrote in it and posted it to John's mother in Plymouth. The clothes shop took ten minutes to find the dress she had ordered, but eventually a young man brought it out to her, unapologetically slow as he put it in a bag. Anna collected her clean car and drove to the supermarket.

Lara texted her on the way. It was a dirty joke that made her snort. She replied with a laughing face.

In the supermarket, she grabbed a basket and filled it with chicken and fresh vegetables for dinner and a green salad for lunch. She also bought some spinach and a bag of walnuts for the baby to get its omega-3 oils. As she was deciding whether to get some ice cream for dessert, Anna suddenly stopped and looked down at her basket.

Tears started to stream down her face.

*My baby.*

Anna's legs felt like they couldn't support her, and she had to lean against the freezer to stop herself from falling over. From nowhere, a wave of guilt and dread hit her at the thought of having an abortion. She was doing her best to be a good mum, buying foods that she knew the baby needed. Why had John put the idea in her head? she thought with rising anger. She was going to have the baby whatever happened. Wasn't she?

She had tried so hard to get pregnant, and she didn't think she could ever go through with the operation to remove her baby. Anna couldn't stop herself crying, and silently cursed her hormones. The hot tears poured down her face.

Her bum became cold from the freezer door, and she was aware of other shoppers dutifully ignoring her and awkwardly walking around her. Nobody seemed to want ice cream.

A passing old lady touched Anna on the arm. The lady

had a wrinkled face, neat grey hair and wore a pink coat. She reminded Anna of the queen.

"Don't worry, my love. It will be all right."

"Can't believe I'm crying in the supermarket."

"I don't have a tissue on me, but the toilet is just back there."

Anna nodded her thanks, left her basket of food on the floor and headed to the ladies' toilet. She locked herself in a small cubicle and sobbed. It stank, and there was no tissue in the roller, but at least she was alone.

She heard the main door open and someone knock on the cubicle door.

"Hello? Cleaner here, I'm just going to…"

"Give me a minute!" Anna shouted.

"I'll come back."

After a short while, Anna calmed down. She wasn't sure why the thought of having an abortion had just come to her, and especially in the shop. As the tears stopped, Anna noticed how dirty the cubicle was. She clenched her fists and left the toilet. Her basket was still where she had left it, in the middle of the supermarket, although the queen lookalike had left.

With mascara streaked down her face, Anna went to the checkout.

"Your make-up has smudged," the checkout girl informed her.

"I know."

"A lot."

"Thanks."

She paid and made it back in the car. She flung the shopping in the boot and sped home.

---

As Anna entered the house, she could hear the television was on and sensed John was in the lounge. Anna went into the kitchen and slammed the bags of food onto the counter before going into the lounge. John was standing in the middle of the room, remote control in one hand, cup of tea in the other, watching the large flat-screen television. He was blocking the screen, and Anna couldn't see what he was watching.

John turned to her as she entered, and he looked shocked at the sight of her.

"What happened to you?" he asked.

"I can't have an abortion," she announced.

"What?"

"Abortion. Can't do it. I'm not doing it. And you're an arsehole for even suggesting it. How could you be so insensitive? I know you have your doubts about being a dad, and we should definitely have talked about that more. And I know there's this issue with Doyle, but we don't even know..." She halted at the look of horror on John's face.

"Oh, Anna," he whispered.

"What?"

John stepped aside so she could see the television, and time seemed to slow. There was a picture of Doyle Kennedy on the screen. Below his picture was a headline: 'Bath architect arrested for murder'.

Anna felt faint. Her head swam, and for a moment she didn't know where she was; all she could see was Doyle's handsome face on the screen. Once again, tears threatened to come, but this time, Anna stopped them. She had cried too much recently.

"They have arrested Doyle," John said.

Anna opened her mouth to speak, but her voice abandoned her.

John was there, hugging her, and his embrace felt life-saving to her floundering mind. He gently directed her to the sofa and sat her down. Her eyes never left the screen. A reporter was standing outside the building on Westmoreland Street, where Anna had been the day before. The sight of the building sent a piercing chill down her ribs and stomach.

John left her and reappeared with a cup of fruit tea. She took it from him but didn't drink it. Doyle had been arrested, a voice in her mind repeated. He was in jail for murder. In a way, she had been expecting the news, but it was still a shock to see it being announced.

Eventually, the screen went black as John turned the television off. Anna blinked and felt herself snap out of a daze. The tea in her hand was untouched and had gone cold.

"Are you alright?" he asked.

She looked at her husband and noticed he was still in his golf clothes. She cleared her throat.

"How was the golf?"

"It was good. What happened to you?"

"Huh?"

"You've got make-up all over your face."

"Oh, that. I broke down and cried in the shop."

John didn't reply. Instead, he took the tea from her, set it on the table, and hugged her again. It felt good.

After a while, he spoke. "Do you want to talk about Doyle being arrested?"

Anna felt a great sadness envelop her, like a dirty wet blanket.

"What is there to say?"

John sighed. "I don't know."

"I guess he's guilty, then," Anna said. "The police wouldn't arrest him unless they were sure."

"Right."

Anna sat up on the sofa, out of John's arms, but still close.

"I know what you're thinking, but the odds of him passing

on anything to our baby are small. And we could deal with the backlash of people finding out we were raising the child of a serial killer."

"The news said the police are connecting him to three murders, and there could be more. He could have killed dozens of women. What if we have the baby and we find out Doyle has killed twenty people? Then when the baby grows up, it starts acting weird. We would be going out of our minds worrying, wouldn't we?"

"You don't know that."

"Anna, I've never known anyone so precise and controlling as you. I've always said I'm fine with how you are. But think about it. If we find out Doyle has killed loads of people because he is a messed-up psycho, and we are raising his biological kid? You couldn't cope with that. I know you. You would drive yourself crazy with worry."

Anna's eyes threatened to tear up again, but she held them back; there would be no more tears from her.

"Maybe. But I would be willing to try. I can't just..."

"We could find another sperm donor. Maybe in a year or two," John suggested.

She looked at his face, and he seemed as unsure as her.

"You want to wait?"

"I'm just saying..."

"Do you want a baby or not?" she asked.

He looked away, unable to meet her gaze.

"Why do you ask?"

"John?"

"Just think about the abortion. I know it's not a nice thing to go through."

"But everything could work out okay," Anna said.

"Are you willing to risk it?"

IN THE AFTERNOON, Anna lay on the sofa, exhausted by the past few days. She had had a shower and cleaned the mascara from her face. John was out with some friends, watching a game of rugby in the pub. He had offered to stay with her, but she had waved him out of the house. He would be gone for hours, and when he did eventually return, he would be drunk. Painting the baby's bedroom was up to her, but she couldn't be bothered.

God, she wanted a coffee. She'd heard a hundred times that it was an addictive stimulant without really listening, but now she understood how addictive it really was.

Instead, she made a fruit tea. A sudden image of being a student came to her. She was at a house party, wearing a pink cowboy hat, and drinking from a large bottle of vodka.

"Turn that music up!" she had shouted.

After being so sensible with her mum, Anna's student years were wild, especially when she had met Lara.

Now she wasn't even able to have caffeine.

She sipped her fruit tea and sat at her desk in the home office. The room was turquoise with framed pictures of the world's best beaches on the walls. John had put them up as inspiration for their holidays.

From her handbag, Anna pulled out the two documents on Doyle she had printed out from Dr Cole's computer. She spread them out neatly on the desk. One document was the student housing tenancy agreement for the shared house in Bath, and one was the water bill from the house in Dublin.

The address on the water bill was in Ballymun, Dublin. Anna searched for the place online and thought she wouldn't feel safe walking around there. Rows of grey buildings stood bunched together as if they were huddling from the cold Irish weather.

Anna read about Ballymun through several websites, but the only thing she really learnt was that Doyle had come from a rough neighbourhood. She thought back to his voice. There was no hint of a working-class background there, just a polite Irish accent.

She searched the names *Kennedy* and *Ballymun,* but nothing of interest came up.

Switching to the second piece of paper, Anna looked at the names listed: Doyle Kennedy, Ron Elliott, Michelle Howells and Uri Rana-Bennett.

The four students had lived together in a shared house in Bath, eight years ago. Eight years ago was when the first victim, Ruth Collins, was found. It sent a shudder through Anna at the thought of a student being a murderer, especially as every day at work she was surrounded by so many students. When Doyle was supposedly out killing Ruth Collins, these four had lived together.

The student house address was listed, and Anna typed it into the computer. It was a four-bed terraced house in the Twerton area of Bath city. Again, it was interesting to look at, but didn't really tell her anything.

Looking at the names, she entered Doyle's first. It came up with his architect practice in the city, which she had looked at in depth several times already. Below that website listing, one of his social media profiles came up. She clicked on it and saw Doyle's profile picture had changed from the last time she had looked. It was now a photo of Doyle and a woman; they were arm in arm, standing at a bar. Anna wondered who she was.

Anna searched for 'Ron Elliott – Bath' and several articles came up that he had written. It looked like he was a journalist. The articles were from when he had written for a local magazine in Bath. Following through the links, she came to his personal profile in a freelance journalists' website. Anna saw an email address link listed. The tiredness she had felt earlier evaporated, replaced by a buzzing energy as she clicked on the email link.

A new message box came up.

*What shall I say?* Which in turn led her to think, *What am I doing?* She didn't really know, but at that moment, she didn't want to stop and think about it.

*Hi Ron,*

*I want to talk to you about your time at Bath University. Are you free for a phone call over the next few days? If so, what is the best number to contact you on?*

*Regards,*

*Anna Wilson*

Anna clicked 'send'.

What would she say to him if he replied? *Hi, Ron, was Doyle weird when you lived together at university? Do you think he could be a psycho killer?* Maybe something along those lines? Or maybe not. She would just have to think about it when the time came.

Anna then searched for 'Michelle Howells, Bath', but nothing came up on the search engine. She tried the name on its own, and several other variations. Still nothing came up.

Her phone rang, which made her jump.

She picked it up from the desk and pressed the answer button.

"Hi, Lara."

"Anna, where are you?" The voice was faint, and there was a lot of background noise.

"Just at home, doing a few chores."

"Fancy a little non-alcoholic cocktail? I'm in the Elbow Room."

"The Elbow Room? Aren't you a little old for that place? Don't tell me you are wearing a tracksuit."

Lara laughed.

"I'm with Katie. Her new boyfriend is working behind the bar."

"Jeez, how old is he?"

"You don't want to know." Lara laughed. "Come on, we can meet you in the Rum Distillery across the road. It's quieter there, and you can listen to what happened on my date with Dave last night."

It sounded great, like something Anna would normally jump at, but she didn't want to be distracted. As far as she was concerned, the clock was ticking over the next two weeks. She had to get clear in her mind what sort of man Doyle was and if he was capable of committing murder. Then she could think about what to do next.

"I can't, darling. I need to get a few things done here."

"Boo. Call me later, then. I miss you."

"I miss you, too. Call you later."

Anna hung up the phone and replaced it on the desk. A part of her wished she could go to the pub, drink cocktails, and gossip with the girls, but it was a small part of her. Mostly, she wanted peace of mind about her baby.

She looked down at her scribbled notes and sighed. She was getting nowhere. Anna decided she'd had enough and needed another fruit tea.

On the sheet, she saw she still hadn't searched the last name. Anna typed 'Uri Rana-Bennett, Bath' into the search engine.

Several links came up. The first was an article that had been written about Uri and how she had passed top of the class on her MBA. She was a doctor. Dr Uri Rana-Bennett.

Anna clicked on the article and felt a little jolt of excitement as she saw that Uri had a doctorate in psychology.

Uri had passed the course with a perfect grade, which was a big achievement in any university, especially one as prestigious as Bath. Certainly, it was a better result than Anna had achieved.

Anna went back to the home page and searched 'Dr Uri Rana-Bennett'. Several links came up, the first being a Spanish website. She opened it, but everything was written in Spanish. However, the pictures showed it to be a hospital website: 'El Instituto de San Villegas'.

A sudden thought occurred to Anna.

If Uri was a psychologist, and she had lived with Doyle for a year, then she would surely have a great understanding of what sort of man he was. Uri would know how his mind worked. Anna could ask Uri questions in the framework of genetic make-up.

With Uri, she would be taking her research on Doyle to the next level. Uri would know if Doyle was capable of killing those women; Uri Rana-Bennett was the key.

Anna sat up straight, unable to stop the grin that had spread on her face.

Clicking through a few links on the hospital's website, Anna found a 'Contact Us' page, which she clicked on to reveal an email box and a phone number. She clicked on the email box and then hesitated.

"Sod it," she muttered and went back to the 'Contact us' page on the site.

Anna picked up her mobile phone and dialled the number listed on the screen. It didn't work. She tried another version with a different dialling code, and the phone began to ring.

"*Hola?*" a man's voice asked.

"Hello? Do you speak English?"

"*Ay, muy poco*...very little."

"I'm looking to speak with Dr Uri Rana-Bennett?"

"*Quien?*" The question was asked with a note of impatience.

Anna gently cradled the phone between her shoulder and head to free her hands for the keyboard, and she searched for a language translator website on the computer.

"Is this a hospital?"

"*Manicomio, si.*"

"Errr, one moment..." She quickly typed *Manicomio* into the translator website. It read *Mental Hospital.*

Perfect. It was a psychiatric hospital. Anna felt sure talking with Uri was going to be useful, as she would have such a good insight into Doyle and his state of mind. Anna didn't expect for one second that Uri would know if Doyle *was* a murderer or not, but she would know if he was capable of it. If Uri had lived with Doyle for a year and she convinced Anna he was a good, sane man, then that would be enough for her.

"There is a doctor there, umm, *medico. Si. Medico?*"

"*Si. Cual Medico?*"

Anna translated the words. The man on the phone was asking 'which doctor?'

She was making progress, and tried to keep the excitement from her voice.

"*Medico* Uri Rana-Bennett."

A tirade of Spanish came back to her on the phone. It was too quick and sounded aggressive. Her grin faltered.

"*Medico* Uri Rana-Bennett," Anna repeated.

The voice tutted at her. "*Imposible.*"

"Impossible? Not possible?"

"*Si. Rana-Bennett es un paciente.*"

Anna typed the word *paciente* into the translator. The word came back as 'patient'.

"Wait. Patient? She's a patient? Uri Rana-Bennett is...a *paciente?*"

"*Si.*"

Anna dropped the phone.

## 12

J ohn was thirsty. As he woke up, he felt sick with a hangover, and it took a while for his eyes to focus. Squinting in the sunlight, he stumbled out to the bathroom and relieved himself before he drank cold water from the sink tap. Feeling better, he made his way back to the bed and buried himself under the duvet cover.

From what he could remember, it had been a good night. They had started in the Crown pub to watch the rugby before heading down the road to the Mall wine bar to drink tequila shots and more pints of beer. After that, his memories of the night became hazy.

A sudden thought occurred to him that he had told Chris and Andy about using a sperm donor, and under the covers of the bed, he started to blush and sweat with embarrassment. The three of them had worked together in a sales office in their early twenties, and they had been close friends ever since. His hangover started to feel worse.

"Great news about the baby, mate," Chris had said.

"Well, it's been a nightmare. I've been firing blanks, haven't I? Don't tell anyone" – Chris and Andy nodded drunkenly – "but we had all the tests and that. My swimmers ain't swimming straight."

"Fucking hell," they said in sympathy.

"I know, so we had to get some sperm donor around to shoot his load in a jar."

They sniggered at this.

"You help him out with that?"

"No chance. Anyway, it's done the job, 'cause she's pregnant now."

"Job done, then." Chris nodded at him.

"Thought you didn't want kids?" Andy asked.

"Well, I don't. Or didn't. Like my dad always said to me, 'Don't ever have kids; just enjoy your life.' I'm still not a hundred percent sure, but I'm thinking I might give it a go. It's what she wants, so why not? Anyway, it's still not a definite we're having this one."

Now that John thought about it, one of the main reasons he'd never wanted children was because his father had always warned him against it. His parents had been poor, and John had grown up sharing a room with his older brother in a tiny three-room house in Plymouth. It was never said openly, but John's dad had always implied that the reason they had no money was because of the kids.

"What do you mean?" Chris asked.

"It might have a few issues." John tapped the side of his head. "We need to decide what the hell we're doing. If we're keeping it or what."

"Sounds tough."

Before he could reply, a few of the other lads had turned up. There were hugs all around and drinks ordered, and the subject was forgotten. Thank god he hadn't told them about Doyle being a suspected killer. But even so, it had been a big admission from him to tell them as much as he had. He felt embarrassed, but strangely, a little happier with the situation now that he had spoken about it, albeit half-heartedly and while he was drunk.

John noticed the silence of the house.

Anna was usually up before him on a Sunday morning, but she was normally in the kitchen with the radio on, pot of coffee on the go and a magazine being devoured. *If she's out shopping, she could pick me up some breakfast on the way back home,* John thought. A bacon roll and orange juice would help relieve his hangover no end.

He reached out to the foot of the bed and found his jeans in a pile. John picked them up and dug out his mobile phone from the side pocket. There were no missed calls, just several texts from Chris, who had sent him photos of the night before. John briefly looked through the images, which showed the three of them arm in arm together, looking happy and drunk.

He found Anna's number in his contacts and dialled her. He yawned as the phone dialled out.

"John?" she answered.

"Hey, are you passing the deli on your way back?"

"The deli? Didn't you get my note in the kitchen?"

"I'm still in bed."

"It's ten thirty."

"Yeah, but it's a Sunday."

"I won't be back for a while. Read the note I left you," she instructed.

An alarm bell started to ring in John's mind. Even with his hangover, he knew something wasn't right.

"Where are you?"

She didn't reply. He could hear something in the background, as if she was driving.

"I'm on a plane, just about to take off."

"You what?! A plane?"

"Yes, we're just taxiing on the runway. I'll have to turn my phone off in a sec."

"A plane? Where are you going?"

"Barcelona."

---

BEFORE JOHN COULD REPLY, she hung up the phone as the plane began to pick up speed. The shock in John's voice told Anna all she needed to know about how crazy her actions were. But at that moment, she didn't care. Anna needed to know about Doyle. It had become like a mantra to her: *I need to know.* Of course, the police were working hard on the case, and not for one minute did she think she would find any evidence or actually solve a crime.

But at the same time, she needed to talk with Uri Rana-Bennett. On one level, she would be able to tell Anna about Doyle's state of mind, because they had lived together. But Anna also thought it was a strange coincidence that Uri and Doyle had been roommates when Ruth Collins had been murdered. Uri, who was now a patient at a psychiatric hospital. Was Uri somehow involved?

The note Anna had left in the kitchen would tell John everything he needed to know. It said that she was travelling to Barcelona, she was going to visit a psychiatric hospital, and she would be back in a few days.

The plane shot up into the air. After the burst of power to get off the ground, the plane eased off and levelled out. Her stomach hadn't liked the takeoff, and as she was hit with a wave of nausea, she checked that there was a sick bag in the front pocket of the seat. She usually enjoyed flying, and she wondered if it was the baby that was making her feel sick.

Anna sat back in her seat and opened her green plastic folder with all of Doyle Kennedy's information in there. It contained the research she had done on Doyle, plus the new sheets of information she had taken from Dr Cole's office. Early that morning, Anna had also printed some news articles on the murdered girls and added them to the folder. There had been three murders in Bristol that Anna thought were relevant to Doyle: Rachel White was the most recent at nine months, Abby Hammond had been killed two years ago, and Ruth Collins's body had been found eight years ago.

Anna didn't actually know if these were the murdered girls Doyle was supposedly responsible for, but her father had said 'three murders', and over the past twenty years, the only murders in Bristol or Bath that could possibly be linked to the same killer were these three girls. The media had reported that these girls had the same bite marks covering their lifeless bodies, and had been strangled in a similar manner.

Of the three dead girls, Ruth Collins was the one that interested Anna the most. It had happened eight years ago, which was when Doyle had been living in Bath. It was also when he had been living with Uri. Ruth's body had been dumped behind a restaurant in Bristol's city centre.

Doyle, Uri and Ruth had all been students at the same time. Doyle and Uri were in Bath; Ruth was in Bristol.

The two cities were a twenty-minute drive apart, two cities that were cosy neighbours. For Doyle to visit Ruth was only a twelve-minute train ride away. It was entirely possible that they had met, or even been dating. The police would probably know if that was the case, but there was no way for Anna to know the details.

It was a macabre way to spend a two-hour flight. She should be thinking about her teaching plans, organising a trip to Plymouth to see John's parents, or thinking what to get Lara for her birthday next month. Instead, she was reading through stories of pain and suffering. She couldn't begin to imagine the horror that these poor girls had gone through. Was it suffering caused by the father of her soon-to-be-born baby?

As she read through the news articles, she felt herself becoming more frustrated with the information before her. Anna really didn't have any facts or background to the killings. Her only hope was that she could get an insight into Doyle's mind from Uri. Was he capable of killing these three women?

---

EVENTUALLY THE PLANE LANDED, and the passengers disembarked. Dark clouds and drizzling rain welcomed Anna as she left the terminal. Her memories of Spain were of holidays in the sun, so the gloomy January weather felt particularly chilling. At least she had brought a denim jacket, which she pulled on over her black jumper, although a proper coat would have been better.

She had no real plans other than to visit the hospital and talk to Uri. It felt strange to Anna not to have a complete itinerary mapped out for her trip. It was a new experience for her to be making up her plans as she went along, and she wasn't entirely comfortable with the feeling. She took a taxi from the airport to the city centre, paid and got out. With her mini-overnight bag slung over her shoulder, Anna walked through the city and found a café to stop in and get her bearings.

The café was small, with only a dozen tables in it. It felt rustic, with dark wooden furniture and a grey tiled floor. Anna sat on a small table at the back of the café and admired the walls that were covered in paintings and pictures of lobsters. The pictures were a mix of styles and sizes, but all centred around the lobster. The walls looked like they had been splashed with blobs of dark orange paint, as the pictures covered every inch of wall. Anna also noticed each table had a small stone lobster statue that held a pot of cutlery and napkins.

She ordered a lemonade and, turning on her phone, was flooded with texts from John. Perhaps her note hadn't been so thorough after all.

Anna replied to John's texts with a short message that said she had landed, all was well and she would call him later. As she clicked 'send', a waiter passed her, holding some little plates piled up with dark and smoky meats. The food looked and smelt amazing, and Anna decided she could quite happily eat.

A thin barman with a dark tan and playful eyes approached her.

"Menu?" he offered.

Anna took the menu and scanned what was on offer. She couldn't eat shellfish while pregnant, but given her surroundings, Anna was perplexed to see that the menu didn't have any listed.

"No lobsters?" she asked the young waiter.

"Lobsters? No."

Anna tilted her head in confusion at him before forcing herself to look back at the menu.

She ordered a dish of roasted peppers, another of meatballs and a bowl of patatas bravas. When the food arrived, it tasted delicious. For a moment, it felt good to sit at the back of the café, hidden from the world but enjoying its delights, like some old artist seated in the shadows, watching the world pass by the café windows.

"You would like some wine?"

"No, thank you. Just the bill, please."

The handsome waiter smiled in reply, and she watched him retreat to the bar. *Maybe I should have invited Lara on the trip,* she thought with a smile.

When the waiter returned, Anna reached into her bag and pulled out her website printout on 'El Instituto de San Villegas'. She motioned for the waiter to look at the address.

"Do you know the best way to get here?" she asked slowly, trying to keep her English clear and concise.

He looked down at the name and address on the paper, and his bright smile faded. He looked at Anna and back at the paper several times with a mixture of curiosity and anxiety.

"Bad place. You want to go there?" he asked her with his basic English.

"Yes, please. I need to know how to get there."

He looked again at the address and slowly shook his head.

"Bad place."

"I'm going there to visit a patient. An old friend."

"You need a train. Station ten-minute walk. Train take you Torre Baro. There taxi into mountains. Maybe thirty minutes."

As he spoke, he pulled out a small pen from his apron and wrote on her printout.

"*Gracias.* Thank you."

He nodded, the smile gone.

"Be careful."

Anna wanted to laugh at his overt warnings, but instead just smiled at the waiter with appreciation, paid her bill and left.

---

THE STREET WAS full of glass-fronted shops and small cafés. She would have loved to stop and shop, but it seemed like most of the shops were closed. It was a cosmopolitan city, she noted, just not on a Sunday.

The walk was short and well sign-posted, but the rain still got her drenched. Of all the things she had thought to pack for Spain, an umbrella hadn't been one of them. Her thin denim jacket became soaked through, and by the time she made it to the train station, her hair and nose were dripping with rainwater.

As Anna walked down the steps and into the station, she was met with a cacophony of noise. Her descent revealed a long platform filled with football fans. There were thousands of men dressed in football T-shirts, waving flags and talking loudly. They smelt of wet dog and beer, and Anna was momentarily disoriented after coming from the quiet street to the busy underground station.

Looking around, she spied a policeman standing on a bench at the edge of the station, silently watching the football fans. Anna made her way over to him.

"Where can I get a ticket?" she called over the noise.

He looked down at her from his vantage point. "Ticket," he said, and pointed with his baton to an automated machine at the end of the platform.

Fixing her resolve, Anna pushed her way through the throng of bodies. They were wet and boisterous, and it was a relief to make it to the machine.

Digging out the paper in her pocket, Anna typed the station name the waiter had given her into the machine. She paid the ten euros with a wet note from her jeans pocket and gratefully collected her ticket.

Next to the ticket machine was a large screen showing the arriving trains' details. With a sinking feeling, Anna saw that the platform she needed was the one she was currently standing on, which was the one with the football fans covering every inch of floor space.

Anna made her way around to the back wall and waited for her train, hoping that she didn't stand out too much.

She received a few curious looks but, thankfully, was left alone.

She wasn't normally claustrophobic, but the underground station being so full made her feel uneasy, and she couldn't help but keep glancing back up to the staircase. After twenty minutes of the oppressive noise and sour smell, she decided she'd had enough, and would try to get a taxi, when a cheer went up from the crowd, signalling the train's arrival.

The train slowly screeched alongside the platform, and the mass of men surged forwards. Anna hesitated. The crowd was shrinking before her as the bodies moved into the carriages. Taxi or train? Finally the platform emptied. The train was full, but Anna could see some space in the doorway for her to stand. In thirty minutes, she could be at her station. So, taking a firm grip on her bag, Anna stepped up into the train and held onto a rail near the door.

As the doors locked and the train slowly started to move, instantly Anna knew she had made a mistake. The carriage was so full that men were standing in the corridors. The stink of beer was pungent in the cramped space. There must have been fifteen men in football shirts swaying in the doorway, and all of them were staring at her. She was acutely aware of her wet clothes and hair.

Anna didn't know what to do, so she turned her back to them and looked out of the window. The train began to pick up speed so that it creaked and rattled. Eventually Anna could sense that the men surrounding her became bored and started to quietly chat amongst themselves. Apart from three of them, whose reflections she could clearly see in the train window.

The three men continued to stare at her with drunken grins.

"*Como se llama?*"

Anna turned to them and smiled politely in reply, shaking

her head no. They were young, maybe in their early twenties. All she could see of them were tattooed arms and leering eyes. They looked mean, and that meanness was focused on her. Turning back to the window, the reflection showed her their drunken swaying and dark smiles.

"*Como se llama?*" another of the young men repeated.

Her legs started to shake with the need to run away, but there was nowhere to run to. She was penned in like a mare on the way to market. Anna didn't think it would help if she explained she didn't speak Spanish.

Her mind started to race. What could she do? Would they attack her on the train? Would anyone else help if they did jump on her? Fear was crawling all over her body like she had fallen into a spider's nest. She just wanted to run and scream.

"*Responde la pregunta!*" another of the three chimed in.

In the reflection of the window glass, Anna could see the men starting to move towards her, although their drunken legs and the rocking train made their progress slow. The sound of laughter from another group of men echoed down the train.

Without looking back, Anna began moving away from them, heading for another carriage. Surely there would be someone who would help her? She could hear the three drunks following and calling out to her. The smell of rain-soaked men was making her nauseated.

She pushed through the crowd of men packed into the corridor.

At the end of the carriage, Anna saw a toilet that looked free. Hope drove her on to it. She tried the handle. It was open and unoccupied. Stepping into the toilet, Anna turned just in time to close and lock the door before the three young men reached her. They banged on the door and called out again.

"There's no way I'm opening that door," she whispered to herself.

The toilet was small but surprisingly clean. She sat on the toilet lid and realised her hands were shaking. The banging on the door became harder and louder. She could hear what she assumed were insults and slurs in Spanish.

Men started to argue on the other side of the door. New voices joined in the shouting. The volume grew louder, and within seconds, Anna could hear the sounds of a fight break out. A man screamed in pain. Something smashed into the door, and Anna pushed against it with her whole weight as she was flooded with adrenaline.

The sounds of violence pounded through the corridor.

Anna trembled as she pushed against the door, using her feet against the toilet as a counterbalance.

After a few moments, the sounds of fighting seemed to move further down the train, and then it ceased altogether. The silence was almost as terrifying as the sounds of violence.

Minutes passed, and the silence continued.

Her arms started to throb and ache from holding the door, and she eased her grip and sat back on the toilet seat, listening and waiting.

The train stopped several times before eventually she heard the tannoy faintly call out, *Terra Bora.*

When the train stopped, Anna clenched her fists and jaw, quickly unlocked the door and sprang out, ready to punch and kick any drunken football fans to save herself.

Much to her relief, the carriage was empty. Anna noticed a long, thin splatter of blood on the toilet door as she stepped off the train and onto the small station platform. Her fists slowly uncurled at the sight of the empty station.

It was still raining.

## 13

The taxi bumped along the thin country road as it drove up into the Spanish mountains. The car's wipers struggled to cope with the heavy rain that continued to pour down from the dark clouds above them.

"Is it much further?" Anna called to the driver over the noise of the drumming rain.

She wasn't sure if he spoke English, but as he chose to ignore her, she thought it didn't matter anyway. He was mute and bald and looked like he might fall asleep at any second. Anna thought how dogs and their owners sometimes looked like each other, and she applied the same notion to the driver and his car. Both the driver and the car were squat, old and slow.

The car had steamed up, and Anna could make out little through the windows, just steep mountains and sparse trees. She had no idea where they were. The car was cold, and as Anna was still wet, she shivered on the back seat.

Checking her watch, she could see that they had been driving for over an hour. Surely the waiter had said the hospital was only thirty minutes from the train station?

For the tenth time, Anna looked at her phone, but it still showed no signal.

Had the driver understood her request to go to 'El Instituto de San Villegas'? She could only hope so. Through the steamy windows, Anna could see that it was starting to get dark, and she wondered what time the hospital would close for the night. Instinctively, she placed her hands protectively over her stomach.

"I like to plan things," Anna told the driver, who ignored her. "My husband usually laughs at me, at how organised I am. I won't go to the shops without an itinerary and a shopping list planned out in order of where the shops are." She looked out to the gloomy mountains. "But I came here last minute, so I don't have any plan at all."

The only response she got from the driver was a long sigh.

"How the hell do people live like this? Just going somewhere and hoping for the best? It's ridiculous..."

Without warning, the taxi lurched to a stop.

"*Estamos aqui.*"

"Why did you stop? Are we here?"

Anna wound down the window and peered through the rain. She could see some steps leading up to a large stone building. It had high, grey walls and looked more like an ancient castle than a hospital. The windows on the building were small and thin and protected by black metal bars. Above the front door, there was a small light on.

The driver tapped his meter, the red digits informing Anna she owed him forty-five euros for the trip. Anna pulled out some wet euros from her jeans pocket and paid the driver. In return, he gave her a business card with what looked like his mobile number on it.

"*Para luego.*"

She didn't know what he was saying, but she took the card and thanked him.

Anna stepped out into the rain. As soon as she closed the door, the taxi pulled away. She watched forlornly as it performed a U-turn on the road and set off back down to the town.

Looking around her, Anna could only see mountains, trees and the hospital. Surrounding the hospital was a world of pale yellow mountains and faded green bushes, as if the rain were slowly washing the country of all colour.

She wished John were there with her.

Anna climbed the steps, holding onto the single rusty rail. Either side of the steps, the ground was covered in dying hibiscus plants and razor-sharp yuccas. Thankfully, there was a small porch over the entrance that protected her from the rain. Looking at the peeling brown paint on the front door, Anna wondered if the hospital was still occupied. She shivered with the cold as she pushed the buzzer on a plastic box next to the door.

There was no answer.

She pushed the buzzer again and looked around for any sign of life. There was a small wooden sign above the door that read 'El Instituto de San Villegas'. At least she was in the right place.

Anna checked again, but there was still no signal on her phone.

"*Si?*" the intercom cackled out.

She spun around and pressed her face into it.

"*Hola?* Hello? I'm here to visit a patient."

"A patient?"

"You speak English?" Anna couldn't keep the relief from her voice. "My name is Anna Wilson. I emailed last night; I want to see one of your patients."

"I'm sorry, there is no visiting today."

"Please. I have travelled from Bristol. From England. I need to come in."

There was no response, just an ominous silence.

After a moment, the intercom buzzed as the front door was unlocked.

"Oh, thank God."

Anna pulled it open and stepped into a dimly lit hallway. She had made it. Despite shivering with the cold and feeling unwelcome, Anna was proud of herself; she was in. The only issue she had now was what was she going to say to the doctors? How was she going to get in to see Uri Rana-Bennett? Desperation clung to her like her wet clothes.

The sound of footsteps echoed around the hallway. They were heading for her. From around the corner a woman appeared. She was short and wore a white doctor's coat with her hands casually tucked into the pockets. Her dark hair was pulled back into a bun, and she gave Anna a friendly, warm smile.

"Hello, I am Camille Alves. I am the head nurse here. Would you like to follow me for some coffee?"

"Yes, please," Anna replied through chattering teeth.

---

ANNA ENJOYED the hot steam in her face from the cup of coffee. She shouldn't really be drinking caffeine with the baby, but, given how wet and cold she was, Anna thought one would be allowed. As well as being warming, the coffee tasted amazing.

She moved her chair closer to the radiator so that the hot metal was touching her legs. They were sitting in Nurse Camille's office, which had a high ceiling and thin blue carpet. The room was sparse, with a desk and two chairs. There was damp creeping across the ceiling, but it was so high Anna had to squint to make it out.

"This coffee is amazing."

"Good. You look like you need it. So tell me, who is it you want to visit?"

"Uri Rana-Bennett."

Camille tilted her head as she considered this answer. She was sitting behind her desk with her own cup of coffee.

"Are you a relative of Uri's?"

"No."

"We have no record of a visitor coming to see Uri before. Did you make a booking?"

"No."

Camille smiled. It was warm and seemed to illuminate the room.

"As we only allow visitors on a Saturday, and it is a Sunday, I was assuming you hadn't booked a visit with us."

Anna realised what she was being told, and her heart sank.

"Oh, Saturdays only?" Anna was momentarily lost for words. She looked around the office, hoping for some inspiration, but there was little to see in the barren room.

Camille was watching Anna. "This hospital is closing. It is a very old building, and the government is building a new site nearer to the city. In two months, this whole place will be emptied and then torn down. My team of nurses are looking forward to getting out of this place."

"It is an old building."

"El Instituto de San Villegas was built when the world believed people with mental problems should be treated like prisoners. It was designed to lock them up and keep them out of society. Of course, we have moved on since then. Now we treat them like patients, with care and support to help them."

"England is the same. It's only been in recent years that we changed the way we look after our mentally ill."

"So you are from Bristol? I studied in London for a year."

Anna nodded. "I teach at Bristol University, at the School of Psychological Science."

"I am curious: Did you say you flew from England to be here?"

Anna sipped her coffee and thought about what to say. She looked at Camille and concluded she seemed reasonable. Anna decided that honesty would be her best approach. As a rule, she didn't trust strangers and had to fight the urge to keep her distance. She forced her face to unfreeze and her body language to relax.

"I'm pregnant."

"Congratulations."

"My husband and I had been trying for a while, and we discovered he couldn't have children. So we used a donor. A sperm donor."

Camille nodded that she understood, and Anna continued.

"I spent months finding the right person to be our donor. We finally used a man called Doyle. It worked. He got me pregnant, and we were so happy."

Anna drank more coffee. She was still feeling cold despite the drink and the radiator. She shifted in her seat, ignoring the growing feeling of embarrassment at discussing her private life.

"A few days ago, we discovered that Doyle is a murderer. Possibly. Not just a murderer, a serial killer. The police have linked him to at least three deaths."

"I am sorry to hear this."

Anna opened her mouth to speak and then closed it. Every inch of her wanted to close off and stay behind her walls. She stared into her coffee cup, blinking rapidly. Steeling her resolve, Anna continued.

"I found out that this man, Doyle, lived with Uri Rana-Bennett for a year. So I want to talk to her. I want to ask her about Doyle, to see what sort of man he was. She is a trained psychologist like me, and I think she would have a good insight into his mind. I need to know. I need to know if this man is capable of doing these things, as the police don't seem sure yet."

"Why is it so important to know about Doyle?"

Her throat felt tight as if a rope were around her neck. She took a deep breath, trying to keep calm.

"My husband thinks we should have an abortion. Maybe I do too. I don't know. We don't know what to do."

"But because the father is a killer doesn't mean the child will be. There must be a very small chance?"

"The chance of it is very small, as you say. But it is still there. It would still be on our minds, forever."

Camille nodded, deep in thought.

"That is a lot of information to take in," she murmured.

Anna sat back in her chair and waited. After a moment, Camille turned her attention to her computer and began tapping away on the keyboard and mouse.

"I have Uri's file here." She peered at the screen as she spoke. "She is bipolar. We have her heavily sedated at the moment. She was admitted here six months ago and has not had a visitor since. You would be her first visitor."

Camille continued to read in silence.

"Yes, she is heavily sedated. Alright, I am allowing you a short visit with Uri. But you must keep everything relaxed. I suggest you do not mention what this man is accused of. Just ask her some simple questions about him."

Anna breathed a big sigh of relief, knowing that sharing her situation with Camille had been the right thing to do.

"Thank you so much."

"I hope you get the answers you want."

THE DOOR to Uri's room was metal with thick, re-enforcing bolts all around it. As Camille unlocked the door, Anna tried to control her rising nerves. She had removed her jewellery and left it in the office with her overnight bag. Her hair had been tied back, and she had been given a quick drill on what to do if attacked, which simply involved running out of the room and calling for help. If she couldn't do that, there was a call button inside the room to bring help.

"How are you today, Uri?" Camille asked as she entered the room.

Anna followed Camille in, noting where on the wall the call button was located. She looked around and was surprised at how empty the small room was. It had a high ceiling and a long, thin window with metal bars across it. The walls were plain white, and a metal bed had been screwed to the floor. Camille motioned for Anna to sit on a small plastic chair, which stood beside the bed. Uri was hidden from view under a brown woollen blanket, which covered the bed. A smell of urine caught in Anna's nose, making her eyes sting. She had to stop herself from pinching her nostrils closed.

"You have a visitor, Uri. Isn't that nice? This is Anna. She has come from England to see you."

Camille turned and must have caught sight of the horror on Anna's face.

"Like I said," Camille whispered, "this is a very old building, and we are moving to a much nicer complex soon."

Fear had stolen Anna's voice, so she just nodded mutely.

Under the bed covers, Uri stirred.

Slowly she sat up. Anna's eyes were glued to her.

Uri looked relaxed. She had high cheekbones and big brown eyes; in another situation, she would have been considered pretty. But her hair was a mess, and Anna noticed missing patches, as if clumps had been torn out. Uri's skin was so translucent, Anna could see the thin blue veins beneath.

"Hello, Uri, I'm Anna," her voice croaked.

"Hello." Uri sounded English, with no Spanish accent.

A high-pitched scream came from the corridor outside the room, and Anna jumped in fright. It hadn't sounded human, and she had to force her hands to unclench. Uri seemed oblivious to the noise.

"I hope you don't mind, Uri; I want to talk to you for a little while."

"Alright."

Nurse Camille seemed happy enough, and with a quick squeeze of Anna's shoulder, she left the room. *I hope she stays close by,* Anna thought.

"How are you feeling today?"

"I'm tired," Uri replied.

*With all the drugs you must be on, I'm not surprised.* She looked at Uri and felt a sense of sympathy for her. It was sad for any young girl to be locked up like this.

"Why did you come to Spain, Uri? Was it for a holiday?"

Uri frowned and seemed confused by the question. "My mum is Spanish, and I grew up there." She paused. "Am I in Spain?"

"Yes, Uri, we're near Barcelona."

Uri didn't respond. Anna watched her, unsure what to say. She had been so determined to get here and talk to Uri that she hadn't actually thought about what to say, or how to ask about Doyle. Uri looked to be a million miles away, and with a sinking feeling, Anna started to think it had been a wasted journey.

"I had the strangest dream." Uri spoke slowly, her eyes struggling to focus on anything.

"Really?"

"I was flying a kite in Bath Park. Have you been to Bath Park?"

"Why, yes. I live in Bristol, very close to Bath. Actually, it's about your time in Bath that I wanted to ask you."

"I love Bath. I'm going to go back there soon."

Anna didn't think Uri was going anywhere soon, but decided it was best not to say anything. Another whiff of urine hit her, and she fought off the instinct to cover her face, especially as she could feel the pungent smell at the back of her throat.

"You went to university in Bath, didn't you?"

"Yes. I'm a doctor." She sounded like a child role playing.

"I know. A doctor of psychology. When you were at university, do you remember living in Twerton in Bath? You were in a shared student house with Ron, Michelle and Doyle?"

"Doyle?"

Anna felt a thrill of excitement go through her as she saw a flicker of recognition cross Uri's face.

"Yes, Uri. Doyle Kennedy. Do you remember him?"

Uri's mouth grew into a big grin, and her face lit up like a child who had just been given a big ice cream.

"I love Doyle. He is so nice. Is he here?"

"Sorry, Uri, Doyle couldn't come today."

"He is lovely. When is he coming to see me?"

"I can ask him to come soon." Anna tried to remain calm. "Uri, what do you remember about Doyle? What was he like when you lived together?"

"Oh, he was lovely. He worked hard and looked after us all. He was always cleaning the kitchen."

Anna felt like she was talking to a child, and wasn't sure how much insight she would get from Uri. Anna's eyes roamed around the small room. It made her sad to see how sparse and empty it was. There was only the metal bed and the plastic chair Anna was sitting on. The brown tiles covering the floor were flecked with peeling paint that had flaked off the walls. Beside the bed were several photos stuck to the wall; they were near the pillow so Uri could look at them.

"Were there times when he wasn't lovely? Did Doyle ever snap at you?"

Uri frowned at the question although she seemed to be considering it. Anna focused on the photos on the wall. There was one of an older lady on her own, another of a dog and a third one with a group of people in it.

"No. Doyle never shouted. Doyle was lovely." Her voice was slow and measured, as if she hadn't spoken for a long time and was getting used to speaking again.

"Did Doyle ever do anything strange, Uri?"

If he did, Anna thought, it would be hypocritical of Uri to comment on it, given she was currently locked up in a mental hospital, but she had to ask the question. As Uri considered the question, Anna squinted at the group photo, and her hand suddenly flew to her mouth in shock. There were three people she recognised in the photo.

A young Uri stood next to a handsome young man, and that man was unmistakably Doyle Kennedy. Standing between them was an attractive young woman with dark hair. Anna recognised the woman instantly, because she had been looking at a photo of her all evening. It was Ruth Collins, the girl who had been murdered eight years ago.

"Strange? No. Nothing strange. He was lovely. Is he coming to see me today?"

"No, not today," Anna repeated as she dug out her mobile phone from her pocket.

She casually swiped the camera on and zoomed in on the photo on the wall. For a second it was blurry, but then the camera focused on Uri, Doyle and Ruth standing together, and Anna quickly snapped several photos of the old photo on the wall.

The phone wasn't on silent, and the sound of the camera clicks filled the small room. Uri suddenly tensed.

Anna watched in horror as Uri's childlike frown disappeared to be replaced by an angry, screwed-up face. Her brown eyes suddenly became alive and focused. Focused on Anna and her phone. The eyes were piercing, and a wave of dread poured over Anna, causing her scalp to feel itchy from the hairs standing up on her head.

"Where is Doyle?" Uri demanded. Her voice had changed from that of a dazed little girl; it now sounded hard and vicious.

The feeling of terror made Anna stand quickly and move away from Uri and the bed. She was shocked at the transformation in front of her. A sudden thought occurred to Anna. A clear, cold thought that slapped her in the face.

"Have you ever been to Bristol, Uri?"

"Of course I've been to Bristol," Uri snapped with impatience.

"Do you get jealous? Jealous of other women?"

"Why?" Uri spat in anger.

Uri was still sitting on the bed, but the knowing, menacing look she now gave Anna made Anna feel like the child.

"Have you ever attacked another woman? Perhaps women in Bristol?"

Uri burst out laughing.

It was a chilling sound. Anna instinctively stepped back further. The door behind her burst open as the laugh echoed up to the high ceiling.

"I think that's enough now," Nurse Camille said quickly behind her.

Anna didn't need to be told twice, and swiftly stepped out

of the room. Camille followed her out and, without hesitating, locked the door behind them.

"Did you get what you needed?"

Anna exhaled and placed her shaking hands on her stomach. "I think so."

---

JOHN HAD SPENT the day worrying. He had cleaned the house, done the food shopping, cleaned his golf clubs and watched two films. Everything was done to try to stay calm, but it was difficult. He was worried about Anna and what she was doing. Flying to Barcelona to go and visit a hospital and talk with someone who had lived with their sperm donor years ago sounded ridiculous to him.

Every hour, he had tried her mobile. There had been no answer to his calls and no reply to his texts. As the faint January sun set, and the dark night finally descended, his phone buzzed. It wasn't Anna's number, but an international caller.

John snatched up the phone.

"Hello? Anna?"

"John?"

"Oh, thank god. Are you okay?"

"Yes. I'm alright. Sorry I haven't called sooner; I didn't have any reception on my phone."

"Where are you?"

"Actually, I'm still at the hospital. I'm staying here tonight."

"You're staying in a hospital tonight? Are you okay?"

"Yes, it's nicer than it sounds. It's late, and the head nurse here has offered me a room in the staff quarters. They're actually nice. Bit small, but I've got a bed and bathroom, and I'm totally knackered. It would have taken ages to get back into the city and find a hotel."

John felt the tension in his shoulders ease a little with this information.

"So you're finally where you belong: Locked up in some mental hospital."

Anna laughed.

"Sorry I rushed off here with just a note for you. But I wanted to get straight out here. Like I said in my note, I wanted to see a patient who had lived with Doyle."

"Did you see this mystery patient?"

"Actually, yes. Her name is Uri, and it was an interesting meeting."

"Look, Anna, I don't mind you going there. I just worry about you."

"You shouldn't worry."

"I know. But you're my wife, and I love you. I just want you to be safe."

"Thanks, Johnny boy."

"When are you coming back?"

"Tomorrow. I'm going to sleep here tonight; then there's a flight in the afternoon. Should be back about seven o'clock."

Before John could reply, a pulsating wail came from the phone.

"What the hell is that?" John asked.

"It's an alarm. There's an alarm going off here." Anna sounded unsettled.

"What does that mean? Anna? Hello? Why is the alarm going off?"

There was no answer.

The phone had cut out.

## 14

"John? Hello?" The phone had cut out. Anna replaced the handset.

The hospital's main alarm had been triggered. What did that mean? She didn't know, but she guessed it couldn't be good news. The alarm was a shrieking wail that she imagined had probably been fitted during the war; it sounded like she was in some old German prisoner-of-war camp.

Anna got out of bed and got dressed. Thankfully, her jeans and jumper had dried on the old radiator. It felt nice not to be wearing wet clothes.

There was a knock on the bedroom's wooden door, and Nurse Camille opened it and poked her head into the room.

"This is not good. Stay in your room, please, and keep your door locked." The earlier warmth had evaporated, leaving her looking worried and businesslike.

"There is no lock on this door," Anna replied, but Camille was already gone, the sound of her feet pounding the corridor amongst the alarm's wail.

She looked out of the room to the long corridor outside. There was a row of closed doors and no sign of anybody else.

Anna closed the bedroom door and double-checked it. There was definitely no lock on either the door or the small silver handle. There was one small window in the room, but it was barred from the outside, to stop people getting into the room. Or out of it.

"Jesus Christ."

*Now what?* She thought about dragging the bed up to the door to block it, but the bed was screwed to the concrete floor. There was no chair or furniture to use either. When Nurse Camille had invited her to stay in the staff quarters, it had seemed like a good idea. Now it felt like one of the worst decisions she had ever made. There was an alarm going off in an old mental hospital, and she was all alone in an unlocked room.

"This is ridiculous."

She tried the landline phone again, but there was no dialling tone. Anna picked up her mobile phone, but it still didn't have any signal. She could feel panic rising in her and tried to stop it from taking over. Surely she was overreacting, she reasoned with herself. There was nothing to worry about.

From the corridor outside, there came a crash. Anna froze in fear, listening intently like a startled deer. What was that noise? The alarm continued to bleat out around the old building as she strained her ears.

There was another crashing sound from the corridor.

Anna recognised the sound now. It sounded like someone was opening the doors. No, like someone was *smashing* the doors open along the corridor outside. She waited, without moving, trying to sense what was happening from the sounds coming from outside the bedroom.

It happened again, another door being flung wide and crashing into the wall.

Anna realised the crashing sound was getting closer. It was as if someone was working their way down the long corridor of bedrooms, looking into each room. *Who is it? What are they looking for?* Could it be a security guard searching for someone?

Another crash. This one louder.

But why would the security guards force each door open in turn? They wouldn't want to damage the place if they were searching for someone. So perhaps it wasn't the hospital security looking into each bedroom. But if it wasn't them, then who was it? Could it be one of the residents?

Anna started to move now, frantically looking around her room for somewhere to hide. Her breathing became shorter, and sweat covered her face. There were four walls, a bed with some white sheets on it and an old phone screwed to the wall. She got on her hands and knees and crawled under the bed and curled up to make herself as small as possible. It was dusty and dark. The alarm continued its relentless blaring.

Under the bed seemed too obvious. Was it too obvious? Anna crawled out from under the bed and stood in the middle of the room. The feeling of panic was rising again.

She got down on her knees and crawled under the bed for a second time. Grey dust covered her clothes and hair. If someone came in, they would likely look under the bed, so it was a poor hiding place. She got back out from under the bed and stood up again. She felt lost, as if she were a blindfolded child in a bad dream.

Anna walked to the door and checked it, in case she had somehow missed a bolt or switch, but there was definitely no lock on the bedroom door.

There was another crash of a door being flung open. This one sounded like it was next door to her. Her room would be next. Anna looked around for a weapon. Anything to protect herself with. There was nothing.

It had to be an overexcited guard, banging the doors open, she told herself. The alternative was too frightful to comprehend.

Anna stood by the side of the bed, feeling exposed and praying it was just a security guard about to burst into her bedroom. Her eyes felt six inches wide as they were glued to the wooden door.

The light of the corridor was blocked out as a shadow filled the door frame. Someone was outside her room.

The door burst open.

It was worse than Anna could have imagined.

Standing there, wild-eyed and destructive, was Uri Rana-Bennett. She was wearing a dirty white nightgown, and her hair was sticking up in a matted clump. Uri's face was contorted and purple. Her hands were bunched like claws, and her bare feet were black with dirt.

Uri's eyes locked onto Anna. A look of twisted triumph came over her. She pointed a clawed hand at Anna.

"YOU!" she screamed.

"Oh, shit!"

With a scream, Uri charged at Anna, her feet slapping on the concrete floor.

Anna screamed.

Uri was on her, her filthy nails digging into Anna's arms. Anna fell onto the floor, Uri on top of her.

"Where's Doyle?" Uri screamed into her face. Her breath was like rotting flesh.

Anna tried to wrestle Uri off her, but she was locked on too tight. Anna's thin arms burned with pain as Uri's nails dug into her skin. The grip felt wet, and Anna realised it was blood.

Uri was too heavy for her. She couldn't move, couldn't breathe.

All Anna could see were feral eyes and stumpy, yellow

teeth that were growling at her. Without warning, Uri snapped at Anna, trying to bite her. Anna managed to push her head to the side to avoid the bite. She felt like she was wrestling with a wild dog.

The clawed hands scratched deeper into Anna's skin.

"Help!" she screamed into the empty room.

All she could hear in reply was the hospital's alarm still bleating around the building.

Uri bit again, and this time her jaw, full of rotten teeth, chomped into Anna's shoulder. She screamed with the pain, the sound drowning out Uri's growls and the pulsating alarm.

The yellow stumps were boring into her flesh.

Anna wept and struggled, unable to move. Her energy was dropping fast, and she wished she were stronger. It felt as though her arms were trying to lift a car. Uri writhed and growled and tore at her.

She was trying to kill Anna.

For an instant, Anna thought about the baby she was carrying. Her baby. It was the size of a pear. The baby who was relying on her. Relying on its mum.

*Mum.*

The word was like a lightning bolt.

With a scream, Anna headbutted Uri in the face.

Anna felt the grip on her loosen just enough for her to get her arm up for a strike. Her fist curled like a stone. She punched Uri in the face. The grip on her weakened further. She struck again, catching Uri in the ear. Anna looked where she wanted to strike. She punched, landing squarely on the nose. Uri's face became dazed, her bloody grip on Anna becoming weaker.

Suddenly there was another arm there. It was wrapping around Uri's throat, pulling her away. It was a huge, hairy arm; it picked Uri up like a child. Anna was free.

A security guard had arrived; he was so tall and wide his frame seemed to fill the sparse room.

Anna sat up.

"I've never hit someone before," she blurted out without thinking.

The guard called out something in Spanish before whisking the struggling Uri away. Anna was on her own, her body pumped full of adrenaline.

She stood up.

Her whole body shook. It wasn't like being cold; it was the body shaking from shock. Her hands, kneecaps, legs, arms, breasts, face and neck all shook uncontrollably. Anna had never felt anything like it. Tears poured down her face.

Anna looked at her arms. They were smudged with blood.

Her arms and head hurt, but despite the shaking, her stomach felt fine. She prayed the baby was okay.

There was a small mirror on the far wall, and Anna stumbled over to it. She pulled down her blouse at the neckline and looked at Uri's teeth marks on her shoulder. She had seen these exact marks before. They matched the ones on the missing girls of Bristol.

---

ANNA DIDN'T SLEEP that night. After the alarm was turned off, Camille appeared, apologetic and sympathetic, reassuring Anna that Uri was now heavily sedated. There was no mention or explanation of how Uri had managed to escape, but Anna suspected the old building offered ample opportunity for breaking out. Camille cleaned and bound Anna's wounds and offered her another coffee. Anna declined the drink, but did move to another room that had a lock on the door. She checked the lock three times to make sure it was secure.

Before lying on the bed with its thin white sheets, Anna spent time in the mirror, studying the bite mark from Uri. It sent a chill down her just to look at it, but Anna couldn't take her eyes off the wound. It definitely looked like the bite wounds she had studied in the news articles on the murdered girls, with the same distinct shape and layout of teeth marks.

It looked like a piece of evidence.

Anna dug her phone out of her pocket and switched the camera so it was facing her. She took a dozen photos of the wound from different angles and distances.

Should she tell the police about it? Her first instinct was to notify Detective Wright, but how was Anna going to explain her presence in Spain, visiting Uri? Could Anna be accused of withholding evidence? If her father had any input into it, Anna would certainly be in trouble. The old bastard would twist everything to make her look guilty.

Throughout the remainder of the night, the hospital remained quiet, but Anna couldn't sleep despite feeling utterly worn out. The slightest sound made her jump. She thought about Doyle and Uri and tried to imagine the two of them living together. For a long time, Anna stared at the photo she had taken of Uri, Doyle and Ruth Collins.

How did they know each other? The photo showed three young and happy people standing together, perhaps at a garden party or beer garden. The sun was shining, and they were all smiling and holding drinks. They looked like they had their whole lives ahead of them, and it was saddening to think that one of them was dead, another was in a psychiatric hospital and the third had just been arrested for murder. What a tragic turn of events for all three of them. As Anna studied the photo, it raised only more questions for her.

Was Uri the crazy one the police should be talking to? Was Doyle innocent? Would her baby be okay?

---

ANNA THOUGHT about John and his reluctance to have a baby. Their world was built around the both of them, around their wants and needs. They had nothing to worry about apart from each other. Anna had changed that. She had upset their balanced lives with her need for a baby. Not just a baby, she wanted a family of her own. She wanted playtime in the park, kids' movie nights, shopping trips and holidays together, painting pictures and reading stories, bedtimes and bath times. Cuddles and kisses with her children.

Anna was so tired, and the scratches on her arms ached. Faces blurred in her mind. She thought about Doyle standing next to John. Uri's crazy face would forever be burned into her memory, and every time her eyes drooped, the feral bitch appeared in her mind and Anna's eyes flew open, fervently scanning the small room.

The night slowly faded to be replaced by a pale sun, bringing a suggestion of daylight. Eventually, Anna thought it was an appropriate time to wake Nurse Camille. She silently walked down the corridor and tapped on her bedroom door.

"Yes?" The door was opened by a tired-looking Camille.

"Can I have a lift to the train station, please?"

---

JOHN JUMPED up from the sofa at the sound of the key in the front door. He stood in the doorway as Anna walked in. She looked terrible, but he was happy to see her.

"Wow, look at you. Is that a black eye?"

Anna stepped into the house and dropped her bag onto

the hallway floor. She stepped into John's arms, and he hugged her tightly. John thought she stank, but he decided not to mention it. He held his wife firmly, feeling her breathing into his shoulder.

"When you said on the phone it had been a long night, you weren't lying."

"Honestly, John, she was crazy. I'll never forget the sight of Uri running at me."

Although Anna had filled John in on the details of her trip to Barcelona on the phone, he still had a lot of questions, but it didn't feel like the right time to ask them.

"Shall I run you a bath?"

"Yes, please," she said into his chest.

He pulled her back and kissed her forehead.

"You look like you've been in a boxing match," he said gently.

"Feels like it."

He softly kissed her again.

"The black eye suits you."

She smiled and hugged him again.

"Come on, let's get you in the bath."

Anna gasped at the hot water. It felt amazing on her tired and bruised body. Slowly she started to relax. The grime of the past two days was scrubbed off; her hair was washed and conditioned twice. It became difficult to stay awake, so she got out and dried herself with several towels.

Anna put on her pyjamas and got into bed.

Before she fell asleep, Anna reached for her mobile and scrolled down to Detective Wright's number. She pressed the call button and waited for the detective to answer.

"Detective Sergeant Wright speaking."

"Hi, this is Anna Wilson. You came to see me a few days ago about Doyle Kennedy."

"Yes, hello, Mrs Wilson. How can I help?"

Anna's eyes felt heavy, and she had to work hard to stay focused.

"I'm not sure how to say this, so I'm just going to come out with it. I think I have some evidence for you. You know, in the case. For the case. Whatever you call it."

"What evidence?"

"I'll come and see you tomorrow. But just you. I'll come to the station lunchtime."

"If it's important, you –"

Anna cut the call and turned her phone off. She was too tired. It was only seven thirty in the evening, but, with a sigh, Anna fell into a deep sleep.

## 15

"Sit down, please. Everyone sit down."

Anna watched her class slowly find their seats. There was a low drone of inane chatter as a parade of students with hoodies and backpacks shuffled around the auditorium.

"Today we will be looking at some sociobiology topics, including genetics and political views."

Anna slouched, leaning on the front podium, bracing herself for two hours of teaching a class of fifty students. She had on a thick layer of make-up to cover her black eye and hoped that none of the students noticed it.

Despite twelve hours' sleep, she still felt a little spaced out, as if she were watching the world through binoculars. It hadn't helped that her dreams had been filled with the snarling face of Uri Rana-Bennett, and she had woken up covered in sweat. Her left shoulder and both arms still ached, and she was wearing a long green blouse to cover her bandages. In particular, her left arm throbbed; she wondered if it had become infected. Infected by a madwoman's dirty fingernails and yellow teeth. The thought made her stomach drop like a stone.

"Sit down!" Anna snapped at the students.

The class fell silent and quickly became seated. Anna blushed at her own harshness. All she wanted to do was get through the two-hour lesson without showing the pain she was in, or losing her mind and screaming at her students.

"Alright, thank you. So, we will start with an overview of the lesson plan."

Anna clicked her laptop on, and the screen behind her brought up her first PowerPoint slide.

"We have been speaking about nature versus nurture and the various factors that influence these. But today's lesson will look at these arguments from a different angle. A political angle."

She could see the students trying to quietly get their notepads and laptops open to take notes. Anna would normally allow them time to get set up, but that morning she didn't have the patience, she just wanted to get through the lesson as quickly as possible.

"Let's start with a few basic notions. If you believe that social conditions, namely your environment, are critical factors in shaping a person, then you would want people to be living in equally good conditions. So what would your political leaning be?"

Silence.

She tutted. "Anyone? Come on, this is an easy one." Anna was shocked by her own scathing impatience.

The students looked wary and cautious; a few even looked worried. Anna took a deep breath and tried to stay calm. It felt like the pain in her left shoulder and arm was getting worse.

"Would you be left wing, Ms?" a young man towards the front called out.

"Correct."

She could sense a mental sigh of relief from the class.

*Must relax,* she told herself.

"Now, if you believe that, through evolution, humans possess selfish, competitive tendencies naturally –" she sipped from her water bottle "– and social outcomes are accounted for by inherited variations, what would your political positioning be?"

"Right wing, Ms." It was the same voice from the front, but Anna couldn't identify who it was. It was just one student who was more awake than the others.

"So left-wing and right-wing views tend to be linked with whether you believe more in nature or nurture. Science is supposed to be above opinions and emotions. Science is the study of facts. It doesn't care what your political views are, which is why this area of psychology is so fascinating. To study what makes us who we are can open a whole world of dangerous paths and ideas. Today, we are going to look at the darker side of the debate to help us get under the skin of human behaviour."

She touched her left shoulder. It was roasting hot to the touch. Anna remembered the dirty fingernails digging into her skin, ripping at her flesh. She clenched her fists against the memory and the pain.

"Does anyone have any painkillers?"

The question was met with blank stares. Thankfully, a girl at the front of the hall stepped forward and handed Anna a small packet of pills.

"Sorry, class, I fell over on the weekend and hurt my arm." Anna wanted to add, 'and I'm in absolute agony here', but didn't.

She quickly put two painkillers into her mouth and drank the last of her water.

"Thank you." She nodded to the girl.

It had probably broken the university rules; technically, she had just accepted medicine from a student, which wasn't allowed, but at that moment, Anna didn't care.

Her mind was suddenly blank, and she couldn't remember what she had been saying. Anna looked at the screen, but it wasn't much help, so she just started talking, hoping there was some logic to what she was teaching.

"Alright, who can tell me what eugenics means?"

Again there was silence, but this time Anna let them off the hook.

"Eugenics is the science of improving a population by controlled breeding to increase the occurrence of desirable, heritable characteristics. That's the dictionary definition, anyway. Does anyone know what 'controlled breeding' means. Any examples?"

"Abortions?" someone called out.

The answer caught her by surprise, and the word was like an electric shock through her body. She had totally forgotten that she had a whole section on abortions as part of her eugenics lesson. Anna gripped the sides of the podium so hard her fingers became numb. The fifty students watched her in curious silence.

"Well, yes, but let us first look at the stage before being pregnant."

She had wanted to drag these points out more, to keep them thinking and encourage discussion, but instead she gave them the answers.

"Sterilization is one way people tried to improve a population."

The students made notes. It felt difficult to breathe, and she couldn't stop her eyes from darting back and forth. For some reason, she had to keep checking that no one was near her.

"Selective breeding is another way to achieve eugenics."

There was more note taking from the students.

"How about murder, Ms? Is that one?"

Anna felt sick. It was a large hall, but it felt like it was getting smaller around her. Had someone dimmed the lights?

"Technically, yes, murder is a form of eugenics."

She picked up her bottle of water, but it was empty. Her hands and back felt clammy.

"Let's concentrate on forced sterilisation. Modern eugenics was started in America in the 1890s with a compulsory sterilization program. The Americans believed that mental illness was hereditary, which led them to surmise that if the mentally ill were forcibly sterilised, it would reduce the number of people born with mental illnesses. They even included blind and deaf people in the programme. It was social engineering."

Anna was mostly on autopilot as she continued to speak. It was a lecture she had given a dozen times.

"Back then, the line of who was or wasn't mentally ill was blurred, so that some women who were deemed 'mentally feeble' were forcibly sterilised."

Anna paused. Then: "What the hell does 'mentally feeble' even mean?"

The class tittered in response.

"America forcibly sterilised over sixty-five thousand people at the turn of the century, the worst area being California. Arguably, a terrible knock-on effect was that America inspired many politicians and scientists in another country in the 1930s. Anyone want to guess where that was?"

"Germany?" several people called out.

They were listening now, engaged with what she was teaching them. She ploughed through the slides, not stopping for the debates she usually encouraged. This was a lazy form of teaching, but at that moment she didn't care.

"Correct. Germany. The Germans took forced sterilisation

to a whole new level. They set up two hundred eugenic courts and forcibly sterilised close to a million people in the 1930s and '40s."

Anna continued to talk through American and German sterilisation programmes. The students continued to take notes.

"The Germans called it 'Racial Hygiene', and the reasons given ranged from being homosexual to being manic-depressive, which today we call bipolar."

An image of Uri charging at her came to mind, and Anna paused again. Her eyes flicked left and right, and she realised that she shouldn't have come into work. She lifted the water bottle to her lips, but it was empty. The clock told her they were only twenty minutes into a two-hour lecture.

"We need to...today we will..." She couldn't breathe. It felt like someone had their hands around her throat, squeezing out the air.

Anna tried to focus as she held on tightly to the podium. An image of Uri in her nightgown flashed into her mind. Anna could see the stumpy, rotted teeth and black feet rushing at her.

"Lesson is finishing early. Read the three chapters of Plomin for next week."

Anna turned off the laptop, picked up her bag and left the hall. She stumbled through the building's main corridor and out an emergency exit. The fresh air felt good, and Anna was surprised to feel so much sweat on her face. In fact, she was completely drenched in sweat. She sat on a low wall by the exit, taking deep breaths of cold air.

Down the corridor, she could hear the students starting to filter out of the teaching hall. With a great effort, she picked herself up and headed up to her office.

She walked through the building and up the stairs to the tenth floor with her head down and bag clutched to her chest. Her corridor was empty, and the other lecturers had their doors closed. Once inside her office, she closed the door, threw her bag on the desk and slumped down on her chair. It was a small room, but it was her own private space.

Anna wheeled her chair over to the window and opened it to let in the fresh January air. She stared out at Bristol's skyline from the tenth floor, looking across to Redland and, in the distance, Clifton. It was a Tuesday morning, but the city seemed peaceful. The serenity helped her to calm down.

As her heart rate eased and her breathing slowed, she felt a surge of embarrassment at stumbling out of a lesson midway through it. Anna blushed and wished she were at home and in bed. She knew the students would be down in the canteen and library, laughing at her.

"Bugger."

Anna wondered if she should take a few days off from work. But what would she say to her boss, Dr Coldfield? 'I need some time off after a crazy woman attacked me in a mental hospital' didn't sound like something she wanted to announce.

Anna rolled the chair back to her desk. It was only ten thirty in the morning, and she didn't feel like going anywhere. Instead, she pulled a pile of coursework papers from her bag and started to mark them. It felt good to be doing something normal, and Anna began to relax as she read through the papers.

Her phone buzzed with a text.

It was from Lara.

*Hey, are you feeling fat yet?! Keep eating your greens! xxx*

Anna still couldn't believe she was pregnant, and despite everything, she smiled at the message and replied:

*Not fatter than usual, just feels hard around stomach.*
*Thanks for asking! Call you later. X*

Whatever was going to happen with the baby she was carrying, she was glad she had come this far. Even with an eighteen-week baby, it had given her a small taste of the experience of caring for someone else, and she had loved it.

Anna held her hands over her stomach to see if she could feel anything, hoping for the little one to move for the first time. But there was nothing, just a warm stillness.

ANNA PARKED outside the Chinese takeaway on Straits Parade in Fishponds. The road was quiet for a Tuesday, although the cafés along the street all seemed full with students and mums having their lunch.

Getting out of the warm car felt like jumping into an icy lake, so Anna pulled on her large black overcoat as her breath steamed in the air. She winced at the pain in her arms and shoulder, especially the left one. It was only a short walk up the road to the police station, but she also put on her scarf and gloves.

The police station itself was a plain, cheery building with blue panelling on its outer walls, and a border of frozen shrubs lined the entrance.

Anna pressed the buzzer on the front door.

"Yes?"

"Anna Wilson to see Detective Wright."

The door buzzed, and she pushed it open. She stepped into a small reception area with three plastic chairs, two doors and a glass panel. Behind the panel, a young female police officer smiled at her.

"She's just on her way down for you," the officer called through the thick panel to Anna.

"Okay, thanks."

Anna sat on one of the chairs and dug her gloved hands into her coat pockets. She avoided reading any of the posters and signs, knowing they would be too depressing; police stations don't have happy things to warn you about.

She sat in the reception for less than a minute before one of the internal doors opened and Detective Wright emerged. She was dressed in a dark blue suit with a cream shirt. The bright red lipstick Anna remembered was still in place. So were the warm smile and the cold eyes.

"Mrs Wilson, thanks for coming in. Follow me, please."

Anna followed her through the door. They took a few steps along a corridor and stepped into a small interview room. Luckily, there was no sign of her father. The last time she had been in a police station was when she was fifteen years old, telling the police about her abusive father. Anna pushed the memory from her mind.

The interview room had a table and four chairs, two either side of the table. The walls were cream coloured and clean. There was an old-fashioned tape recorder on the desk and nothing else.

"Take a seat."

Anna sat down, and Detective Wright sat opposite her.

"Thanks for seeing me on your own."

Wright nodded, seemingly understanding that Anna didn't want to see her father.

"Detective Gleadless is following up on a lead," she said, pulling a cassette tape out of her suit pocket and putting it into the old machine on the table.

"I would have thought you'd be digital by now."

"Some of our resources are very advanced. Some are tape recorders."

Anna smiled at the joke.

Detective Wright clicked the 'record' button.

"This is Detective Sergeant Wright, badge number one-four-one, conducting an interview with Mrs Anna Wilson in connection with the murders of Rachel White, Abby Elford and Ruth Collins. The date is the nineteenth of January, 2018. Time 1 pm."

Detective Wright seemed to remember something and pulled her mobile phone out of her pocket and switched it to silent before replacing it.

"So, Mrs Wilson, you called me yesterday and said you have some evidence you would like to share with us about an ongoing investigation. What is it you would like to tell us?"

Straight into it. No preamble. Where to begin?

"Well, I remembered Doyle mentioned he used to live with a girl called Uri Rana-Bennett in Bath when he was at university there." Anna licked her lips at the lie.

Anna really knew about Uri because she had hacked into Dr Cole's computer files on Doyle. She was lying to a detective. On tape. She could feel icy eyes boring into her as she spoke.

"This is Doyle Kennedy?"

"Yes."

The detective pulled out a small notepad and pen from her pocket.

"That name again?"

"Uri Rana-Bennett."

Detective Wright wrote the name down. "Go on."

"I was going through the file I have on Doyle, and the name..."

"You have a file on Doyle Kennedy?"

"Because of the sperm donations."

"For the record, Mrs Wilson, please can you explain your relationship to Mr Doyle Kennedy?"

Anna told the tale again, the same tale she had told her father. They had wanted to get pregnant, John couldn't conceive, they needed a sperm donor, and they chose Doyle.

"Thank you, please continue with Uri."

"I don't know why, but I did some digging on Uri and discovered she is a patient at a hospital in Barcelona. Just outside Barcelona, actually. It's a psychiatric hospital. Anyway, I went there on the weekend..."

"You went to Barcelona this weekend?"

"Yes."

"To visit Uri Rana-Bennett?"

"Yes."

Detective Wright stared at her in thoughtful silence. Anna stared back at the red lips and icy eyes and decided the detective was one of the toughest women she had ever met.

"Go on."

"Well, I was fortunate enough to be able to interview Uri and found that she is quite unwell. Very unstable. She is bipolar, and the treatment she is on doesn't seem to be helping her much. I thought you would want to know about her. Uri has only been in Spain for six months. Before that she lived in Bristol. She was living with Doyle at the time of Ruth Collin's death. Maybe..."

"Please don't speculate, Mrs Wilson. Just stick to the facts of what you know."

"Sorry. Well, Uri lived here. And she is unstable."

"Okay, we'll check her out. Thank you for the information. But a word of warning, Mrs Wilson. You shouldn't be getting involved in a murder case. As soon as you had this information on Uri Rana-Bennett, you should have reported it to us. I'm also going to need a copy of this file you have on Doyle Kennedy."

"Sure."

"I need to report your involvement to my boss. You'll

probably be okay, but they may want you to come back and talk through some more details."

"There's something else."

Detective Wright leaned back in her chair and folded her arms. "Go on."

Anna pulled out her phone, unlocked it and brought up the photo she had taken in Uri's room. She laid the phone on the table and slid it across to the detective, who stared down at the screen.

"That's Doyle Kennedy," Detective Wright said as she leaned forward, "and next to him is Ruth Collins. Who's the other girl?"

"The third person in the picture is Uri Rana-Bennett."

The detective looked up at Anna and then back to the photo. For a moment, the only movement in the room was the slow roll of the cassette tapes.

"Where did you get this photo?"

"There was a photo on Uri's bedroom wall. I took this snap of it."

Detective Wright looked like she was going to ask another question, but instead, she picked the phone up and used her fingers to zoom into the faces. She stared at them for a long time.

"I need a copy of this," she said, and before Anna could reply, Detective Wright started typing away on the phone and sent herself the photo. She dug out her own phone from her suit pocket and made sure the copy had arrived.

Detective Wright asked Anna to repeat her actions over the weekend. Anna talked her through what she had done, from finding Uri's name in the file, the trip to Spain and the visit with Uri.

"Okay, this really isn't the way to do things. But this photo could also prove helpful to our investigation, so thank you for bringing it to us."

Anna knew the response from her father wouldn't have been so grateful.

"I'm not finished yet."

Detective Wright smiled with a clenched jaw and, once again, leaned back in her chair with folded arms.

"Alright, Mrs Wilson, go right ahead. What else do you want to tell us?"

"When I was with Uri, she attacked me."

Anna had decided to leave out the details of her staying at the hospital and Uri's attempted escape from the ward. She thought it would be best to keep it simple.

"Attacked you?"

Anna didn't reply. She stood up, unbuttoned her coat and slipped it off. Her green blouse had a loose neckline, and it was easy enough to pull it to one side.

"What are you doing?"

"She bit me."

"Uri Rana-Bennett bit you?"

"When she attacked me, Uri bit my shoulder."

Anna leaned down and revealed her shoulder to Detective Wright, who slowly sat up in her chair.

"For the record," she said into the tape recorder, her eyes never leaving the bite marks, "Mrs Wilson is showing me her left shoulder, which has a clear bite mark on it."

Detective Wright paused, transfixed by Anna's shoulder.

"Wound is consistent with the murder victims' bite marks."

## 16

A fter the interview with Detective Wright, Anna couldn't face going back to campus, so for the rest of the day she worked from home, planning her mid-semester lectures while swallowing painkillers. By late afternoon, she'd had enough of work, so she changed into her gym clothes, went into the lounge and put on a yoga DVD. Anna was just starting her breathing exercises when something occurred to her. Could she do yoga now that she was pregnant?

It was strange, but Anna still didn't think of herself as a pregnant woman. She stopped the DVD, got her phone from the kitchen and searched for 'pregnant yoga'. The information online was conflicting, but Anna thought she would be alright as long as she avoided a few poses. She returned to the lounge and resumed her yoga session. Her breathing slowed, her body stretched, and she could feel the stress seeping away. Her arms and shoulder still ached, but she managed to ignore them. After an hour, she finished, and felt much better for the workout. Anna switched off the DVD player and showered.

John was away with work for the night, so she made a chicken salad and ate it alone in the kitchen. Afterwards, she took more painkillers and lay on the sofa to watch the TV. Her guilty pleasures were dating shows, and there were plenty to choose from on her planner.

By ten o'clock, she was ready for bed. As she switched off the bedside lamp and closed her curtains, she saw a large black car parked on the opposite side of the road to the house.

Their street, Orchard Close in Winterbourne, only had six large houses on the estate, and Anna knew all of her neighbours, but she didn't recognise the vehicle. It looked vaguely familiar, but she couldn't remember where from. In the dark bedroom, she squinted and thought she could see someone in the driving seat, but it was difficult to tell from where she was standing.

Anna was too tired to give the car much more thought. The burglar alarm was set on the house, and all she wanted was her bed. She curled up under the covers and was sleeping within minutes. Her dreams took her back to Barcelona. She dreamt that she was running through the psychiatric ward, being chased by Uri, who was, quite literally, snapping at her heels.

———————

The following day Anna got out of bed early. She showered, put on a French navy polka-dot dress and skipped breakfast. She slipped on a new pair of pink ankle boots; they felt good.

Her Mercedes roared down the dark country lanes to the city, where Anna arrived at the university building as the security guard opened the glass doors.

"Morning," he greeted her.

He was a stooped, old Jamaican man with a friendly smile.

"Morning," she replied without breaking her stride.

In her office, Anna threw her bag and coat onto the spare chair and sat at the desk. Her to-do list covered three A4 pages, so, without hesitating, Anna began by pulling a pile of papers towards her and started to work her way through it. She worked all morning, chewing through papers like a rubbish truck on New Year's Day.

Dr Aitkin, the finance lecturer, put his bald head around the door and offered her a drink.

"Fruit tea, please," Anna replied without looking up.

Just before eleven o'clock, she stood up. Leaving the papers on her desk as they were, Anna picked up her laptop bag and set off for the lecture theatre. She had a two-hour lecture on 'Memory as a Psychological Process', and before her students had sat down, she started talking.

"Who can tell me the three stages of memory?"

A young man was still shrugging out of his coat as he replied.

"Encoding, storage, and retrieval, Ms?"

She nodded at him. "Good. Now, let's look at each of these stages and how unreliable they can all be."

Anna didn't stop talking for two hours. The only other sound in the lecture hall was the sound of the students frantically typing. At the stroke of one o'clock, Anna unplugged her laptop and thrust it into her bag.

As she headed for the door, she called out to the dazed cohort, "Read chapters eight and twelve from the Groome text for next week," before leaving the hall.

Anna was out the door before they had risen from their seats.

Back in her office, she sat at her desk and continued with her work. The January sun hung low in the sky behind fat purple clouds, and despite it being midday, Anna had to turn on the office light to see her planning papers. She had barely picked up her pen before her mobile buzzed on the desk.

"Hello?"

"Anna? It's Marianne."

"Hi, how are you?"

"Great. Listen, I've been thinking about our conversation the other day. I have a free window in about an hour if you want to come to the surgery?"

"In an hour?" The surgery was only a ten-minute walk along Whiteladies Road.

"Yes, I don't have long, but we can talk."

"Thanks, Marianne, that would be good. I'll see you in an hour."

Anna ended the call and looked down at her lesson plan. The clock on the wall ticked at her as she reread the same passage of text over and over without processing it. Her concentration had been shot, so Anna dropped the pen and stood up. She put on her coat, picked up her bag and went down to the university canteen for lunch.

---

An hour later, Anna waited in the reception area of the doctors' surgery. It was a GP's on Whatley Road, between Clifton and Bristol University, just off the main strip of Whiteladies Road. It was early Wednesday afternoon, but the waiting room was already full of sick young professionals and dozy-looking students who had likely just rolled out of bed.

Anna watched the screen on the wall, waiting for it to flash her name, when a door leading to a long corridor opened and Marianne was standing in the doorway.

"Anna," she said quietly.

Anna looked across the waiting room and smiled at her old friend. Marianne was plump and tall. She wore a blue-and-red rugby jersey, and her dark hair was cropped short. Marianne wore no make-up, which Anna thought was a shame, as her face had red blotches all over it. Anna had met Marianne through Lara when they had all been at university together. Marianne couldn't have been more different to Lara in every way, but Lara was like that; she had a kleptomaniac's habit for eclectic friends.

Anna followed Marianne down the long corridor and into her surgery. The room was small and sparsely decorated. There was a desk with a computer on it flanked by two chairs, a dark green bed with a paper covering and a filing cabinet in the corner.

"Take a seat."

"Thanks. God, how long has it been?"

"Six months, when we went out for Lara's birthday."

"Oh yes, the Naked Butler night."

They both smiled and blushed at the memory.

Anna took off her coat and took a seat. Marianne shifted some papers on her desk.

"Is that a black eye?" Anna asked.

"Yes, I'm still playing for Bristol Ladies Rugby Club. We had a game against Worcester on the weekend."

Anna couldn't help but raise her eyebrows, unsure what to say. Her own black eye was covered in a thick layer of make-up, but Anna didn't feel the need to start comparing wounds.

Marianne smiled at Anna's look. "It's great for relieving stress from work."

Anna snorted. "I should give it a try."

"If you fancy it, I'll email you the details, and you can come and train with us."

Anna smiled politely as way of an answer. They both

knew she wouldn't survive a game of rugby and would never really join Marianne in the mud and cold.

Marianne put on a pair of spectacles and typed on the computer's keyboard on her desk. Anna couldn't see the screen, but assumed Marianne was bringing up Anna's medical file.

"Before we get started, can you have a look at this?" Anna asked.

She rolled up her sleeve and revealed her bandaged arm. She peeled away the bandage to show Marianne the scratches that were now bloody welts. Amongst the red cuts in her skin, yellow pus was forming.

"Do you think this is infected?"

Marianne peered at Anna's arm. "Yes. I'll write you a prescription for some antibiotics. Make sure you keep it clean and dry, and it should clear up okay. How did it happen?"

"I'd rather not say."

"No problem."

Marianne made a note on the computer; a printer delivered a prescription slip, which she signed and handed to Anna, who put it in her pocket.

"So," Marianne said, taking off her spectacles and looking at Anna, "have you had any further thoughts on the termination?"

Anna swallowed. "I think –" she paused "– we think it's still very unlikely, but it's worth getting more information."

"You're eighteen weeks pregnant?"

"Yes. Eighteen weeks. So –" she paused again "– how does it work?"

Marianne leant forward in her chair, the blue-and-red rugby jersey stretching against her big arms.

"The first thing to say is that, by law, you can have a termination up to twenty-four weeks. But like I said on the phone, in reality a lot of doctors won't go past the twenty-week mark;

they will refuse to perform the procedure. Obviously, I don't do the termination..."

"You don't?"

"No, I would refer you to a specialist, but I would need to register the referral as urgent, as it can take up to two weeks to get an appointment. The hospital will then contact you and interview you. Then the hospital's gynaecologists will either perform the termination or refer you to another doctor if they won't do it."

"I don't understand. It's legal up to twenty-four weeks, but the doctor may refuse?"

"You need to understand, by twenty weeks the baby is really well developed; it has kidneys, a brain and a heart. They have taste buds. Twenty weeks is a big jump forward in the baby's development; it's not just a little sperm in there anymore. A termination is not an easy thing for a doctor to do, and most won't do it, whatever the law says. Doctors have the right to refuse a termination and will conscientiously object."

Anna felt a cold sweat over her head and neck. She pictured the baby growing and sleeping inside her. As Marianne spoke, the room started to spin, and her ears filled with a rush of white noise. Anna felt like she was falling.

After a moment, she found herself looking up at Marianne from the bed in the corner of the room. Marianne looked down at her, mostly concerned, slightly amused.

"What am I doing on the bed?" Anna asked, her voice sounding strange to her.

"I think you fainted. I managed to catch you and get you onto the bed."

"I'm so sorry."

"Don't be sorry. These things happen."

Anna was feeling thirsty, and she was ready to be sick. The blood had drained from her head, leaving her woozy.

"Good job I'm used to throwing people around on the rugby field." Marianne smiled. "It helps that you are as thin as a chopstick."

Anna tried to smile in return, but thought it might have been a grimace smudged across her face.

"I know this is a difficult subject to talk about. We can leave it there if you want."

Anna took a few breaths through the nose. With one hand on her stomach and the other holding the side of the bed, she managed to focus her eyes on Marianne.

"No, let's keep going. I need to know this stuff."

"Alright." Marianne nodded. "There are two options for having a termination. Either it's a medical abortion, which is done with medication that induces a miscarriage that flushes out the foetus –" the words 'flushes out' caused Anna's stomach to flip "– or you can have a surgical abortion. It's a minor surgery, and you can normally go home afterwards. I think at your stage, it will be the surgical option."

Anna knew that hundreds of women had an abortion every day, so she was not sure why she was so squeamish about it all. Perhaps it was because she had never even considered it before. Everything about being pregnant and having a baby was new to her. As a teenager, Anna had made the decision that she was never going to have children, and since then, the world of pregnancy and babies had simply disappeared for her. It was like a hidden world with its own codes and language that Anna simply did not know.

"Go home and try to forget about it," Anna mumbled.

"If you're lucky," Marianne replied.

Anna looked up at her.

"You need to know that they are not risk-free. There are possible complications."

"I've heard it can make it harder to get pregnant again?" Anna whispered.

"It's rare, but yes, it can happen."

In the silence that followed, Anna stared up at the cream ceiling. So those were her choices: Have a baby fathered by a potential serial killer, or have an abortion and risk never getting pregnant again.

Marianne coughed, and Anna realised she had been lost in her own thoughts.

"Do you need some time to think about this? Maybe talk it through with John?"

"Yes, but I think a termination is..." She took a deep breath. "Am I able to book the appointment now and cancel if needed? It sounds like time is really tight."

"Of course. Let's get it booked in."

"Thanks."

Marianne sat back at her desk and began typing on her computer. "The gynaecologist will give you another interview before they do anything, just to make sure you are one hundred percent."

Anna's mobile phone began to ring in her polka-dot dress pocket.

"Sorry, Marianne," she said as she reached down for it and dug it out.

Anna searched for the silence button on the screen and stopped. It was Detective Wright.

"I need to take this, but don't trust my legs."

Marianne waved amiably at her without looking away from the computer screen. "This will take a few minutes to organise, so go for it."

"Hello?" Anna said.

"Mrs Wilson? This is Detective Sergeant Wright."

"I know. I saved your number."

"Right. Well, I'm calling you as a courtesy. I wanted to let you know that as of this afternoon Doyle Kennedy is being released from custody."

Anna gripped the phone tighter. "What? Why?"

"I can't go into too much detail, as it's an ongoing investigation, but what I can say is that the interview you gave yesterday certainly made an impact here."

"Oh."

"I need to be honest with you. I'm not sure how much your interview exonerates Mr Kennedy. He is still a person of extreme importance to our investigations."

"What does that mean?"

Detective Wright sighed, and Anna could just imagine her bright red lips talking through the phone.

"It means he is still our lead suspect despite this new information."

"But he's being released?" Anna asked.

Impatience seeped through the phone. "Look, I'm letting you know Mr Kennedy has been released so that you can be vigilant. This is a warning, Mrs Wilson. I would not have any further contact with this man, in any capacity. You could be risking your life if you even go near him."

"I understand. Thank you for letting me know."

Anna thought the call would end, but Detective Wright stayed on the line.

"There is something else I wanted to tell you." The detective's voice had dropped to a whisper.

It sounded strange to hear the powerful detective talk so quietly, and the tiny hairs on Anna's neck stood up.

"What?"

Anna listened to Detective Wright breathing, and she could sense that a decision was being wrestled with. In the room, Marianne continued to quietly type at the computer's keyboard. Anna waited.

"Your father hasn't taken the news of Mr Kennedy's release very well...he's a good colleague and a solid detective...but I've never seen him get this wound up over a case before." She paused again, struggling to find the words. "For your own benefit – " Anna could hardly hear her now "– you might want to stay out of his way."

"Stay out of his way? What do you mean? He's a police officer; he should be..."

Detective Wright hung up.

Anna's mind was spinning with the news. What was her father going to do? He clearly still hadn't forgiven Anna for breaking up his marriage. Now she had added fuel to the fire by helping have Doyle released.

In that moment the image of Doyle came to her. In her mind, she could see his blue eyes and broad shoulders, his big smile and broken nose. After being in a prison cell, he would travel home; she wondered if anyone was waiting for him, or would he be all alone? Should she call him?

Anna sat up on the bed, the paper covering sticking to her damp back. She put her phone on the bed beside her.

"Marianne, thanks for seeing me today, but there's no need to book the appointment. I've made my decision. I'm not having the abortion."

## 17

"Hello?" Anna called out as she walked through the front door.

There was no answer as she walked through the hallway and into the kitchen. She opened the internal door to the garage and found John forcefully punching the boxing bag. He was wearing tight black shorts and an old blue T-shirt that clung to his sweaty body. Drops of sweat flew from him as he skipped around the big, old punching bag. The garage smelt damp.

"Hi."

"Hi. You alright?" he said, panting with effort.

"Long day. I was going to make a chilli for dinner. I feel like something spicy."

"I'm not here for dinner. I need to go to Leeds tonight. Got an early morning meeting there."

"Leeds?"

"Yeah." He didn't stop moving around the bag and punching it, the strikes echoing around the empty double garage.

John tap-tapped a few left jabs before smashing in his

right hook. Anna found it slightly hypnotic, watching him move.

*Tap-tap bang.*

"When are you back?"

*Tap-tap bang.*

"Tomorrow night."

"I had a call from the police today."

"Your dad?" he panted.

"No, Detective Wright. She said that Doyle has been released on bail."

John stopped moving and turned to Anna. He wiped the sweat from his face with the side of his T-shirt. He was breathing hard, as if he had pushed himself to his limit.

"How come? Does his release have something to do with your Barcelona trip?"

"I think so. Like I said, last night I gave her all the details and showed her the teeth marks." Anna touched her left shoulder. "Detective Wright asked a lot of questions about it. Took a lot of photos of the wound, too."

John stared at her, silently computing what Anna was telling him. "So they think this Uri woman is relevant enough to release him?"

"It looks like it."

"What does this mean for Doyle?" John asked.

"I think it means Doyle is innocent. Which means we can have the baby without worrying too much."

Anna smiled at him, but John's face remained sullen.

"So you still want this baby? I thought we were talking about an abortion?" His voice was neutral, his eyes guarded.

Anna folded her arms and leant on the wooden door frame like an old gunslinger. She took a deep breath to control her rising anger and could taste the dust in the air. She decided not to tell him about her visit with Marianne that afternoon.

"That was just one idea, which I wasn't happy with anyway. If Doyle was a serial killer, I thought we should consider it as a last resort. But I don't think he is now. And even if he's guilty, should that really be an option?"

John stared at Anna. Their eyes locked, but he seemed distant, like he was deep in thought.

"What?" she asked him.

"I told the guys about us having a baby, and they were really pleased for us. And it got me thinking –" he paused "– I think I've finally come around to being a dad. I want a family with you."

"Good."

"It's just that, I'm still not sure about Doyle being the donor."

Anna kept her arms folded as her fists clenched.

"John," she said slowly, "I can't have this argument again. You need to decide what you want to do, but I'm having this baby." There was a slight tremor in her voice.

John didn't reply. He didn't move. Sweat dripped from his nose, but he didn't wipe it away.

Anna walked out of the garage.

Behind her, she could hear the *tap-tap bang* of the punching bag being hit again.

---

DR LYN COLDFIELD was short and old; her wrinkled face and grey hair gave her the appearance of a kindly old grandmother. However, Anna knew Lyn's appearance was deceptive. Her dark, ambitious eyes were a more accurate reflection of the woman she was. Anna watched as Lyn addressed the gathered management team, her thin lips and brown molars barking mandates to the wary managers. She had a Midlands accent, low *O*'s and high *A*'s.

"As vice-chancellor of the university, I have made certain promises to the board. Chiefly, that we will improve the grades. Better grades mean we can charge higher fees."

Anna looked around at the faculty heads sitting at the long mahogany table, a line of checked shirts and tweed jackets. A few took notes, but most sat still and attentive as their boss addressed them. Along the table were notepads, bottles of water and plump little cupcakes. The cakes had been a gift from Lyn, but they were untouched, as no one had dared to eat one. The room was hot and musty, and Anna was longing for some fresh air.

"The three-year plan I've set out is progressing well. Our planning application for a new swimming pool has just been submitted. The new campus in China is reporting a huge uptake in students. And as you all know, the additional funding plan from the board has been agreed."

Lyn leaned forward, her dark eyes on them. Anna admired the trick, how it seemed like she was looking all of them in the eye at the same time.

"But none of it matters if we can't get the grades up. That's why you all have the top positions. You are all in the top tier of teaching at this university." Her small frail hand pointed at them. "Grades are your responsibility."

Dr Aitkin sat forward, his bald head and grimy spectacles turned towards Lyn.

"The problem with the finance department is that we've had..."

"I don't want to hear it," Lyn barked, annoyed that someone had dared answer her back. "Every department here has issues. Look at Anna, her department is missing two lecturers, but she is getting on with it; she's not moaning."

Anna felt herself blush and tried not to shift in her seat as a few of the gathered lecturers turned to her. She had already learnt that it was better to go unnoticed in these tense management meetings, that a compliment was almost as bad as a reprimand.

"We need a year of strong results. A minimum of five percent improvement on bottom-line grades."

Dr Aitkin shrank back into his seat.

"Better grades mean higher fees. Higher fees mean we can invest back into the university."

It was a line they had all heard many times before.

"Alright, that's all for today," Lyn said, dismissing them.

Anna watched as all of the managers stood up, barely concealing their relief that the meeting was over as they walked out of the claustrophobic room. Anna stayed seated as the room quickly emptied, although she wished she were leaving with them.

"Annabelle Wilson," Lyn said once they were alone.

The two of them sat opposite each other on the long table.

"I wanted a quick chat, Lyn."

Lyn leant back in her chair, her eyes on Anna. "Of course. How are you finding the new job?"

"It's been good. As you said, the paperwork is vast, but I'm on top of it."

"It's nice to have another woman on the team. Far too many men around here."

Lyn smiled at the joke she had made, but the comment surprised Anna, as she had always thought of her boss as gender-neutral. Certainly, she didn't see Lyn as a fellow woman.

Anna managed a smile in reply, but she kept her hands hidden under the table. "I have some news, Lyn. I've always wanted to be open with you, and thought I would give you as much notice as possible."

Lyn's smile dropped. Her black eyes were burrowing into Anna, like a maggot eating out a rotting apple.

"I'm pregnant."

Lyn didn't move.

Anna had to look away; the gaze was too much. Instead, she stared down at the little pink cupcake on the table in front of her.

"Pregnant?" Lyn's Midlands accent was more pronounced.

"Yes, John and I..."

"When are you due?"

Anna looked up. "The end of May."

Lyn's eyes flicked down to Anna's stomach and seemed to notice the loose blouse she was wearing.

"In the middle of exam time?"

"I suppose so, yes."

Lyn digested this news in silence. Anna shifted in her seat, her arm wound still aching, her stomach feeling heavy. It was an effort to stay in the chair and not leave the oven-like room.

Finally, her boss leant forward in her chair.

"When I promoted you, we talked at length about the plans for the psychology department, did we not?"

"We did."

"I explained there are issues with the department. Issues you have been tasked with sorting out. Twenty percent of the university student intake falls under your department."

Anna nodded.

"Twenty percent."

Anna looked down at the cupcake, but she could still feel the anger bouncing off Lyn like sonar radar, pulsating towards her.

"The month of May this year is an important time for the students. Have you considered that?"

"Well, I can still –" Anna began.

Lyn suddenly stood up. She snatched her water bottle

and notepad from the table and clutched them to her small chest. Anna looked up at her.

"Congratulations on your news," Lyn announced loudly. "On behalf of the university, we are pleased for you, and thank you for letting us know."

After this sound bite, Lyn left the room, leaving Anna sitting alone in the boardroom. She let her breath out and, despite herself, snorted at the tension. Telling Lyn the news had gone better than expected.

Now that she was alone, Anna picked up her pink cupcake and took a big bite from the top of it.

It tasted stale.

---

THAT EVENING, Anna arrived home to an empty house. She put the chain on the front door and went into the kitchen to flick the kettle on. The ache in her left arm and shoulder reminded her to take some of the antibiotics Marianne had supplied, and she washed them down with a glass of water. When the kettle boiled, Anna made a fruit tea, then sat at the breakfast bar in the kitchen and sipped it.

She picked up her phone and dialled John, who was still in Leeds.

*Hi, this is John. Sorry I missed your call. Leave me a message, and I will get back to you.*

Anna scrolled through to Lara's number and pressed the call button. Lara's phone was off.

What a crap day.

The fruit tea just tasted bitter, and Anna suddenly longed for a normal cup of English breakfast tea. Or a cup of coffee. Or a large glass of wine.

Feeling restless, she went upstairs and took off her clothes. She ran a shower and stepped under the hot water, the stress of the day beginning to seep away. Her injured arm throbbed again, and she took off the bandage to let the hot water blast onto the wound.

The doorbell chimed.

"Son of a bitch," Anna spat through the torrent of water.

Anna turned off the shower, gave herself a quick rubdown with a towel and put on her white dressing gown that was hanging on the back of the door.

With her hair still dripping wet, she made her way downstairs to the front of the house and peered warily through the spyhole on the front door.

Anna froze at what she saw.

Standing casually outside the house was Doyle Kennedy.

She hesitated, totally unsure.

He pressed the doorbell again.

Doyle looked relaxed. And handsome. And humble.

"Hello?" Anna called out. Her heart hammered; her spine shuddered.

"Hey, Anna, it's Doyle. Sorry for the late hour, I just wanted to come over and say thanks to you and John," he called out to the front door.

"Thanks?"

"I understand you guys had something to do with me getting out of prison."

Anna shifted from foot to foot, clutching the dressing gown to her chest. The silence lingered. She continued to watch him through the spyhole in the door and suddenly realised how much she'd been thinking about him over the past few months.

He started to step backwards. "Hey, sorry if it's a bad time. I'll leave you guys in peace."

Before she could think about it, Anna opened the front door.

A rush of cold air swept into the house and swirled

around her legs and up the dressing gown, bringing out goose bumps on her bare skin. Doyle was halfway down the drive. He turned and moved back towards her, out of the darkness and into the light of the house. His blue eyes sparkled at her.

"I didn't think about the time. Sorry." He smiled. "I just wanted to thank you and John. They wouldn't tell me what happened, only that new evidence had come to light, and I wasn't the only suspect now. I overheard them mention your name."

"Oh, it was nothing really." The high-pitched words spilled out of her.

She was half-hidden by the front door, half exposed to him. Her left hand gripped the front door handle while her right hand was still clutching the dressing gown closed across her chest.

The light from the hallway shone on his face as he stood in the cold night, the beam making his cheekbones seem even higher, his jawline even more defined.

"It's been a crazy couple of days. I don't even know what the hell has happened." He shook his head in disbelief.

"It's fair to say John and I were a little shocked, too."

*You should close the front door,* her mind said, but her body ignored the advice. 'Stay away from him,' Detective Wright had warned her.

Doyle chuckled. He was wearing dark trousers and a cream polo shirt. The cold had made his nipples hard. In the yellow hallway light, he looked topless, like a Roman gladiator.

"I bet. You let some guy into your house, and he's then accused of being a murderer. I would have freaked out."

"Well, we did a little."

He laughed, and she couldn't stop the smile appearing on her face.

There was a muscle on the outside of his big arms. A thin, bulging muscle that she hadn't noticed before. The word *rippling* ran through her mind. Anna pulled her dressing gown tighter, aware of her naked body underneath it.

"Look, I won't keep you. I really just wanted to say thanks. I was thinking about it on the way over here, of how to repay you both. I've got an apartment down in Cornwall. I want to offer you and John a weekend down there if you want it. Use it like your own. It's a cool little place, overlooks the sea and mountains."

"I think John is away for most of the weekend."

Anna silently cursed herself; should she have told Doyle that?

"Oh, shame. Well, if you want to go on your own, you're welcome to it. Get some alone time."

He ran his hand through his wavy hair as he spoke. It was dark and thick. Her wet hair dripped onto her shoulders.

"Thanks for the offer, Doyle. I'll have a think and let you know."

"I need to meet a client for the day on Saturday down in Cornwall, so if you are around, I could show you some local restaurants to try." He smiled, his face open and hopeful, like a puppy trying to please.

Anna didn't know what to say.

They would be alone together in Cornwall? She was too aware of being naked under her dressing gown and couldn't think clearly. The cold night air had seeped through the thin material, and her breasts and nipples became pert. Anna told herself it was just the cold that was making her body tingle and shudder.

"I'll let you know." Her voice was husky.

"Anyway –" he stepped backwards, down the drive and into the darkness "– thank you so much for what you did. I'll see you around."

He gave a small wave, and with that, he was gone.

Anna felt a tug of disappointment. She closed the front door, bolted it and walked back to the warm bathroom. She sat on the edge of the bath, and her robe fell open in the steamy room. The thought of Doyle's muscles and hard nipples flashed in her mind, and before she knew what she was doing, her hand dropped between her legs. She touched herself. Slowly at first, and then quicker.

Her body tingled, and goose bumps spread further across her naked skin. There was an image in her mind, playing over and over. It was Doyle, using his huge arms to gently open her dressing gown. His blue eyes watching her and lusting after her.

Anna gasped as she orgasmed.

## 18

The following day was a Friday, and Anna wasn't teaching until the afternoon, so she drove down to Eastgate Retail Park in Bristol, just off the M32. Cautiously she walked into the Mamas & Papas baby shop on the edge of the retail park, thinking she would buy some items for the baby. Anna was wearing a grey herringbone skirt, a black blouse and a white single-breasted blazer: work wear ready for the afternoon's teaching.

The shop was huge, and instantly, Anna felt lost. She passed a young couple looking at cots who were whispering like they were in a library, and Anna could sympathise, because it felt like that sort of place.

There was a long line of pushchairs and car seats running through the middle of the store. Along the walls were various pieces of equipment. Some of them left her feeling puzzled as to what they were. Anna walked around the large store, trying to take it all in. The colours of the products were pale and soft. Everything seemed to have baby rabbits or baby foxes on. On the walls were large posters of contented mums and sleeping babies. She tried to place the strangely sweet smell in the shop but couldn't.

Anna came to the baby clothing section. She tentatively picked up an all-in-one baby suit. It looked tiny and felt strange to hold; she was half expecting someone to tell her to put it back. The baby suit was pastel blue and soft to the touch. Would babies need something so small? She hung it back on the rack and looked around at all the clothes. They were different sizes, but she wasn't sure what size she would need to buy. How big were babies when they were born? she wondered.

She kept her slow-moving pace around the store and came to the breast pumps. Was she going to breast feed? It hadn't even occurred to her. Instinctively, Anna held her boobs through her black blouse. A few years ago, Lara had had a breast enlargement operation, and she had tried to convince Anna to have one with her. She smiled at the memory and felt relieved she hadn't gone through with it.

Anna realised she was standing in the middle of the store, smiling and holding her breasts, so she dropped her hands and moved on.

There were baby baths and cots and toys and bottles and steamers.

Anna looked at the price ticket on a pram.

"Six hundred pounds!?"

"Can I help you?" a voice asked behind her.

Anna was startled and turned to be greeted with a short, plump woman dressed all in black and wearing a lot of make-up. Her gold name tag said 'Maureen'.

"I'm just looking, thanks."

"I'll be over here if you need anything." Maureen shuffled back to the counter, where there were two other ladies watching her.

Anna realised the three of them must have been watching her confused meander through the shop.

She turned back to look at the prams. They had large tags on them with long product specifications. The information didn't make any sense to her. As she read the tag, she could feel the three women staring at her from the counter. *They must think I'm an idiot,* Anna thought. Which, in a way, was true; she didn't have a clue about babies or what they needed.

Anna left the pram and walked back to the entrance. She could feel the stares following her and could almost sense them rolling their eyes.

It was a relief to get back in the car.

Anna sat in the driver's seat, running her fingers around the steering wheel. She wanted to call John, but knew he would be working.

How the hell was she supposed to learn about this stuff? How did other women do it? They probably got told everything by their mums, like an ancient tradition, knowledge passed down from mother to daughter. The mums would know what their daughters needed to do, what to buy, how they would be feeling.

Once again, Anna wished her mum were around. Her mum would know what to buy and would be able to help her. The thought brought a lump to her throat. Her mum would have loved shopping for baby things with Anna. She would have loved being a grandmother and giving advice on how to look after a baby. If she were still alive, they would shop and talk; her mum would hug her and tell her everything was going to be alright. A hug from her mum would have been great right now.

Tears started to build up, but Anna stopped herself from crying. She didn't want to feel any self-pity. Instead, she did what she always did; she took control.

Anna took a deep breath, checked in the rear-view mirror

that her mascara wasn't smudged, and got out of the car. She locked the door and strode back to the shop.

The three women in black were still at the counter, their eyes watching her as she approached them.

"I need some help, please."

"What are you after?" Maureen asked her.

"Everything."

Maureen considered this with a tilt of her head before nodding. "Alright, my love, come with me."

From the front of the store, Maureen fetched a trolley, and they set about filling it.

"Are you having a boy or a girl?"

"I don't know. Does that matter?"

"Depends. Do you like yellow and white?"

"Yes, I suppose so."

Maureen smiled at her. "Then you'll be fine."

Anna picked a pushchair with a matching car seat, a high chair, a bath, a breast pump, a box of six feeding bottles, two bottle steamers, three blankets, three swaddles, eight baby grows of different sizes, ten vests, two hats, two sets of gloves, a sleeping bag, a night light and one large yellow rabbit. Everything was yellow and white and soft and clean; Anna was surprised at how satisfying it was to fill the trolley.

"That should be enough to get you started," Maureen told her as she ran everything through the till.

"Thanks, Maureen."

"That'll be one thousand and six hundred pounds, please."

"No problem."

Anna paid and, with Maureen's help, loaded everything into her Mercedes. The car's boot and back seats were filled with the baby equipment. Anna wondered how John would react at seeing it all.

"Good luck with everything, my love," Maureen said.

"Thanks," Anna replied with a proud smile.

---

WITH HER CAR full of baby's things, Anna drove through Bristol city centre and up to the university campus. She parked around the back of the main building, bought a sandwich from the university canteen and headed to her office on the tenth floor. With an hour to spare before teaching, she ate as she marked some coursework papers. Normally, she would have skipped lunch, but with the baby she wanted to make sure she was eating properly. As she ate, Anna held her hands over her stomach, again wondering when she would feel the baby move.

Looking at her workload, Anna could see that she was getting behind on marking deadlines. She would have to work hard over the weekend to get back on top of everything. It felt strange to be behind on her work, she was normally so efficient, and she felt a pang of annoyance at seeing her standards slipping.

With a sigh, Anna texted Lara to cancel their planned lunch for the following day. She also texted John to let him know she was going to be working all weekend. Finally, she typed out a message to Doyle that read:

*Thanks for the offer, but I need to work this weekend. Take care. X*

Anna read the text back before she sent it and decided to delete the kiss at the end of the message.

She paused again. It had been an innocent invitation from Doyle, but it was still an invitation, just the two of them, alone in Cornwall together. Anna could imagine the two of them in an apartment overlooking the sea, drinking wine, talking and getting close. The idea was tempting, and the thought of it gave her another thrill, but she knew it wasn't fair. Not fair to John. Not fair to her.

She clicked *send* on the message to Doyle, put her phone down, and got back to work.

After an hour of lesson planning at her desk, the clock told Anna it was time to head down to the auditorium. It was a Friday afternoon and the final lecture of the week. The campus and surrounding university buildings were quiet. Clearly, students and staff had better things to do on a cold Friday afternoon in January than hang around the university.

She arrived at the auditorium, and it looked sparse. She should have had fifty psychology students in her class, but there must have only been twenty of them casually spread out in the large hall.

"You can move forward if you want. There's plenty of empty seats down here at the front."

A few students got up and moved closer to the front of the hall, but most stayed where they were. There were a few at the back of the hall who didn't move, which didn't really surprise her.

Anna plugged her laptop into the podium, and her lesson slides appeared on the overhead screen.

"Today, we are going to look at a key question in psychology." She checked they were all listening. "Why are people becoming nicer?"

There were a few whispers and chuckles from the students.

"I know it doesn't seem like it, but humans are becoming a nicer species. The number of wars around the world is declining, humanity is less violent, less racist and less sexist. Of course, you can argue that the twentieth century saw a lot of war and suffering, but studies show that the number of people dying from conflicts has dropped by ten percent in some countries. In Britain, murder rates have dropped by ninety percent in the last few hundred years."

Anna could feel the shift in the room as they started to listen and become engaged with what she was teaching them. It was a subtle change, but one she loved seeing. It meant they were thinking and learning.

"Humans are increasingly outraged by the killing of innocent people. Civil rights have increased, and there is equality for the LGBTQ community. It was only in 1986 that corporal punishment was banned and children couldn't be struck by their teachers in school. From women's rights to the treatment of animals, things have gotten better."

She looked around at them. They were hanging on to her every word.

"So, the question we will consider today is...why? Why are people becoming nicer?"

---

THE HOUR FLEW BY, and it wasn't long before she was dismissing the class.

"Have a good weekend, all of you, and please do the textbook reading for next week's lesson."

As the class left, Anna closed her laptop files. She loaded her bag, turned off the projector system and dug out her keys to lock the hall for the weekend. She started to turn out the hall's lights from the podium.

Anna looked up and froze.

There was still one student at the back of the class, sitting on the back row of seats. From where she was standing, Anna could just make out a dark shape hunched in the shadows.

"Time to go," she called out.

The student didn't move.

The silence was unsettling. Had they fallen asleep?

"Hey!" she called, her voice echoing around the empty hall.

Anna squinted up to the back of the hall, trying to make out who was sitting there, trying to see if they were awake. She thought she could see a pair of eyes watching her.

She reached out to turn the lights back on when the shape at the back of the hall slowly moved. The person stood up and stiffly walked out of the back row of seats and down the steps to the front of the hall.

"Interesting lecture," the dark shape called to her.

The gravelly voice gave her a shock. It was her father.

"What are you doing here?"

He didn't reply, just kept walking down the steps towards her. As he got closer and moved into the light, Anna could clearly see his gnarled face. He wore the same long black coat and crumpled suit that he'd worn previously.

Her father reached the bottom of the stairs and stopped on the other side of the podium to Anna. His face was still surly. His eyes still lacked any white in them.

"Thought it was a load of shit myself, though. People aren't getting nicer."

She frowned at him. Anna knew he was trying to get a reaction from her, so she remained silent. She folded her arms across her chest.

"You can't just attend lectures here."

"I wanted to see the great Anna Wilson in action." His voice grew louder. "Wanted to see the clever fucker who thinks she knows better than the police." Spit flew out of his mouth as he swore at her.

Anna instinctively stepped back at the hostility even though the podium was between them. Her arms dropped to her sides.

"Do you know what you've done?"

"Don't swear at me."

"We've been working on these cases for over a year." He glared at her. "A year!"

His face was turning red as his anger rose. Veins bulged in his neck and across his bald head. Anna looked around to the door in the hope that someone else was near, but the place was deserted.

"Detective Wright and me, we've been working day and night on this, and last month, we finally found our man. All that work led us to him, to Doyle Kennedy."

"I didn't do anything wrong," Anna said without conviction.

"You fucking idiot," he hissed.

He paced around the podium towards Anna. Without thinking, she moved in the opposite direction to keep the distance from him. They began to slowly circle the podium.

"Stop swearing at me."

"You used the evil bastard to get you pregnant 'cause your husband ain't up to the job."

"That's nothing to do with you," she snapped at him.

"Of all the people out there, you pick Doyle Kennedy. He gets you pregnant, and then you find out he's a killer, so you decided to get involved. You're a control freak. You always were. Sticking your nose into other people's business. Just like with me and your mum."

Anna stopped. "That was different. I watched you beat the hell out of her all the time, and I wasn't putting up with it." She pointed at him. "Getting social services onto you and getting you out of the house was the best thing I ever did."

"You broke up my marriage," he snarled.

"You didn't deserve to have a marriage!" Her voice echoed around the empty hall.

His face was pure menace.

Anna fought to keep control of herself, but she was struggling. It was like she was riding a wild bull of emotions. Her father always had a way of making her lose her self-control. He made her so angry, and right then, she felt rage boiling in the pit of her stomach in a way she hadn't felt since she was fifteen years old.

"And now, after all these years, you come out of nowhere and mess up my case," he continued. He kept moving around the podium, getting closer to her.

"I didn't do anything wrong," she repeated.

It was hard not to feel like a petulant child again. Like a young daughter arguing with her father. It was a horrible feeling.

"Yes, you did. You stuck your nose in where it didn't belong. You put another suspect in the frame. The wrong suspect."

"All I did was…"

Before Anna could finish, he lunged at her. For an old man, he was quick, and before she could stop him, his left hand was clamped onto her right arm. His breath stank of tea and cigarettes.

"Let go!" she screamed.

His right arm tore at the neckline of her blouse to reveal the bite mark from Uri Rana-Bennett. Anna struggled to get out of his grip.

"This is it? This is your evidence?"

"Let go!"

She felt herself going red in the face as rage and blood rushed to her head. Anna gasped as she tried to pull her arm away from her father. His iron grip was painful, and for a moment, Anna understood the helplessness her mum must have felt, having to live with this horrible brute.

He hunched over her and stared at the wound.

"I've got news for you. Bite marks can't be used as evidence. They're useless."

Anna stopped struggling. She looked into the eyes of the man she hated.

"Can't be used in court. Experts will tell you, you can't get an exact match off a bite mark to a person's set of teeth. It may look the same. May look an exact match. But it's not a fingerprint. It doesn't count for shit."

He relaxed his grip, and Anna seized her chance, yanking her arm away from him. She stepped back and, with shaking hands, felt her blouse, which was now ripped at the neckline.

She was breathing hard. "You arsehole."

"Courts can't use a bite mark. But do you know who can?"

He stood still, leaning on the podium and panting heavily after his lunge. His ugly gaze never left her.

Anna didn't reply to his question.

"Solicitors. That's who. A bite mark like that gives them enough ammunition to throw doubt on Doyle's guilt. Enough to get him out of jail. But all it's doing is wasting time. Means we need to get a judge to write off this so-called new evidence, and he'll be right back in lock-up."

Through the hatred and pain Anna was feeling, her mind told her there was truth in what her father was telling her. Was Doyle guilty after all? Or was her father just trying to mess with her?

"I'm not a detective. I don't know how cases work. Or evidence. All I know is that there is a crazy woman locked up in Spain who likes to bite people. She was living in Bristol when these murders were committed. If you were working this case for so long, why didn't you interview her?" she said.

He shook his head defensively.

"We have only had Doyle as a suspect for the last few weeks. Typical bloody Anna. You just had to stick your nose in."

Anna's arm and neck hurt where he had grabbed her, and more memories of her childhood flooded back to her. Her mother screaming. Her father standing over her with a belt, stinking of whisky and full of rage. For the first time, Anna realised that she had probably saved her mum's life. If the abuse had continued, he would eventually have killed her.

Shakily, Anna took a deep breath, calming herself down as much as she could. Her hands were still trembling. She remembered they were in the auditorium, in her place of work.

She stood tall and met his gaze.

When Anna spoke, the calmness of her voice surprised her.

"You might be right. It's not for me to say. But I'm pregnant with my first child. It could have been your grandchild. But it won't be. You will have nothing to do with this baby. You won't even exist in its life."

He tried to keep any emotion from his face, but Anna could see the words hurt him. His face changed from anger to hurt and back to anger almost imperceptibly.

"You were a terrible father, but you'll never have the chance to be a terrible grandfather."

"You bitch," he wheezed.

"Now leave. I need to lock up."

Her father stepped away from the podium and walked past her. He was close enough to reach out and grab her, but Anna didn't move, didn't flinch under his murderous gaze.

He reached the auditorium door and turned back to her.

"You can't get rid of me that easily. You're going to regret this."

Anna didn't know what he was referring to, but as her father walked out of the door, she didn't care. She was just glad that he was gone.

## 19

Anna left the hall, locked the door and looked around her. The corridors were deserted, and there was no sign of her father. It always felt strange seeing the university empty after being so full of life during the day.

She walked back to her office with the torn blouse clasped tightly in her right hand. As she walked up the stairs to the tenth floor, Anna didn't see another soul. The building was silent and empty, as if it had been closed to the outside world and nobody had thought to tell her. It was always like this on a Friday evening. Normally, she liked the peace, but that evening it felt unsettling.

Anna walked the ten flights of stairs, pushed through the swing door to her floor and continued down the long, thin corridor. She passed a dozen offices; all had their doors closed and lights switched off. The last office along the corridor was hers.

In her office, Anna dumped her bag and laptop on the spare chair and sat at her desk. She leant forward in her swivel chair, putting her head in her hands, and breathed deeply. Her foot tapped on the thin blue carpet with nervous energy.

Eventually, the adrenaline drained from her body, leaving her feeling tired and heavy. Her wrist still hurt where he had grabbed her.

She had meant what she'd said to her father; he would never be a part of her life or the baby's. That aside, Anna thought about what he had told her, that they still thought Doyle was the killer. Her head was feeling like it was in a washing machine. Should she tell John what her father had said? Should she be having this baby? Her head was spinning with indecision again.

Anna suddenly felt like she was being watched. She straightened and listened. Through the open doorway, all she could see was the corridor wall. It was deathly quiet. The corridor lights were on a motion sensor, and as if on cue, they suddenly clicked off. Anna surmised that there couldn't be anyone out there; otherwise the lights would have stayed on. But the skin on her neck and arms still felt like a spider was scuttling over them.

To take her mind off her father, Anna opened a folder with some coursework marking that needed doing. She picked up a green pen from a pen pot on the desk and began scanning through the text. After the first paragraph, she stopped reading and looked up.

There were eyes on her. She was sure that she was being watched.

Anna had her back to the window, and she swivelled her chair around to look out into the dark evening. The Bristol city lights twinkled below her. On the tenth floor, the angle was wrong for anyone to be able to see up into her office, but just to make sure, Anna pulled the blinds closed before turning back to her desk.

Her office was small, with just a desk and two chairs. There was no way someone could be in here without her knowing. Through the open doorway, she looked at the corridor outside again but couldn't see or hear anyone in the darkness.

"Hello?" she called through the open doorway from her desk.

Silence.

She tried to concentrate on her work.

Anna began reading again, but her brain was tired, and the information wasn't going in. Normally, she would drink a large coffee and plough through it, but caffeine was off the menu for her. Instead, Anna counted through the papers; there were still seventeen that needed marking by Monday. She really wanted to get her work done, but she admitted defeat and decided to review and grade her students' work over the weekend instead. Slowly, Anna gathered the course-work papers spread across her desk.

Suddenly, in the corridor outside her office the lights came on, illuminating the long, thin corridor.

They had been triggered by the motion sensor.

Anna looked up from her desk, but couldn't see what had set them on.

She listened but couldn't hear anything. "Hello?"

Silence.

Anna stood up and walked to the doorway of her office. She peered down the long space. At first, she couldn't see anything. Then she did a double take, squinting towards the end of the corridor. There was a thin shadow at the far end. It looked like someone tucked into a doorway at the end of the corridor.

"Hello?" Anna called out.

The shadow moved. It shifted out of the corridor and through the exit door to the stairs.

Startled, Anna stepped back and gripped the door frame.

"Hey, stop pissing around out here," she yelled in shock.

Her voice echoed before the stillness returned.

Anna stepped back into her office. Was that a student messing around, or was it something more sinister? Could it be her father? Or worse, could it be Uri? Had Uri Rana-Bennett escaped from the Spanish psychiatric ward and come looking for her? The thought was like an ice-cold blade running down her skin. She couldn't help but tense.

She picked her mobile phone up from the desk but didn't know whom to call. John was away. She tried Lara's number to see if she wanted to come and meet her, but there was no answer. For a moment, Anna thought about calling Doyle to come and escort her home; he would make a good knight in shining armour. Her fingers hovered over his name on her phone before she stopped herself from calling him.

*I don't need this crap,* Anna thought. Would her father still be in the building? It was unsettling to think of him lurking around the university this late. What had he said to her? 'You're going to regret this.' Was that a threat?

Yes, Anna decided, that was most definitely a threat.

She had taken the man's wife away from him, and now she had apparently messed up an important murder investigation. Anna knew that he was petty enough and mean enough to want revenge on her.

She stuffed the coursework papers, phone and laptop into her bag, grabbed her keys and left the office. Anna set off down the corridor. Walking along, she peered into each dark office, but they were all empty, having been abandoned for the weekend.

As she reached the end of the corridor, Anna slowed and peered through the glass panel on the main door to the stairs. The doorway, landing and staircase were empty. All she could see were the plain white walls and light brown lino flooring.

There was an elevator on each landing, but it was reserved for disabled people who were given a key to use it. Everyone else used the stairs.

She pushed the door, and a creak resonated through the stairwell as she stepped out onto the landing. It was cold and silent and smelt of disinfectant. Her skin started to itch again, like she had just fallen into a bath of nettles, and she wanted to tear at her skin.

Anna began her descent down the stairs, unaware that her right hand was placed protectively over the bump of her stomach. She tried to keep as quiet as possible. Her flat Kurt Geiger shoes only made a light tap on each concrete step. In the hushed stairwell, Anna listened for the sounds of anyone else, but there was nothing to be heard. She wished she were at home.

Her mouth felt dry and stale. Her torn blouse flapped against her chest, and she thought about her father's painful grip on her; he was strong for an old man. A sinking feeling trickled through her stomach. Her eyes were bouncing around the stairs and corridor. She strained her ears as her heart hammered. There was a security guard on the ground floor. The friendly old Jamaican man. She just wanted to get down to him. Then she would ask the security man to walk her to her car. Then she would drive home. Then lock the doors and curl up on the sofa.

Anna suddenly heard a scraping sound above her.

She stopped.

She heard it again. Like a shoe scuffing the floor.

It sounded close.

Anna looked up, and a mountain of dread fell on her.

There was someone on the floor above her, looking through the metal bars of the staircase. They wore a black hooded jumper and had a black scarf covering their face. The face was in the shadows, but Anna could make out dark, glaring eyes focused on her. Their black gloves gripped the stair rail. The person was only one floor above her, level with her head on the higher floor.

So close they could reach out and touch her.

It was a terrifying sight. She was glued to the spot.

Their eyes met. The eyes looked strangely familiar. Where had she seen them before? It couldn't be her father, could it? She didn't blink. Didn't breathe.

The person looked menacing and terrifying and ready to hurt her. They were here for *her.* Her adrenaline suddenly kicked in. The fight-or-flight part of her brain did its job.

Anna ran.

Her body moved before her brain could comprehend what was happening. Anna needed to get out of the building.

She had nine floors to get down.

Her feet pounded on the concrete stairs as she took them two at a time. Above her, she could hear the person in black running after her.

Her mind raced, torn between panic and trying to process what was happening. Someone menacing and dressed in black was chasing her? Then the reality hit home: She was running for her life.

Anna pleaded silently that someone else was there, but she knew the building was empty in the evenings, especially on a Friday. She reached floor seven.

Her face was hot, and sweat ran into her eyes.

She pumped her long legs, and her heels hurt as she bounded down the hard steps.

Should she try to get off the staircase and into one of the corridors? But would they be empty too? Was her best chance the security guard on the ground floor?

"Help!" she cried out, hoping that somehow her voice would reach the guard or anyone else who might still be there.

Anna risked a quick glance above her and screamed when she saw how close her pursuer was. They were only one staircase behind her. As she was reaching the bottom of one set of steps, her pursuer was reaching the top of them. She caught sight of a stubby metal pole in one of the black-gloved hands.

Anna tried to run faster. She still had five floors to go.

"I know that's you, Dad," she shouted over her shoulder, somehow hoping that if it was her father, it would snap him out of his thirst for revenge.

Desperately, Anna dug into her bag to get her car keys out, thinking that they would make a good weapon. She couldn't find them, and rummaging around in the bag was making her slower. In her desperation, she threw her bag behind her.

The sound of it hitting the person in black filled the corridor, and they wheezed in shock and pain. The sound gave Anna a sliver of hope as she continued to run.

"Help," Anna shouted again, her voicing echoing down the empty staircase.

Could she fight? Was she strong enough to fight whoever was chasing her? She'd never had a fight in her life before the one with Uri, and that had been enough. Her pursuer looked strong and determined, and at that moment, nothing was going to stop Anna from running out of the building.

Four floors to go. Surely the guard must be able to hear her? Why couldn't she remember his name? He always did a slow walk around the building with a friendly smile.

"Anyone..." she gasped, but she couldn't finish.

She could hear the person keeping up with her, but their breathing was as laboured as hers.

Three floors to go.

Her legs kept pumping, her feet slapped the steps, fear driving her down to the ground floor and the hope of safety.

Behind her, she could sense the bastard in black getting close. Their breath was almost on her back. She pictured a hand reaching out to grab her.

Two floors to go.

Anna could see the ground-floor exit, a set of large double doors that would lead out to the main foyer, where there were bright lights and security cameras. Surely there must be people still in the building?

She was close. She was going to make it.

A pain shot through Anna's back as she was hit.

The air left her body as she gasped and fell. Instinctively, her hands went to her stomach, to protect her unborn baby. *My baby!* her mind wailed.

Anna lay panting on the floor, desperately gasping for air after her mad dash. A bolt of agony was shooting through her back where she had been hit. Her knees had taken the brunt of her fall, and she could feel hot blood on them. Sweat trickled into her eyes as she blinked and tried to focus. She had nearly made it, with only one floor to go.

Standing above her was the person in black.

Anna took a breath to scream for help, but a gloved hand clamped down on her mouth. It was a hard grip, and pain shot over her cheeks and mouth. The black leather threatened to choke her. She struggled for air.

Tears mixed with the sweat in her eyes. Frantically, she breathed through her nose.

Slowly, her attacker pulled down the black scarf covering their face.

It was Doyle. Doyle Kennedy was staring down at her.

Except it wasn't the Doyle she knew. This was a different man; the difference was in the eyes. They were wild. Madness seeped through his face and eyes and smile. The bulging muscles that Anna had admired before were now pinning her down like a doll.

He leant in so that their noses were touching.

Anna couldn't breathe.

"You're mine now," he whispered.

Before she could react, Doyle punched her on the side of the head, and the world went dark.

# PART III

## 20

J ohn arrived home Saturday morning to an empty house. He was pleased that he had done the journey from Leeds in just under three hours. If he had done the drive on Friday afternoon, it would have taken at least five hours to get home. He got out of the car and stretched.

Anna's Mercedes wasn't on the driveway, so he assumed she had gone into the office to catch up on her work. John went into the house and put the kettle on. He'd had a large breakfast at the hotel, but he still stuck his head in the fridge to see what he could find. Grabbing a sausage roll and his fresh coffee, he went into the lounge and flicked the television on.

He ate his sausage roll and sipped his coffee.

There was nothing worth watching, so he turned the television off. He checked his phone, but there were no messages or missed calls. Maybe he should have organised a game of golf?

He finished his drink and put the empty cup in the kitchen.

It seemed he had the day to himself, so he decided to have a workout on the boxing bag. John headed upstairs to get changed into his T-shirt and shorts, but he paused on the landing. He was standing outside the room they were going to convert into the baby's bedroom.

For the first time in weeks, John stepped inside. It was empty apart from a flat-packed baby cot, a tin of paint and some painting equipment.

He picked up the paint pot and read the label 'Sunshine yellow'.

John replaced the tin of paint and turned to leave. He hesitated. Months ago, he had promised Anna he would decorate the room. But he hadn't. A few days away with work had done him good. It had given him a chance to think, and his main conclusion was he had been an arsehole recently.

Why was he still reluctant to have a baby? The question was like a mole in his brain, digging to get out. He had told Anna that he was coming around to the idea, but that wasn't entirely true. He still wasn't entirely comfortable with any of it.

There were the obvious issues with the sperm donor, Doyle, but something else was holding him back. It was a half-formed thought and something he couldn't quite grab onto. Why *not* be a dad? People did it all the time.

He thought of his own dad, who had always told him, 'Don't have kids, son; enjoy your life.' The words rattled around in John's mind.

Growing up, they had been poor and had never been out to restaurants or away on holidays. The kitchen cupboards had always been empty, and his dad had taken the bus to work because they couldn't afford a car. Life had been tough.

A picture of his dad came to mind: looking downtrodden with a furrowed brow, counting out his pennies on the kitchen table to buy some milk.

John had approached him: "Dad, can I have…"

"No!" The reply was harsh, upsetting and a regular occurrence.

Thinking back to that moment, John's face flushed red with anger.

He turned to leave the spare room, but didn't. Instead, he thought about Anna and how desperate she was to be a mum, for them to be a family.

God, he loved her, even after all these years. She made him so happy; he wanted to make her happy, too. Wasn't that what marriage was all about? Supporting each other?

John had been in his early twenties when they had met. For eighteen years, they'd been a couple. He felt they were well balanced: Anna had a need to be controlling, and John was easy-going. When she needed support, he was there for her; when she needed a protector, he took on that role. In return, Anna never moaned at John or stopped him from doing anything that he wanted to. They enjoyed each other's company, whether in silence or deep in conversation, and they had always been a contented couple. Until Anna's sudden need to have a baby.

John sighed. Would it be so awful to be a dad?

He opened the paint pot, and the fumes filled his nose. The yellow was a light tone, soft and warm. He looked at the thick paint and thought about Anna and making her happy.

John unwrapped the plastic covering of a roller tray and poured some of the yellow paint into it. He took some of the folded dust sheets and laid them around the edge of the room to protect the cream carpet. With the sheets in place, John began painting the first wall. He was applying the paint straight onto a white wall, so the colour shone out brightly. The yellow looked great, and John knew Anna had chosen the right colour. It was a perfect choice for the baby's room.

ANNA WAS COLD. Her body was needled all over with pain, and it dragged her out of a deep and dark stupor. Her arms were hanging above her head and had turned numb. Her knees throbbed and felt bloody.

The skin on her face felt stretched, as if it was swollen where she had been struck. She could taste blood on her teeth and on her tongue. There was something stuck over her mouth, so that she could only breathe through her nose, which felt full of bloody snot, making her breathing ragged and thin. Of all the distressing injuries to her body, her bound wrists were the worst. They convulsed in throbbing waves of agony.

She realised she was hanging up by her arms, so her wrists were holding her body weight. Her limp frame was pulling down on the bonds, which was causing the sharp pain in her wrists. Slowly, Anna put weight onto her legs. Blood began to flow back to her hands and wrists, which helped a little, but it also made her aware of the lacerations in her knees. She was a mess.

Anna blinked and looked around.

She was in some sort of garage. There was a bare concrete floor. Grey brick walls surrounded her. The room was dark, but thin lines of light shone through two large doors, giving her just enough light to take in her surroundings. It was a double garage. In front of her, the garage doors were white and covered in cobwebs. The light beneath the doors looked like daylight. Had she been there all night? On the floor, against one of the large metal doors, Anna could see her handbag. To her left, there was an old wooden table with nothing on it. It had thick legs and a grimy top.

Anna looked up, causing a spasm of pain to run down her spine. She could see her wrists were tied with a length of chain that had been secured to the wooden rafter on the ceiling of the garage. The chain around her wrists was held in place with a stubby brass padlock. Behind her, there was a small window, which had been covered with a torn piece of cardboard. It was too small for a person to fit through, and offered little light or salvation. There were no sounds outside the garage. The only thing she could hear was her own breathing as she struggled for air. Even if she managed to stretch her legs and arms out, there was nothing for her to reach; the place was empty.

As the situation began to sink in, Anna began to weep. Warm tears ran down her cheeks and dropped onto the concrete floor. She tried to call out, but the tape over her mouth turned the noise into a groan.

Slowly, Anna looked down to her stomach. Her own suffering was suddenly forgotten as she thought about her baby. Anna made herself become aware of her own body and where she was feeling the pain. There was agony or discomfort in a lot of places, but her stomach felt okay. She could only hope the baby was unharmed.

Tears continued to pour from her eyes.

She was thirsty and cold.

Her body began to shake from the cold and the shock.

There was a strange smell in the garage. It was partly old engine oil and partly something she couldn't identify. Anna realised she didn't want to know what it was.

To try to ease the pain in her knees, Anna alternated putting her weight on each leg. She thought back to what had happened the night before. The memory of her running down the stairs came to her. Being chased. Being hunted. It had been Doyle.

Was it all true? she asked herself. The accusations – was he really a murderer? A serial killer? The look in his eyes had been horrifying. Anna thought about the three women who had been brutally murdered, and knew then that Doyle had done it. Doyle Kennedy was a crazy, psychotic killer. And he had Anna locked up in some dank, horrible garage.

Tears continued to pour down her cheeks.

Anna screamed into the tape covering her mouth.

---

JOHN STOOD BACK and admired his handiwork. He had done the first coat of yellow paint, and the room looked great. It had been transformed from a plain room to something warmer and much more pleasant. A little sunlight shone through the winter clouds and into the room, giving the space a soft glow.

He dropped the roller onto the dust sheet and went into the bathroom. John scrubbed his hands and arms of paint and walked down to the kitchen.

His phone was on the counter. Still there were no messages, so he made another coffee and rooted through the cupboards. There wasn't much to eat, but he found a leftover lasagne in the freezer. Normally, it would be too much for lunch, but as he'd been working all morning, he thought he could get away with it. After four minutes in the microwave, it was bubbling hot.

John turned on the radio and sat at the breakfast bar. The lasagne tasted rich and cheesy, and he happily ate it while listening to some old rock songs on the radio. He finished his lunch, belched and put his plate in the sink.

He unplugged the radio and took it upstairs with him. He plugged it into an outlet in the baby's room and picked up his roller. Two coats of paint should be enough, he thought. John continued with his painting, this time whistling along to the radio.

As ANNA SHIFTED her weight from one leg to the other to ease the pain, she realised she was only wearing one shoe; the other one must have fallen off. Looking down at her knees, she could see they were scraped and crimson, as if she had been dragged along a road. Maybe she had. She wasn't sure what had happened after Doyle had jumped on her in the staircase of her office building. At least twelve hours must have passed, but she couldn't account for any of that time.

She could see that her black blouse was torn from when her father had lunged at her. The moment it had ripped felt like a year ago instead of just the previous evening. The white blazer she had been wearing was gone. Her grey herringbone skirt was plastered in mud and grime, and Anna knew she was looking a complete mess.

What was she going to do? What could she do? Anna felt awful, and her mind couldn't focus on anything. She couldn't think straight as her eyes flitted around the room she was being held in. There was nothing to look at except the two garage doors, her handbag on the floor and the empty wooden table to her left. The thin slices of light coming through the garage doors stayed still without any sign of movement from outside the garage. There was nothing she could do except wait and hope.

She was a university lecturer. She was a psychologist. Her world was being on campus, in the library, writing papers on theories, eating in nice restaurants, yoga classes and the theatre, music, paying her taxes and luxury holidays. She didn't belong here. Locked up and chained like an abused animal. Panic dug into her. Her body shook harder so that the chain around her wrists started to rattle.

Anna suddenly felt something. It was the baby moving.

She looked at her stomach with wide, unbelieving eyes.

After wishing to have the feeling for so long, her baby was finally moving. It felt amazing, as if the little one was saying hello to her.

For a second, the delight made her forget where she was, but when Anna tried to touch her stomach and say hello, the chain on her wrists and the tape on her mouth gave her a crashing reminder of where she was.

She wanted to speak to her baby, but couldn't. She wanted to touch her stomach, to feel the movement. For weeks, Anna had been thinking about feeling the baby move, and now it had happened at the worst possible moment. Instead of feeling joy, Anna just felt a deep, dark depression pour through her.

For a while, she just stared down at her stomach, thinking how sorry she was. How sorry she was that they had gotten into this mess. It was a terrible place to be, especially for a pregnant woman.

Distantly, she could hear a car engine. It was a sound that filled her with both alarm and hope. Surely someone must have seen her being dragged into the garage and called the police? But she knew that was wishful thinking. As the sound of the car grew louder, Anna could only feel a sense of dread coursing through her battered body.

The car came closer and closer until it was outside the garage. Anna could smell the engine fumes drifting under the garage doors. The motor engine was switched off, and the sudden silence was chilling.

She heard a car door opening and closing. There were footsteps on gravel. They were walking towards her. A door within the large garage door opened, and her eyes stung as the outside sunlight burst into the garage.

Anna squinted as a figure stepped into the garage.

The door closed with a clang. As her eyes readjusted to the darkness, Anna could see Doyle standing in the corner with his back to the door. He had his arms folded and looked menacing. He still had the black hoodie and jeans on, but his face was uncovered.

"Hello, Anna." His voice was still like Irish heather honey, smooth and sweet.

Doyle's blue eyes glistened in the gloomy light, but now they weren't a Mediterranean blue, they were Arctic. Looking at them, Anna felt like she was meeting with some abominable ice monster. Her mind couldn't comprehend him, his face was so handsome, but now she knew it hid a dark soul. A soul that was evil.

He bounced on the balls of his feet in excitement as he studied her, and Anna had never felt so afraid in her life. Doyle smiled at her, and even in the dim light, she could make out his bright, white teeth.

Doyle was carrying a small brown satchel, and he put it on the dirty worktop. He turned away from Anna, opened the bag and began to rummage through it. She tried to look away, but she couldn't; her mind screamed with fear as he rooted through the bag. Anna could hear the sound of scraping metal coming from the leather bag. What torturous tools would he produce?

After a moment, Doyle turned back to Anna. Her eyes tried to focus on what he was holding in his hands. She blinked and squinted in terror. What was it? A toothbrush? Anna thought her mind was playing tricks on her. It was a toothbrush and a tube of toothpaste.

Doyle stepped towards Anna with a grin, like a happy schoolboy.

As she watched, he poured out a long line of white toothpaste onto the brush he was holding.

"My mother was a dentist, you know," he said.

Anna wept.

Doyle started to brush his teeth with great vigour. As he

did so, his wild, glacial eyes never left Anna. As she watched, his face turned to one of pleasure. It was as if brushing his teeth was giving him some kind of sexual delight.

His arm pounded away on his mouth, moving the tooth-brush back and forth. The sound of his brushing filled the garage. Anna could even smell the mint paste. Doyle's arm moved quicker and quicker, his eyes getting bigger and bigger as they watched Anna. She could only watch him in horror through tear-filled eyes.

Finally he stopped with a groan of delight.

He swallowed what was in his mouth and lowered the brush. Doyle flashed a huge smile at Anna. His teeth looked clean and straight and white. It was a perfect smile.

"What do you think, Anna? Are they clean enough?"

Anna couldn't speak through the tape, but even if she could, she wouldn't know what to say.

Suddenly he ran at her, a burst of violent energy.

Anna tried to scream, but the tape over her mouth kept her quiet.

Doyle bounded three paces to her and crashed into her hanging body. Anna tried to move away from him, but the chain holding her was too tight.

Doyle sank his teeth into her neck.

It was agonising. The hard teeth pierced her flesh, and Anna again tried to scream. The bite drew blood; she could feel it pour down her neck and onto her breasts. It was all too much, and Anna felt the room spin, her ears filled with the sounds of crashing waves, and the shock and exhaustion rico-cheting through her caused her to pass out.

---

JOHN FINISHED the second coat of paint and felt pleased with his efforts. It was still an empty room, but it had already transformed into something different, somewhere a baby would happily sleep.

Through the window, he could see that it was late afternoon.

"Still plenty of time," he muttered to himself.

John took the used roller and paintbrush down to the kitchen bin. He washed his hands and arms again; then he grabbed his toolbox from the garage. On the way back upstairs, he checked his mobile phone. No messages or missed calls. With the toolbox in one hand, John used his free hand to type out a text to Anna:

*What time you back? Dinner out? Xxx.*

Back in the baby's room, John set his toolbox down and tore opened the cardboard box with the cot in it. It had been lying in the corner for months, and he finally felt he was ready to assemble it.

John smiled to himself, feeling proud of how the room was looking. He knew Anna would be pleased. John looked forward to her finishing work and seeing his efforts. He knew his wife would love the baby's room.

## 21

Doyle's phone buzzed in his pocket. He stepped back from Anna, panting and aroused. She wasn't conscious, so she couldn't see the look of pleasure on his face. He had been fantasising about this moment for weeks, and he couldn't believe it had finally arrived. He couldn't believe how lucky he was to have Anna Wilson tied up in his garage. He touched his erection. A jolt of pleasure went through him.

In the harsh light, he studied Anna and could see that she was pregnant, but he didn't care. He hated kids, with their crying and demanding requests all the time. The only reason he was a sperm donor was to find and stalk new victims. Over the years Doyle had learnt that pregnant women were desperate and easy to trap. He certainly didn't give a shit if he got them pregnant or not.

Doyle took out his phone and saw the reminder he had set himself.

He swore at the phone and spat out Anna's blood from his glistening mouth. The reminder told him he had a meeting with Detectives Gleadless and Wright. As a condition of his release from jail, he'd agreed to several more interviews with the police, so they could check further details of his background and movements around the times of the unsolved murders.

Anna was hanging from her arms by a length of chain that he had bought from a DIY shop. He had looped it over a wooden beam in the roof of the garage, and the weight of her body had pulled it taut. Anna's hands were turning purple as the blood was strangled out of them, in contrast to her pale face, which had turned luminous with fear. Her black blouse was ripped, and his bloody bite marks on her neck and shoulders winked at him through the torn material.

Doyle stroked her unconscious face. He pulled off the tape covering her mouth, prised her soft lips open with his hands and peered at her teeth. They were neat and clean. The gums were healthy. He stared into her mouth and shuddered with delight.

With a great effort, he walked away from her.

"I don't want to rush this," he said.

Doyle dug into his bag and found his toothbrush. He carefully squeezed some paste onto it and brushed his teeth in the small mirror he had brought with him in his leather bag. He brushed off Anna's blood, rinsed with a bottle of water and spat. His teeth gleamed in the mirror.

"Hey, Anna." He smiled at her lifeless body. "I have to go out for a few hours, but don't worry, we'll continue this when I return." He picked up his car keys.

---

DOYLE PARKED on Straights Parade in the Fishponds part of the city. He gave his teeth a quick check in the rear-view mirror of his car before walking into the police station. The small reception area was empty. Doyle pushed the buzzer on the counter, and a young police officer appeared. She was short and blonde and smiled at Doyle. He returned the smile.

"I know this is a cliché, but you are far too beautiful to be working here," he said, accentuating his Irish accent for full effect.

The young officer blushed and looked at the floor before looking back at him. Doyle knew he was stunning to look at, knew that women couldn't resist his compliments. If he wanted to, he could arrange to meet her for a drink later. It didn't matter if she was married or had a boyfriend; they always agreed to meet him.

"How can I help?" she asked, leaning her body on the counter.

"I have an appointment with Detective Gleadless and Detective Wright."

"Oh, right, let me sign you in." She fumbled with a pen as the blue door to the side of the counter flew open.

"You're five minutes late," Detective Gleadless called into the small reception area.

"Sorry about that. The traffic was bad." Doyle winked at the young officer on the counter. She couldn't help but beam at him.

The door into the station was opened wider. "Follow me."

Doyle walked into the main station and saw the two detectives waiting for him with granite faces. He followed them towards an interview room, aware that there were a dozen police officers staring at him in the main office. It was not every day they came face to face with a suspected serial killer, and he could feel them studying him, as if they would be able to unlock whether he was guilty or innocent by the way he acted.

He turned and smiled at them. "Afternoon all."

They didn't move, and Doyle could almost sense their bated breaths.

"In here," Detective Gleadless barked at him.

Doyle walked into the interview room. It was a small space with a table and four chairs, two either side of the table. As he entered, his solicitor stood up and shook his hand.

"Mr Kennedy, how are you?"

"I'm good, thanks, Bernard." Doyle shook his solicitor's hand with genuine warmth.

Bernard was in his late fifties, and the tone of his grey suit matched the grey of his hair. He adjusted his plain blue tie and smiled at Doyle. The smile revealed false teeth, but Doyle didn't hold it against the man. Bernard cost him a fortune, but after he had helped get Doyle released from prison, Doyle thought he was worth every penny.

Gleadless closed the door and occupied the seat next to Detective Wright, opposite Doyle and his solicitor. The detectives were both as he remembered them; Detective Wright was wearing bright red lipstick and seemed relaxed and focused. Her partner, Detective Gleadless, still looked like a grumpy old bald man; he sat with folded arms, his glare fixed on Doyle.

Detective Wright put a tape in the recorder on the table between them. She clicked the 'record' button.

"It is February the first at 3:10 pm. This is Detective Sergeant Wright of the Avon and Somerset Police Constabulary. With me, I have Detective Gleadless. Interview is with Mr Doyle Kennedy of North Road, Bristol. Also in attendance is Mr Kennedy's solicitor, Bernard Dunbar from White and Cooper Solicitors."

With the introductions done, Detective Wright opened her notepad.

"To start, Mr Kennedy, we would like to ask you again about the night Ruth Collins went missing..."

Before she could finish, Bernard interrupted her.

"It has come to our attention there is a conflict of interest in this case."

The three of them looked at the solicitor in silent surprise. Doyle didn't know what he was referring to. Bernard opened his own, larger notepad and peered at a lined page that had several notes on it.

"Recently, a witness has come forward with evidence on another potential suspect in these cases."

Doyle tried not to smile at the mention of Anna.

"So?" Detective Wright asked.

Bernard ignored her. "That evidence was enough to raise doubt on my client and allowed us a reprieve on his incarceration."

"Get to the point," she told him.

"I understand that the new witness was a Mrs Anna Wilson."

Doyle sensed a slight drop in Detective Gleadless's shoulders. He looked at the old detective, who wouldn't meet his eye. Doyle could feel a sliver of excitement building in his stomach as his eyes moved from Detective Gleadless to his solicitor.

"Detective Gleadless, please can you tell us your relationship with Mrs Anna Wilson?"

"Fuck," Gleadless growled.

He sat back and wiped his bald head with his gnarled hands.

"Dave," Detective Wright warned her partner.

Doyle watched the old detective. He could see a black rage trying to burst through his sagging face. It was bubbling up through the skin, like a deadly disease.

"Well?" the solicitor pressed.

"She's my daughter." Gleadless leant forward. "But she has nothing to do with this case."

The news was orgasmic to Doyle; he couldn't help but

groan in delight. The detectives recoiled at the noise, but he didn't care. Oh, what joy! The old bastard who had made his life hell, the person who had arrested him and had him thrown in jail had a daughter. And she was currently locked up in Doyle's dungeon! Doyle tried and failed to keep the smile from his face as he sat back in the cheap metal chair.

He looked sideways at Bernard. The man was a genius.

"Based on this news, we request a delay to this interview until we can notify the judge and get a new detective assigned to the case. Just so you know, I will be requesting that any evidence Detective Gleadless has been involved in is dismissed from the cases against my client."

Gleadless seemed unable to speak; he opened his mouth, but then clamped it shut and held his bunched fist against his mouth, as if he didn't trust himself to reply.

"The judge won't agree to that. This is a murder investigation. He won't have time for games," Detective Wright said. Her tone was businesslike, but Doyle could tell she was worried.

Bernard shook his head. "There are no games here, Detective."

Although Doyle was thrilled with what his solicitor was saying, he also didn't want Anna's father to leave just yet. There was more fun to be had. Doyle couldn't take his eyes off Detective Gleadless, whose red face seemed ready to explode.

"Bernard, I understand what you are saying," he told his solicitor. "I think you're right we need to bring this to the judge. But I'm here now, and I'm happy to answer their questions."

"You don't have to, at least not today," Bernard replied.

"Why doesn't Detective Wright ask the questions and Detective Gleadless stay as an observer?" Doyle kept his tone friendly and humble, desperately trying not to laugh aloud.

"I've said all along that I'm innocent of these terrible charges, and I have nothing to hide."

"It's up to you, Mr Kennedy." Bernard seemed to consider the suggestion. "The judge will look favourably on you staying to answer their questions."

The detectives looked visibly shaken. Detective Gleadless stabbed a finger at Doyle and was about to speak when his partner laid her hand on his arm to silence him. With a great effort, as if he were straining to push a car uphill, Gleadless clamped his mouth closed and once again pushed his fist against his mouth.

"If that's what you're willing to do, then we appreciate you staying," Wright said to Doyle.

Doyle leant back further on his chair. "So ask your questions. I'm happy to answer them."

Detective Wright looked back to her notepad. She seemed to be composing herself, and it was a long, silent minute before she asked her first question.

"As I was saying, we would like to ask you about the night Ruth Collins was murdered."

The questions came at a steady pace, and Doyle gave them steady answers, but all the while he was staring at Detective Gleadless, who still wouldn't look him in the eye.

Doyle had been watching Anna and fantasising about her for months. So many nights he had sat in his bed and looked at pictures of Anna and thought about what he would do to her. But now, on learning that she was the daughter of Detective Gleadless, he was really going to make her suffer. He was going to torture that bitch for days, until she was screaming for him to stop. Doyle licked his lips and smiled as he stared at the detective and thought about the suffering he was about to unleash on Anna.

As the time wore on and Detective Wright worked her way down her list of questions, Doyle managed to stay relaxed. His lies were rehearsed, and he knew they sounded like natural answers. He also knew the detectives didn't have enough evidence to arrest him, so he was happy to play the game with them.

Eventually, the detectives looked at each other and closed their notepads. Their bowed heads and despondent faces told him that he had done well. Detective Wright put the lid back on her pen and replaced it in her suit jacket pocket. Doyle sat forward, ready to stand.

"You were an only child and raised by your mum, weren't you?" she asked.

Doyle blinked and clasped his hands together on the table, all thoughts of Anna suddenly gone.

"Yes."

"What did she do for a living?"

Doyle unclasped his hands and clenched his fists. Detective Wright's cold eyes watched his hands. With a great effort, Doyle unclenched his fists and put his hands flat on the table.

He swallowed. "She was a dentist."

Detective Wright smiled at him. "Probably why you have such nice teeth, huh?"

"My teeth are awful. Disgusting things," Doyle couldn't help but reply.

He tried to control his voice, and his tone was overly casual. Why were they asking about his mother? He didn't want to talk about her.

The detectives looked at each other.

"They look good to me," Wright said.

"Well, they're not," he replied.

Detective Wright studied him for a moment before she pulled the pen back out of her suit jacket pocket. She opened her notepad again. The room felt like it was becoming stuffy, drained of clean air.

"Was your mum insistent on keeping your teeth clean?"

Doyle couldn't answer. He clasped his hands together and sat forward. Images of his mum came to him. He could almost feel her teeth biting into his neck, and he gave an involuntary twitch as if he were about to get bitten. Doyle's mind left the interview room; for an instant all he could see was his topless mother sitting on the edge of the bath, demanding to see his teeth. He could see himself as a young boy, open-mouthed and scared in front of her. She would push her finger into his mouth and slowly inspect each tooth: 'Molars, canines, bicuspids....why are the incisors looking so dirty?' she would scream at him.

He blinked and looked at the detectives. "You've got to –" he strained to get his words out, like he was talking underwater "– you've got to keep them clean."

"With great teeth like yours, you must have to clean them regularly?" Detective Wright asked.

He thought about his mum stabbing him in the mouth with a toothbrush, about her splitting his lips so much that they bled down his chin. His cries would be drowned out by his mum shouting, 'Dirty mouth, dirty mouth,' over and over again.

Doyle blinked and licked his teeth and lips, his tongue flickering across his front incisors. He couldn't speak. Bernard seemed to sense that his client was struggling with this line of questioning and intervened.

"I think that is enough for today. My client has given you almost an hour of his time, and as stated at the beginning of this interview, there is a clear conflict of interest in Detective Gleadless being here."

"Just a few more questions and then we can finish," Detective Wright tried.

"We're already finished," Bernard told her.

The solicitor stood up and motioned for Doyle to do the

same. Doyle felt light-headed, and it was an effort for him to get to his feet.

"Interview terminated at four pm exactly," Detective Wright said and turned the tape recorder off.

The detectives stood up, both watching Doyle intently.

He felt a rising rage in his body. They had caught him off guard; he could tell they thought they were on to something. There were further interviews planned, and he knew they would now focus on his mother. He tried to push the thought of her out of his mind and concentrate on something else. The image of Anna entered his head, and his flailing anger suddenly centred on her. He needed to punish her. Dirty teeth. Dirty mouth. Dirty woman. He needed to make her clean.

Doyle locked eyes with Detective Gleadless.

He would make her suffer.

"Give my regards to your daughter," Doyle said, the words coming out through a grin.

They frowned at him in silence.

"Let's go," Bernard said, his briefcase pushing into Doyle's leg.Doyle walked out of the room and out of the police station without looking back. Bernard was talking to him, but he wasn't listening. All he could think about was Anna locked up in the middle of nowhere. He was going to make her scream.

He was going to make her suffer.

Anna and her dirty mouth.

## 22

Anna's throat throbbed with a sharp pain. Her mouth was dry and unresponsive, as if she had been made to swallow a gallon of glue. She felt pain all over her body, from her arms and wrists, down her neck and back and through to her knees and feet, but the worst agony was her throat. She was desperate for water.

Distantly, she was aware that Doyle had gone and she was alone. It was little comfort to her, because she knew he would return. What was he going to do with her? Was he going to kill her? It was a terrifying thought; she had never felt such a clinging, consuming fear. Anna tried to think of excuses or reasons why she was there – some kind of logical, sane motivation for Doyle. But her mind failed to find a scenario that didn't involve her being tortured and killed. And if he killed her, then her baby would die, too.

It was her fault. Her fault that Doyle was in their lives. She had wanted a baby, and when they couldn't conceive, Anna hadn't given up. She had thoroughly looked at other options. She had registered with the donor clinic, but had become impatient. It was as if her body clock were actually ticking in her head. So Anna had done what she always did: She had looked for another way. She wouldn't be put off or delayed. Anna wanted a baby now. So she looked online and searched for a private donor. There were thousands on there.

What struck her at the time was that the donors all had reviews and comments from people who had used them. The donors were clearly in demand; clearly there were a lot of women choosing the private donation route. Anna had been thorough; she had emailed the donors questions about themselves, as well as requesting letters from the sexual health clinics to show her they were clear of any diseases and healthy. But for all the research she had conducted, how was she supposed to pick up on someone being a murderer?

As Anna hung in the cold garage, her mind drifted back to her mum and the last time she had seen her.

Her mum had known she had cancer for over a year before she had told Anna.

"I didn't want to worry you," her mum had said.

At the time, Anna thought it was all happening so quickly. From getting the news, to seeing her mum becoming frail and sick from the chemotherapy. Then, getting the news that the chemo hadn't worked. That she only had twelve months to live. Anna had raged. Researched. Cried. A pattern that tens of thousands had done before her. She had gotten a second opinion. Paid a lot of money for a third opinion. But there was nothing that could be done to change the outcome. In the end, the twelve months had been ambitious. Her mum had died within seven.

Anna remembered being at her mum's side at her bungalow in the final few days before her death.

The bed had been moved to the lounge, as there was more space. More space for the daily nurse visit to change the sheets. More space for the television that had kept her mum entertained.

"Your hair looks nice," her mum croaked at her.

Anna sat on the faded armchair next to the bed. Her mum was seated against a bundle of pillows propping up her small frame. She wore her favourite knitted cardigan and held a cup of weak tea in her hands. The television was on with the volume turned low, showing a game show involving a lot of contestants with red boxes.

"Thanks. I had Jackie, the mobile hairdresser, do it. I can get her here for you if you want?"

Her mum waved the idea away.

"How's John?"

"He's fine, he sends his love. Said sorry he hasn't been over this week. He's up in Manchester at some conference."

"Bless him. He works hard. You're lucky to have him."

Anna smiled. "I know, Mum."

"I'm happy for you. You deserve a good one."

They sat in silence for a while, looking at the television but not really watching it.

"Have I been a good mum to you, Anna?"

"Of course you have! Don't be silly; you've been great."

"I always tried to be. It wasn't always easy with your father around causing havoc." They looked at each other, remembering how hard it had been. "But something I regret, something I wish I'd done, is push you to have some kids."

Anna had been surprised at the comment.

"Kids?"

"I'm sixty-three. I'm here on my deathbed..."

"Mum."

"Listen. Of all the things I've done, my whole life, having you was the best thing I ever did. I'm sat here now, and what matters? Family. That's what."

Anna's eyes glistened with tears.

Her mum put her cup of tea down on the small table by the bed and leant back towards Anna. Despite being frail, she took Anna's hand and gripped it tightly. For a moment, her mum's eyes were alight and focused, something that Anna hadn't seen in a long time.

"You've done so well. With your career. And that house, it's huge. I'm so proud of you, Anna. The way you got your father out of our lives and helped us to make a new home together. You saved me. But, Anna, the one piece of advice I can give you, the one thing that will make you feel complete, is a family. Have some kids. One or two or ten. More the merrier."

Anna laughed, causing tears to slip down her cheeks.

"I'll think about it."

"Come here, give me a hug."

Anna leant in and took her mum in her arms. She felt like a child again in that hug. She felt safe and protected.

"You'll be a great mum, Anna," she whispered into her ear.

As Anna hung from her arms in the cold garage, tears dropped from her cheeks and chin to the floor. She felt sick and alone and would have given anything to be back in her mum's arms again. So far she hadn't been a good mother. Her little bump couldn't be happy in her stressed and battered body.

Anna looked down at her stomach. She had such a desperate urge to hold her stomach and talk soothingly to her baby.

Instead, she moved her legs. She stood up slowly, unsteady and shaking, like a baby deer. The pain in her knees caused her to groan, but she stood tall. She blinked the tears out of her eyes. Anna focused her mind. Focused her eyes.

There was nothing in the garage except an empty wooden table and her handbag, which was by the garage door about a car length away from her. It was like being in a stone box. It was cold and unforgiving and smelt of oil and suffering. The bricks and floor were grey and rough and bare.

Anna kept looking. She saw the concrete floor with nothing on it except her handbag. There was the old wooden table to her left. Two garage doors that were closed in front of her. There was the small window covered in cardboard behind her. Above her head, there was a naked light bulb, hanging from a wire, that was switched off.

'You'll be a great mum, Anna,' rang through her mind.

Anna slowed her breathing, relaxed her body and tried to ignore the pain she felt in order to think and focus. She kept looking around her. The wooden table to the left that was oil-stained and empty. Her handbag ahead of her next to the garage doors. The window behind her covered by a ripped piece of cardboard. The chains on her wrists and the wooden beams above her head. The brass padlock holding the chains in place.

*I'm okay,* she told herself. *Just a few cuts and bruises. Just a bit thirsty.*

Anna breathed and focused. She needed to take control.

Her eyes scanned the space again. Grey brick walls all around. Bare concrete floor beneath her. Little window behind and two garage doors in front. Table to her left. Bag in front of her. The beams above her head.

Anna looked up. There were five thick wooden beams above her head that were part of the roof structure, and her chain was looped over the middle one. She looked at the chain on her wrists: it was grey and solid looking. It had been wrapped and locked around her wrists so tightly there was no way she was ever going to undo it herself. She gave the chain a small pull, and it moved.

The chain was tied to her wrists, but it was only resting on the beam above her head. Anna's body weight was pulling it down and keeping it tight. When she stood tall, the chain became slack. It was metal resting on wood. It slid when she pulled it. Anna pulled at the chain and could see the smooth metal slip along the flat wooden beam.

A buzz of adrenaline went through Anna as she realised she could move up and down the garage in a straight line. She could go back to the small window. Or up towards the garage doors and her bag.

Without hesitating, Anna turned so her back was facing the dirty garage doors and pulled on the chain. Slowly, she moved away from the middle of the room and made her way to the front of the garage and the doors where her handbag was.

Anna stopped.

She could hear a car in the distance.

It must be Doyle coming back. Was he coming to torture her?

Anna started pulling frantically on the chain, causing it to cut painfully into her wrists. The metal slowly slid across the wooden beam. As it moved, it dislodged dust and cobwebs that gently rained down on her from above. The chain was moving well when it suddenly caught dead. It wouldn't move any further. There was a burr in the wooden beam that the chain had caught on. Anna pulled with everything she had, so that pain stabbed into her wrists from the chain, but it just wouldn't move. The chain was stuck.

Anna groaned through the tape on her mouth.

She turned around and could see that her handbag was close.

The car sounded louder as it neared the garage.

Anna stretched her bloody leg out and touched the bag with her foot. She stretched and gasped and managed to get her right foot through one of the handles of the small leather bag. Gently, she dragged her foot back with the bag on it.

The car sounded loud as it drew near.

Anna kicked off her right shoe and stuck her foot into the handbag. She yanked her foot back to empty out the contents of the bag. Her purse came out. A lipstick rolled across the floor. Sweat covered her face as she worked. She put her foot back into the bag and came out with a pocket mirror. Anna kicked it away and stuck her foot back in.

She could hear the car pull up outside. Sweat rolled down her back, chilling her in the cold garage. Her wrists screamed in agony as she stretched her body and leg out to root into her handbag.

Anna felt something large and metal against her toes. She managed to get her toes hooked onto the object and gently retrieved her foot with the metal item. She looked down and could see it was her phone that she had prised out of the bag.

She calmed herself. Took a slow breath through the nose. Softly she tipped the phone over so the screen was facing up.

Anna heard the car door open and close outside the garage.

With her big toe, Anna typed her PIN number in, and the screen opened up. The screen light felt huge in the dark garage.

There was a notification that she had a text from John.

Anna clicked on it with her toe.

She could hear footsteps on the gravel outside. Doyle was coming.

Delicately, Anna tapped her foot on the top right of the message. There were three options on the top bar. The third one read 'info'.

Anna tapped it. A list of options came up on the screen of the phone.

The door to her left opened, flooding the garage with sunlight.

Doyle stepped into the room, and Anna looked at the

screen, which said, 'Send My Current Location.' She tapped her toe on it. The phone paused for half a second before it confirmed her location had been sent to John.

*'You'll be a great mum, Anna.'*

"What are you doing?" Doyle screamed behind her.

## 23

J ohn stood in the doorway and admired the room. It had taken him all day, but the walls were painted, and the cot was built. Now, it looked like a baby's bedroom. For the first time, he could imagine a baby being in there, and John smiled to himself at the thought.

His arms and back were aching after the decorating, so he went straight into the bathroom, stripped off his dirty clothes, turned on the shower and stepped in the hot water. It felt good, and he took his time, making sure he cleaned the paint from his hands, arms and face.

Afterwards he dried himself and dressed. He went to find his phone in the kitchen to see what Anna wanted to do for dinner. There were no missed calls, just one text.

He opened the text, read it and frowned.

Anna had sent him a location text a few minutes ago. It had come through as a picture, which John clicked on. Automatically his phone went to the maps application. A small red pin flashed at him in the middle of a map. The information on the bottom of the screen told him that the pin was sixteen miles away. He tapped the screen to zoom out, but there wasn't much to see. Was it a new restaurant where Anna wanted to go for dinner? John zoomed back in to the location on the map, but there were no names there. In fact, there was nothing there at all. It was in the middle of nowhere.

John gave up trying to work out what the location meant and brought Anna's number up to call her. Her mobile phone was switched off. He texted back a question mark and put his phone down. Looking at the clock, he saw it was five o'clock in the evening. John made a large mug of coffee and sat at the breakfast bar in the kitchen. The central heating had come on, and the house was feeling warm and cosy.

He sipped his coffee and looked at his phone.

Once again, he picked it up and dialled Anna; once again, there was no answer. He checked his texts, but he had none.

*Why would she send me a location like that?*

A thought occurred to him. John flicked through his contacts and dialled Anna's office phone line. No answer.

John was usually a calm man, but for some reason he could feel a nagging anxiety building within him as he went online with his phone and found the main switchboard number for the university.

"This is Bristol University. How may I direct your call?"

"Hi, I'm trying to get through to my wife, Anna Wilson, but there is no one picking up on her line. Can I speak to the reception in her building, please?"

"What department is she in?"

"Psychology."

"Please hold."

Instantly the phone clicked twice, and another voice greeted him.

"Psychology department, how can I help?"

"Hi, this is John Wilson. My wife, Anna Wilson, has been

working from her office all day. I'm trying to see what time she left?"

"Hi, Mr Wilson, this is Jackie Lane. I'm the administrator for the Psych department."

The name didn't mean anything to him, but he said, "Hello."

"I've been here since lunchtime, and I haven't seen Anna around today."

"Hmm. Okay."

"My office is next to hers, and she's not been working in there. She may have been working from the canteen downstairs?"

"Yes, maybe."

"Sorry I can't be more help."

"No problem."

"Take care, Mr Wilson."

He hung up the call and put the phone down onto the counter. It didn't make sense that she would be working from the canteen. Anna didn't like background noise while she was trying to work, and if it was a choice between her office and a café, she would always pick her office. If she hadn't been there since lunchtime, where had she been all day?

John drummed his fingers on the kitchen counter and stared out of the kitchen window. It was already dark outside; there was only a thin crescent moon in the sky, and he could barely see to the end of the garden. To the side of the kitchen window, they had a leaking gutter pipe. John could see frozen water covering it like icy lace.

Where was his wife?

*I'll just have to wait until she calls,* John concluded.

He got up and looked in the biscuit tin and found some chocolate cookies. Taking a handful and his cup of coffee, John made his way into the lounge. He put the television on and flicked through his recordings until he found a golf competition and pressed play.

He ate his biscuits, drank his coffee and watched the golf, but something was niggling at him, and the golfers hit their balls without him really noticing. After ten minutes, John turned off the television and went back into the kitchen. He called Anna's number again. There was still no answer.

"Where is she?" he muttered.

Something didn't feel right to him. John peered at his phone and clicked on the location Anna had sent him by text. It was twenty-five minutes away by car. Once again he wondered why she was so interested in this place.

A sudden thought occurred to him that felt like a snow-ball rolling down his back. Anna hadn't just sent him a map of a random location.

It read 'My Current Location'.

She hadn't sent John a location; she had sent him *her* location.

Anna was there. In the middle of nowhere, where the digital red pin stood proudly on the map. It was north of Bristol and Winterbourne, on the edge of the Cotswolds. *Why the hell is she out there?* He thought back to her recent trip to Barcelona and wondered what she could be up to now.

The idea of her being out there on her own left him feeling uncomfortable, and he knew he wouldn't be able to relax now.

John slipped on his shoes, grabbed a jacket, picked up his car keys and left the house.

---

THE FIRST FEW miles were on large, open roads, and it was a pleasant drive in his Audi, especially once the heaters had warmed the car.

John wondered if he should have taken a few photos of the baby's new bedroom to show Anna. He felt proud of how the room looked and knew she would love it too. Not only that, but she would be happy *he* had done the work on it. He supposed it was his way of saying that they should keep the baby, that they shouldn't have an abortion.

"I'm going to be a dad." He grinned.

It didn't feel so bad. He wondered why he had been so worried. The fact that he couldn't conceive was always going to be a source of frustration for him, but John also realised that sometimes in life you just needed to suck it up and get on with it. It had taken him a while, but he had come around to the idea of being a dad. It had dawned on him that it wouldn't be the end of the world, that they would still be happy and have a great life, except there would be three of them instead of just two. As the car cruised along the smooth, empty road, John dialled his parents' house phone, which rang through the car's speakers.

"Hello?"

"Dad, hi, it's John."

"Bit late for you to be calling, son. We're heading out to the pub in five minutes."

It was their one treat every week, a few hours down the local boozer on a Saturday night.

"I won't keep you long. Just wanted to see how you're both keeping?"

"Yes, fine. Doug from round the corner called in, seeing if we wanted to buy his sofa. I said to your mum, 'what do we want with that old piece of crap?' "

"Is Mum there?" He paused. "I've got some news. Can you put me on speaker?"

He had been dreading this conversation, but he now suddenly felt ready to have it.

"What news?"

"Am I on speaker?" John asked.

"Barbara? John's on the phone; he's got some news for us."

"What news?" his mum asked in the background.

"Hi, Mum."

"Hiya, love. What's going on?"

John paused and took a deep breath. Preparing himself for an argument, he shifted in the leather car seat.

"Well, I wanted to visit you with Anna, so we could both tell you, but I can't wait. It's been on my mind for a few weeks now, and it's about time you knew."

The car sped through the dark night, his headlights lighting a path for the car. He wondered why he was suddenly so desperate to tell his parents about the baby. In a way, he wanted to argue with them, he thought – especially with his dad. All his life, his dad had talked him out of having children, and suddenly John wanted to ask him, *Why?* He wanted to tell his dad that having kids wasn't the end of the world.

"John?"

"Anna is pregnant. You're going to be grandparents."

He held his breath.

"Oh, John, that's wonderful news," his mum said.

"Thanks, Mum."

"When is she due?"

"May time," John told them.

"Oh, I'm so pleased for you. Tell Anna we're really happy for you both." Her joy poured out of the car speakers, and John could just imagine the huge smile on her face.

"Thanks, Mum." He hesitated. "What do you think, Dad?"

"Makes no difference to me, John. But if it's what you want, then like your mum said, we're happy for you."

His dad didn't sound happy, but on the other hand, he didn't sound angry at the news either, which was what John had been expecting.

"Really?"

"Of course, son."

"That's nice to hear, thanks."

"How is Anna feeling?" his mum asked.

"She's great, really glowing at the moment. Maybe we can come down next weekend and see you?"

"That would be lovely. I can bake a cake for you," she replied.

"We need to get off, John," his dad interrupted. "We'll call you tomorrow to congratulate Anna, too."

"We'll speak to you tomorrow. Oh, I'm so pleased." His mum laughed.

"Okay, have a good night. I'll call you in the morning."

He hung up and thought about their reactions. His mum seemed pleased, and his dad had been indifferent. On reflection, it was a better response than he'd expected, and he felt a sense of pride warming his chest. Why had he been so worried?

At the edge of his memory, he could recall his dad moaning about the kids. As John drove north, it occurred to him that his father blaming his lack of money and opportunities on his kids was a load of crap. Maybe it wasn't something that his dad really believed either. Maybe he was just having a moan, but kids were impressionable, and his dad's curses had left a lasting impression in his mind.

"She was bloody right," John said to himself.

Anna had told him that the news would make them happy, and she had been right. He couldn't stop smiling.

After the first ten miles of his journey, he left the main road and had to slow his pace as the road changed, and he found himself weaving through a thin country lane.

He had only driven a few miles through the lane when he felt the car slip on a tight corner, and a jolt of adrenaline made him grab the steering wheel with both hands.

"Jesus," he cursed, hitting the brakes.

John flicked on the Audi's full-beam headlights and slowed the car, his eyes scanning the road ahead for any more ice. His speed was averaging forty miles an hour, and he started to doubt himself.

Maybe Anna had sent him the location by mistake. Maybe it was a bit of land she was looking to buy? Maybe there was a little campsite there she wanted to go to in the summer? Was she actually there, or had he misinterpreted the text message?

John didn't have a clue why she had sent it to him, but she was his wife, and he hadn't seen her for a few days, and he missed her, so he ignored the doubts and questions he had, and concentrated on the road ahead.

Eventually, the map on his phone told him he was getting close to his destination, with less than a mile to go. As he turned into a small side road, John's car skidded on the mud and ice that caked it. The road began to slope upwards, and he could feel the grip slipping out of the tyres. Patiently, John pushed his foot down on the accelerator pedal, and the car shot forward and raced up the icy slope. He felt like he was just reaching the top when over the brow of the hill he came to a cattle gate.

John slammed on the car's brake, and the Audi skidded to a stop, avoiding the gate by inches.

The large gate was blocking his route.

"Son of a bitch."

He looked down to the map on his phone, and he could see that the red pin was directing him to the end of the road he was on.

John exited the car. The cold hit him hard; instantly he knew he should have put a lot more layers of clothing on. He was only wearing jeans, a jumper and a thin jacket. He needed a thick coat, gloves, hat and scarf at a minimum. A strong wind was shooting down the lane, whipping icy air into his face.

All he could see beyond the gate was more road and more hedgerows. John walked into the wind and stepped up onto the gate. It shuddered under his weight, but he carefully climbed two of the gate's crossbars and stared along the road and into the distance.

The road curved in a long arc, but from his vantage point he could see the end of it. At the edge of his vision, he could make out a few small buildings where the road finished. He pulled his phone out of his pocket and brought up the map with the little red pin on it. Looking at the distant buildings, then back to the map, he calculated that they were his final destination. The map told him they were just under a mile away.

John climbed down from the gate and checked its latch. As he suspected, it was locked with a thick chain and a padlock the size of his fist, so he got back into the car.

The inside of the car was still warm, and it was a relief to be out of the biting wind. His hands were already red from the winter cold. He held them over the heaters.

John called Anna's phone again, and once again it went straight to voicemail.

He sighed.

Why would she be out here, behind a locked gate? He put himself in Anna's shoes, trying to imagine her opening her phone. He imagined her searching for the location and sending it to him.

His wife was in those buildings.

But why?

John turned the car's engine off. He looked around for anything else he could wear in the car to keep him warm, but there was nothing there, so he made sure his thin jacket was zipped closed as much as possible, and he got out of the car.

He locked it, stuck the key in his jeans pocket along with his phone and climbed over the gate blocking his way.

John clenched his jaw, dug his hands into his jacket pockets and bowed his head into the pounding wind. He set a brisk pace as he walked towards the distant buildings.

It was a terrible wind. One that was icy and fast. It seemed to hit every inch of his body and burrow its way under his clothes and into his skin. It was the worst of British weather. Despite walking quickly, he was shaking from the cold within minutes. His arms and chest and knees shivered. His feet and hands felt numb.

The lane was dark and empty, and John felt like he could have been on the moon. The clouds were thick and menacing in the sky above him, blocking out what little moonlight there was. Hedgerows either side of the road shuddered and bent in the wind. John couldn't hear his own footsteps, couldn't hear anything other than the raging gale in his ears.

John made it through the darkness to the small buildings. It had felt like a long walk, although in reality it must have only taken him fifteen minutes. As he approached the end of the road, he could see there were three buildings in a poor state of repair.

Two of the buildings were dark, but the third and smallest had a thin line of light coming from it. As he neared the building, John could see that it was a double garage, and the light was coming from under the two garage doors.

There was a black sports car parked near the garages. John stopped dead still and stared at it.

He recognised the car instantly. It was Doyle Kennedy's car.

Was Anna with Doyle? Were they having an affair, and his wife had sent him her location by mistake? Was he about to catch them in the act? Anger instantly boiled within him, and he clenched his fists. For a moment, he forgot the howling wind that was threatening to push him over.

Sense cut through his rage. *No, I trust my wife,* John thought. Also, he knew she wouldn't have an affair in some dilapidated old garage. She would be in the best hotel in the city.

So why was she here? John was unsure what to do.

His mind whirled with possibilities, but he couldn't figure out why they would be here together. While his mind was confused, his gut instinct was screaming out to him that this was wrong, especially with Doyle's sports car parked there. He wondered why the lights were on in this little building in the middle of nowhere. He thought about the text from Anna. It all felt wrong.

The more he stood there looking at the car and building, the angrier he became. Primal instinct took over. Blood rushed to his head, energy to his veins.

He set off for the garage. As he approached, he could see a smaller door within the right-hand garage door. John yanked the handle down and burst into the old building.

What he saw in the bright light of the garage stopped him dead. He suddenly felt like a statue as he stood there, taking in the scene before him.

"Oh, God," he whispered.

## 24

A fter Doyle had caught Anna in possession of her phone, he had smashed it onto the concrete floor, screaming with rage. Once he had finished with the phone, he had turned to her and slapped her hard across the face. She could feel blood on her lips as he screamed at her: "You bitch!"

He had hit her again, this time harder. The force of the strike sent shock waves through Anna's head, so that the world turned dark, and she felt herself pass out for the second time.

When she came around, she felt sick and cold, and her head throbbed. The light in the garage was on, and the single light bulb felt harsh on her eyes after the day of darkness. Her handbag and its contents had been removed from the garage floor, and Doyle was sitting on the big wooden table, staring at her. She wasn't sure how long she had been unconscious, and she was devastated to find her ordeal was not yet over.

He chuckled and smiled at her. "Think you're clever, don't you?"

Doyle slid off the table and approached Anna. She tensed as he came closer, but this time all he did was remove the duct tape covering her mouth. As it was pulled away, it stung her skin, but being able to breathe properly felt like a luxury. Anna gulped cold air in through her mouth.

"Water," she croaked at him.

He pulled her head back by her hair, his face so close she could smell his fresh breath. Anna could feel his body touching hers, and he was like a tower of muscle, while she felt like a mound of skin and bones.

"There's no water for you," he whispered in her ear.

Doyle's whispering was more terrifying than his screams.

He strode back to his small leather bag on the table and once again rummaged through it. Doyle turned back to Anna. This time, he was holding two toothbrushes. One was blue, and one was pink. In his left hand, he held the tube of toothpaste.

Doyle carefully pushed out some of the white paste onto both brushes. He put the tube back into his bag and walked over to Anna.

"Time for you to brush your teeth, too."

His voice was sweet and lyrical, like a parent talking to a child.

Doyle put the brush into Anna's mouth. Should she bite down on it to stop him? But at that moment he was being gentle, and Anna sensed it wouldn't take a lot for him to become violent and forceful.

The toothpaste tasted sharp in her dry mouth. She was desperate for some water; the paste only made her mouth feel drier. The mint taste was so strong, and Anna wondered if that was because she was thirsty...or because it was poisoned.

Doyle moved his right hand back and forth to brush her

teeth. He then started to brush his own teeth with his left hand.

Tears dripped out of Anna's eyes as she squeezed them closed to shut out the look of ecstasy on Doyle's face.

"Please..." she mumbled through the brush and paste.

Minty white gunk stuck to her lips and chin. Her whole body shook with fear.

Doyle groaned in delight as he brushed their teeth. He was slow and methodical, working from the molars at the back of the mouth before moving the brush forward to the canines. Once he reached the incisors, he tilted the brush up in order to get the front and back of the teeth. Anna's whole body was tense, and her hands and legs were shaking. The shaking was hurting her knees, but she couldn't control it.

"Oh, yes," he whispered.

Their brushing was done in unison, both brushes moving at the same pace and in the same place.

"Doyle..." she tried to plead around the pink toothbrush.

"Now swallow," he told her.

Anna couldn't swallow. Her mouth and throat were too dry and wouldn't work.

"Water," she begged.

"Come on. You can do it. Swallow and let me see those clean teeth."

Anna tried again, but only managed to half gulp down the foam and paste so that it stuck in her throat, causing a burning sensation.

"Well done. What a lovely smile you have, Anna."

He smiled at her, his own teeth looking bright and clean.

Doyle walked back to his case and carefully put the brushes away. He then pulled out a short, stubby knife and proudly showed it to her.

"Look at this. Lovely, isn't it?"

Anna saw the knife and screamed, spraying flecks of toothpaste across the concrete floor.

Doyle continued: "I know what you're thinking, that it's small. But you see, when I cut flesh, I like to take my time. Nice and slow."

Anna pulled at the chains and tried to move away from Doyle. The metal rattled and dug into her wrists as she pulled.

"Please don't," she begged.

"You know, if I had some big knife, you'd be dead in seconds. The trick is to enjoy ourselves. This blade is only an inch long. That's the perfect size. When I put the blade into you, it's not going to kill you straight away. It's going to take time."

"No...please no," Anna pleaded through her dry mouth.

Blood and snot poured from her nose; her tears rained down onto the concrete floor of the garage. She wanted to remind him that she was pregnant and he was the biological father, but couldn't speak. Looking at him, she knew he wouldn't care anyway.

Doyle approached her and smiled, his mad blue eyes twinkling in the harsh light.

Anna couldn't help but look at his teeth; they were impeccably straight and white. In that instant, it was a perfect smile of pure evil.

The door to the garage suddenly burst open.

A blast of cold wind rushed in as John stumbled through the doorway. He lifted his head up, stopped still and stared at them with his mouth open and eyes wide, taking in the terrible sight before him: His bloody wife hanging by her hands, a madman standing next to her, brandishing a knife.

Anna felt a wave of relief at the sight of him. Her text had worked.

"Oh, God," John whispered.

Doyle turned to John.

"What are you doing here?" Doyle snarled.

He stepped towards John and raised his knife. He seemed annoyed rather than worried at the intrusion.

"Bad mistake coming here, short arse."

"What the fuck?" John whispered.

"John," Anna mumbled, unable to find the words, unsure if any were needed.

John looked at Doyle and then back to Anna. He was wide-eyed and pale-faced; he looked in shock, trying to process what he was witnessing. Anna watched her husband and prayed that he would somehow make it all okay. John stepped back to the door and put his hand on the door handle. Anna's stomach dropped as he turned his back on them.

"Don't leave," she gasped.

But John wasn't leaving. He was just closing the door, which he did gently. He took a deep breath and turned back to face them.

Then he cracked his knuckles.

"Bit cold out there," John said as he rolled his shoulders.

The look of shock and horror drained from his face, and he started to relax. He caught Anna's eye and gave her a small nod, which was oddly reassuring to her. Then he turned away from Anna and focused on Doyle.

Her husband always had a relaxed demeanour. He was a casual man who lived his life in a casual way, but even for him, he looked laid-back.

*Why is he so calm!* her mind screamed.

John's hands hung loosely at his sides.

Doyle spat on the floor. "Probably best you leave, John. This is nothing to do with you."

John smiled.

"I never liked you, Doyle." His voice was so quiet and

calm, Anna had to strain to hear him. "Always knew you were a messed-up bastard."

Doyle brandished the stubby knife at John.

"Yeah? Only reason you know who I am is because you couldn't get your wife pregnant. You're not man enough, so you had to call me round."

John chuckled. The sound of it was as cold as the wind outside.

Anna didn't understand why he was so calm. He looked so relaxed and nonchalant. Had he seen the knife? Did he know how much danger they were in?

She tried to warn John, but her voice and mouth wouldn't work, and both men seemed unaware of her.

"What you going to do with that little thing?" John nodded to the knife.

"Cut your throat. And then your wife's."

John sniffed.

"Go on then."

Doyle hesitated. Anna could tell he was as unsettled with John's demeanour as she was.

Time seemed to stop. She felt like she was in a museum, looking at two ancient statues that had been turned to face each other. The winter wind was the only sound, the only hint that the clocks hadn't stopped and the world hadn't frozen on its axis. Neither of them moved. In that moment, Anna felt civilisation fall away. The animal kingdom had returned to power. Adrenaline and rage were swirling in the room. She wanted John to destroy Doyle.

Suddenly Doyle moved, taking three quick steps towards John, lifted his arm and slashed at John's face. The attack from the blue-eyed Irishman was fast.

But John was faster.

At the last moment, he ducked the strike and stepped to his left. Doyle's momentum kept him going, and his body half-turned so that the side of his torso was angled towards John. In a flash, John punched Doyle in the kidney. The thud filled the garage. Doyle gasped at the blow.

John stayed where he was. Relaxed and focused. Eyes watching the knife.

As she hung from the chains in the middle of the garage, Anna could see pain wrenched across Doyle's face. It gave her a thrill to see him suffering.

"That all you got?" John calmly asked.

Doyle's face turned the pain into rage, and he charged at John.

This time he stabbed rather than slashed, but again John managed to step out of the way of the strike. Once again, Doyle left the side of his body exposed to John, who stepped in and hit him with three fierce kidney blows: right, left, right. The three thuds sounded agonising in the small space.

Doyle quickly spun back to John. but his body was arched, and he looked breathless. He struggled to stand straight and breathe.

"Painful, isn't it?" John asked. "That pain you're feeling is your kidney being ruptured."

Doyle's face was screwed up in pain and thunderous anger. "You motherfucker!" he screamed as he charged at John.

This time, John stepped into Doyle's moving body and threw a number of punches. His first strike batted Doyle's knife away, and the following punches smashed into his face and body. The sounds of grunts and accurate punches filled the garage.

Anna could only see a blur of movement as fists smashed Doyle's flesh and bone. His nose split. She heard cracks from his ribs. A punch to the eye sounded wet. John didn't stop. He skipped lightly to the left, and his hands started their pumping flashes of attack again. Blood splattered onto the concrete floor, fresh and bright and precious. Doyle had been quick, but John looked almost comically quicker, like someone had clicked him on fast-forward.

John struck Doyle in the face, throat and body, a hailstorm of damage that she could hardly see.

Doyle lurched forward, and John sidestepped again, throwing out more kidney punches. The knife fell from Doyle's hand and clattered to the floor.

The tall Irishman managed to turn back towards John and raise his fists, but he looked completely out of it. His face was bloody; his eyes were rolling in his head; his tongue was hanging loosely from his battered mouth. He didn't look handsome anymore.

John smiled, stepped forward and arched his head back. With his back and neck muscles straining, he headbutted Doyle squarely in the face. It sounded like a raw steak being dropped on the floor.

Doyle crumpled into a heap.

It had been a short fight. Anna felt an immense sense of relief at the sight of the unconscious Doyle.

John didn't hesitate, but went to Anna and held her.

"Hey," he whispered to her.

It felt amazing to be back in his arms.

He looked up at the chains wrapped around her wrists and the lock holding them in place. John straddled Doyle's lifeless body and swiftly rooted through his pockets until he found a set of keys. He patiently tried each key in the lock until he found the correct one and unlocked Anna's bindings.

Without the chain holding her up, Anna slumped into John's arms. They felt so warm and comforting. As the blood began to flow back into her arms, she could feel the pain in her wrists more intensely. She managed to place her hands onto her stomach as John held her upright.

"Water."

He held his ear to her mouth to try to understand what she was asking for.

"Water."

John lifted her up and sat her on the wooden table. She could see him look around the garage. He looked in Doyle's bag but only found an empty water bottle.

"There's no water here." John looked at his phone. "You need a hospital, but I've got no signal on my phone."

He went back to Doyle's still body and searched again through the pockets with no luck. Then he returned to the black bag and poured out the contents onto the wooden tabletop.

"There's no phone here. And these don't look like car keys. Did you see what he did with them?"

"No."

John thought for a second before he turned to her.

"Sod it, my car is less than a mile down the road. We need to walk down there, and I'll drive you to a hospital. As soon as I've got signal on my phone, we can call the police on this nutjob." He nodded towards Doyle.

Anna could only nod in agreement.

She was only wearing her ripped blouse and tattered skirt, so John took his jacket off and put it over her. His hands looked swollen and red as he fed her arms through the sleeves of the jacket. He zipped it up and gave her a big embrace.

"Not long now, we'll be safe." He kissed her lightly on the cheek. "Okay, let's go."

Anna felt awful, and her body was a wreck, but hope and adrenaline gave her enough energy to leave the hellhole she had been trapped in, and she stumbled out into the cold night without a backwards glance.

## 25

They only managed to walk a hundred meters before Anna had to stop. She was too weak and couldn't go on. The fear, dehydration, beatings and exhaustion had robbed her body of any energy. Her legs wouldn't carry her, and the world spun in her blurred vision. As she slumped into John's side, she felt his arms wrap around her as he lifted her up and cradled her like a baby. He started carrying her back to the car.

Anna wrapped her arms around his neck and nestled into him. John was panting hard, but his breath was warming her neck and felt comforting to her in the freezing night.

She could see over John's shoulder, but she had to squint against the icy blast of black wind. They were making good progress down the thin road when something suddenly caught her attention.

Anna blinked and looked back to where they had come from.

She could see bright lights from the garage.

No, it was *next* to the garage. It was headlights.

"John."

"Yeah?" he panted.

"Car coming," she managed to say.

John spun around so Anna was facing away from the lights and the garage and instead was looking towards the way they were headed. In the distance, she could see John's car parked behind a gate. It still looked a long way off.

"Shit," he said into the wind.

John put her down. It took all of her willpower to stand. Anna and John looked at the hedges either side of them. They were tall and thick, and there was no break in them that they could see.

"Is it him? I thought I'd knocked him out."

She couldn't answer. The wind carried the noise of the car engine to them.

John quickly lifted her up again and started running and puffing down the road so that she bounced in his arms. Behind them, Anna could see the car getting closer as the headlights lit up the narrow lane.

"John."

"Just a bit further. I think there's a gate up ahead."

The engine was louder now, and Anna watched as the car came closer. The lights illuminated the road and hedges so that the darkness fell away to be covered by the harsh yellow beam. As the car came around the curved road, it washed them with the light. Anna felt completely exposed.

"It's coming," she gasped in his ear.

"Just a little further," he panted.

Anna held on tight as John continued his laboured run down the narrow road. She was looking over his shoulder at the car lights that looked like yellow eyes, and as they spotted Anna and John, the car suddenly sprang into life and picked up speed. In an instant, it was revving down on them, and they were seconds away from being mowed down.

Anna gasped as their bodies knocked together.

"Gap up ahead," John called out.

The car was roaring towards them in the night, like some ancient beast of hell. Anna watched in horror as it came within five meters of hitting them when John suddenly jumped to the side of the road, and the car sped past them both.

Anna could see nothing but black metal and glass roar past them as they fell into a field. They grunted as they landed awkwardly, and Anna instantly felt soaked as she lay on the sodden grass.

The noise of the car screeching to a stop filled the lane and field as she struggled to catch her breath. She could hear John breathing heavily next to her, and for a second neither of them moved.

Anna watched in horror as Doyle suddenly appeared at the gap in the hedge.

In the moonlight, his face looked bloody and wild. His shirt was splattered with blood, and his fists clenched in rage as he came hobbling towards them like some undead creature of the night.

John slowly sat up as Doyle lunged forward and pounced on him. Anna screamed, but her throat was too dry to make any sound.

John and Doyle wrestled on the muddy field, and Anna managed to stand up to step away from them. They quickly became one snarling beast of mud and blood as they rolled and grunted together in the thin moonlight.

Anna looked around, her panicking eyes desperate for anything to help John. The field was wide and dark and empty. She could see a stack of logs at the field entrance, and she limped over to them to try to find something to use as a weapon. On her way to the logs, her foot struck against something solid. Peering down, she saw a stone.

She leant down and hefted it upwards. It was smooth and black, about the size of a brick.

Without any thought or plan, Anna painfully made her way back to the sounds of fighting. She felt completely drained, and it was an effort to carry the stone. The soggy grass pulled at her ankles, making it harder to move. John suddenly yelped in pain as Doyle dug his teeth into his arm.

Anna looked down at the two men. Their limbs were wet and slimy with mud, like some twisted deity of darkness. It was difficult to tell them apart in the dark until one of the heads was raised, and Anna saw a pair of cold blue eyes.

Seizing her chance, she swung down with her black stone. She struck Doyle on the side of the head. For such a big swing, the sound it made was surprisingly small, just a dull crack. Doyle fell to the grass.

For a moment, the only sound was John heaving air into his lungs. His breath was like a train shooting out steam.

Slowly, he untangled himself from Doyle's violent embrace.

"What happened?"

"I hit him," Anna replied.

"Good." He sat up and saw the stone in Anna's hands. "Thanks...I don't think I would have..." He paused. "He was strong."

John stood up, looking weak and muddy.

They both stared down at Doyle. He looked crumpled, like a piece of paper that had been scrunched up, thrown on the floor and then stepped on.

Anna could hear Doyle's ragged breath and realised she could have killed him. She felt a reluctant sense of relief that she hadn't ended his life, but only because she didn't want to risk going to prison.

"He's not leaving here this time," John said.

John bent down and took off Doyle's belt. He had to

struggle and heave to pull it off, but it eventually slid off the prone body. John tied the arms together. He then took off his own belt and used it to tie the legs together.

"He won't get out of that. Should keep him there till we can get the police here."

John looked over to Anna.

"Let's get you to a hospital."

JOHN'S CAR was still warm, and thankfully he had a bottle of water in the drinks holder. Anna guzzled the water as John slowly reversed down the steep slope and back to the small country road.

Anna had never experienced such immediate relief. In seconds, the water made her feel better, washing away the pain in her throat and the dry toothpaste that still coated her mouth.

John programmed the nearest hospital on the satnav, which was Southmead in Bristol. The screen told them they would be there in thirty minutes.

Keeping the car steady with his knees, John dug out his phone from his jeans pocket.

"Got signal."

He dialled the emergency services.

"Police, please."

Anna drank the water and turned the heater up to maximum as the heated seats warmed her back. John talked quickly on the phone as he gave the police the details of Anna's kidnapping. He also gave them Doyle's description and told them to contact Detectives Gleadless and Wright.

Anna looked down at her wrists. The wounds looked nasty; they were swollen red lines with cuts and scratches.

Her head and knees ached too, but despite the pain, she felt lucky to be with John.

Not only lucky, Anna was surprised to feel a little happy too. She knew how close she had been to being murdered by Doyle, and the fact she had survived flooded her with a momentary feeling of being invincible. She sensed later there would be tears and nightmares and emotional outbursts, but despite all of that, Anna knew she would be okay in the end. Most importantly, she felt the baby she was carrying would be alright, too. Anna finished the bottle of water. She wanted more, but it had been enough to ease the agony in her throat.

John hung up the phone.

"The police are on the way. They had his details on screen, knew he was just out of jail."

"That's good." Her voice almost sounded normal again.

"They want to interview you, of course, but I said they'd have to do it from the hospital." He peered down at the screen. "Should be there in twenty minutes."

"Thanks, John."

He turned and smiled at her.

"I don't even know what just happened, but let's just get you to the hospital first."

Anna managed to tell John a few details; how Doyle had chased her through the empty university building, how she had been strung up all day, expecting to be killed at any moment.

John listened in silence.

"Christ, that must have been terrifying."

"It was."

They lapsed into silence as the car came out of the lanes and reached a main road. John began to pick up speed on the wide, empty road.

"John."

"Yeah?"

"I'm having the baby."

He turned to her, a small smile on his face.

"Okay."

"Okay?"

"Sure. Let's have the baby. I don't know what we were thinking about having an abortion anyway."

Tears glistened in Anna's eyes. "What about Doyle being the sperm donor?"

John reached over and took her hands gently in his left hand.

"I've been doing a lot of thinking. Since you've wanted a baby we've had problems conceiving. You've had work and friends giving you stress about it, and you've had me being an arsehole. Let alone all this madness with Doyle. Through the last few months you haven't changed your mind once, you haven't listened to me or your friends, but just focused on having a baby."

He looked over to her. "Seeing you hung up like that was horrible. I don't ever want to lose you. I know I was worried about Doyle being the biological father, but –" he struggled to find the right words "– whatever happens, I think it's worth the risk. I want to have a family with you. You're so determined to be a good mum, and I know you are going to be amazing."

John kissed her hand.

"You'll be a great mum, Anna."

Anna smiled at him and leant into his shoulder.

"Thanks, John. I love you."

## 26

Anna screamed. John watched as her body contorted with pain and her hands twisted the bed sheets into knots. Sweat covered her red face. He tried to smile and offer her support, but she was off in another world, a primal world of nature and agony.

"John!" The screech sounded like it was ripped out of her.

John held her hand.

"One more push, Anna," Lisa the midwife called out, her voice overly loud in the small delivery suite.

John looked between his wife's legs. "I can see the head," he said.

"John!" she screamed again.

She crushed his hand in hers, and he had to work hard at keeping a calm and serene look on his face.

"Nearly there, Anna," Lisa announced.

John watched the baby appearing and muttered, "That is mental."

The midwife looked up at him with her eyebrows raised at his comment.

"Oh, sorry." He turned back to Anna's red face. "You're doing well."

"You fuuuuuuuuuucccccckkkkkking..."

"Here it is, Anna. Baby is out. Well done, Mum."

The wet baby was handed over to the waiting doctor, who placed the newborn onto a padded worktop to quickly check it over. Lisa, the midwife, joined the young female doctor.

"All looks good. Ten fingers and ten toes." She paused. "Breathing is good."

Lisa turned back to the dazed couple with a smile.

"Baby looks perfect, Anna."

Once the doctor had finished her inspection of the baby and left the room, Lisa put on a small nappy and wrapped the baby in a cotton blanket.

"Here you go, Mum, well done. A beautiful baby girl."

"A girl?" John asked.

He looked down at Anna, who was completely exhausted after her efforts. Her hair was wet with sweat and was stuck across her forehead.

"We've got a girl, Anna. A baby girl."

Lisa handed the swaddled bundle to Anna. She and John looked at the tiny sleeping face wrapped in the white cotton blanket.

"She's beautiful," Anna whispered.

"Yes."

John brushed the hair from Anna's face and lightly kissed her on her wet forehead.

"Well done, Mum."

---

ANNA WAS CLEANED up and wheeled across to the maternity ward with the new baby in her arms. John followed, feeling dazed and lost.

They were put in a small private room. John sat on a chair beside the bed, and they both enjoyed the peace after the nine-hour birth. Neither of them had the energy to speak. Instead they both gazed at their new baby in happy silence.

Anna dozed for an hour. John watched his wife and daughter sleeping. The word was strange and exciting to him: *daughter*.

Outside, as the clouds parted, the summer sun peeked through the blinds. Anna shifted in the bed and opened her eyes.

"Hi."

"Hi," he whispered. "How are you feeling? Can I get you anything?"

"I'm okay. I think. Was I asleep?"

"You slept for an hour. The baby has been sleeping, too."

Anna looked down at her daughter and smiled, and John felt a surge of pride in his wife. She had done so well during the birth and throughout the whole pregnancy.

The last few months had been difficult. Since her ordeal with Doyle, there had been many sleepless nights and tears. Testifying in court had been emotionally draining for them both, although seeing Doyle get a life sentence had made it worth the strain. There had been the pregnancy hormones and the after-effects of being kidnapped; John had done everything he could to support his wife. On reflection, she had done amazingly well.

It had been a difficult spring, but over the past month, as the summer had arrived, Anna had blossomed with the baby, and she had started to mellow. The nightmares had become less frequent, and John had sensed that a corner had been turned and Anna would be alright.

There was a gentle knock on the door.

Lara poked her head into the room from the corridor.

"Is it okay to come in?"

"Lara, yes, come in," Anna said.

Lara walked into the room, holding a shiny helium balloon and a large paper bag with a designer logo on it. She wore an electric blue dress and had her long curls tied up.

"Congratulations, both." She beamed. "How are you feeling, Anna?"

Anna looked pleased to see her friend, and John felt the same; it was nice to see a familiar face.

"I'm doing fine," Anna replied.

Lara's perfume filled the room as she set down the bag and balloon.

"A few gifts for the new arrival. So, is it a he or a she?"

"A she."

"Oh, Anna, that's wonderful news."

Anna grinned. "I know."

"I'm so pleased for you both."

Lara peered down at the sleeping bundle.

"Oh, she's gorgeous. John, she's got your nose. Let's get a photo."

Lara produced her phone and shooed John over to the bed.

"Here, John, you hold her," Anna told him.

John hesitated, then: "If you're sure."

Anna handed the baby to John, who sat on the bed and looked at his daughter. It was the first time he had held her. She felt so light in his arms.

Her skin was red and wrinkled, but he could see real strength and beauty in her face. Slowly, her eyes opened, and her black pupils fixed onto John's face.

"Hi," he whispered to her.

Tears of pride and happiness filled his eyes. For a while, he had been concerned about how he would feel once the baby was born. John had worried about connecting with the new arrival; a part of him had dreaded the day the baby arrived and they became a family of three.

In that moment, as his new daughter looked at him, John knew that his fears were unfounded. Everything was going to be great. He had an overwhelming desire to protect and care for the beautiful little gem he was holding. He couldn't take his eyes off her little face.

Eventually, John looked up to see Anna and Lara watching him.

"Sorry, you want a photo?"

They both smiled at him.

"Don't worry, we'll get one later." Lara turned to Anna. "So, what are you going to call her?"

John and Anna looked at each other and smiled.

"We've decided on Lily-May," Anna said, "after my mum."

# THANK YOU FOR READING

Did you enjoy reading *The Donor*? Please consider leaving a review on Amazon. Your review will help other readers to discover the novel.

# ABOUT THE AUTHOR

JJ Burgess has a degree in Economics and lives in Bristol with his wife and two sons. By day he is the Director of a greetings card company, by night he writes psychological thrillers that ask questions about the world we live in. When he isn't writing, he is usually running through the woods around Bristol, thinking of new characters and dark plots.

 twitter.com/JJBurgesso

Published by Inkubator Books
www.inkubatorbooks.com

Made in the USA
Las Vegas, NV
23 October 2021